A

CANDLELIGHT REGENCY SPECIAL

CANDLELIGHT REGENCIES

216 A GIFT OF VIOLETS, *Janette Radcliffe*
221 THE RAVEN SISTERS, *Dorothy Mack*
225 THE SUBSTITUTE BRIDE, *Dorothy Mack*
227 A HEART TOO PROUD, *Laura London*
232 THE CAPTIVE BRIDE, *Lucy Phillips Stewart*
239 THE DANCING DOLL, *Janet Louise Roberts*
240 MY LADY MISCHIEF, *Janet Louise Roberts*
245 LA CASA DORADA, *Janet Louise Roberts*
246 THE GOLDEN THISTLE, *Janet Louise Roberts*
247 THE FIRST WALTZ, *Janet Louise Roberts*
248 THE CARDROSS LUCK, *Janet Louise Roberts*
250 THE LADY ROTHSCHILD, *Samantha Lester*
251 BRIDE OF CHANCE, *Lucy Phillips Stewart*
253 THE IMPOSSIBLE WARD, *Dorothy Mack*
255 THE BAD BARON'S DAUGHTER, *Laura London*
257 THE CHEVALIER'S LADY, *Betty Hale Hyatt*
263 MOONLIGHT MIST, *Laura London*
501 THE SCANDALOUS SEASON, *Nina Pykare*
505 THE BARTERED BRIDE, *Anne Hillary*
512 BRIDE OF TORQUAY, *Lucy Phillips Stewart*
515 MANNER OF A LADY, *Cilla Whitmore*
521 LOVE'S CAPTIVE, *Samantha Lester*
527 KITTY, *Jennie Tremaine*
530 BRIDE OF A STRANGER, *Lucy Phillips Stewart*
537 HIS LORDSHIP'S LANDLADY, *Cilla Whitmore*
542 DAISY, *Jennie Tremaine*
543 THE SLEEPING HEIRESS, *Phyllis Pianka*
548 LOVE IN DISGUISE, *Nina Pykare*
549 THE RUNAWAY HEIRESS, *Lillian Cheatham*
554 THOMASINA, *Joan Vincent*
555 PASSING FANCY, *Mary Linn Roby*

PIPPA

Megan O'Connor

A Candlelight Regency Special

Published by
Dell Publishing Co., Inc.
1 Dag Hammarskjold Plaza
New York, New York 10017

ISBN: 0-440-16825-2

Printed in the United States of America

First printing—April 1980

PIPPA

CHAPTER 1

The night was so black that for the moment the slim figure of a young man hesitating at the top of the stairs seemed only another shadow. But, undeterred by the enveloping darkness of the moonless night, the shadow detached itself from the porch pillar and flitted down the stairs and away down the drive. Such unerring steps bespoke complete familiarity with the line of the grass verge beside the road, for not once was there a break or a stumble betrayed.

The drive was some half-mile long, and just before reaching the gates, the figure veered to the left, ran several hundred yards along the wall to where, aided by a rise in the ground and a convenient tree stump, the wall was surmounted and the young man disappeared without a sound and set off at a run down the London road.

Where a huge elm overhung the road the figure seemed to disappear entirely as it entered the deeper shadow.

"Hsst!"

Only silence answered this summons.

"Jem!" The voice raised itself, something more urgent in the tone now.

"I'm yer," came a laconic reply from the gloom.

A stifled scream escaped from the figure, then: "Jem! For heaven's sake, where are you? And why didn't you answer me the first time?"

"I wuz watchin' 'ee—gallumping down t' road, making

more noise nor a herd 'ee was," came the denigrating reply.

"I was not!"

"Wuz."

"Oh, what's the difference," the young man replied crossly. "Will you stop arguing and come out. Where *are* you?"

"Well, I'm 'ere, behind the tree. Where else could I be? Wouldn't want me to stand out in the middle of t' road, would 'ee?"

"I can't see that it would matter since it's so dark and the road is hardly bustling with traffic at this time of night," came the lofty reply.

"And how so many times did 'ee tell me as to how I was to be kep' hid and make no noise? Not onct, but agin and agin. 'Jem, don't let no one see yer and don't make no . . .' "

"Oh, do be quiet! Now come on out here and let me see what you've brought me."

A great clomping was heard, and then Jem appeared, leading a horse. At least he was visible to eyes now accustomed to the deep gloom of the night.

The young man peered silently for a moment at the animal, then slowly walked around it.

"Well, of all the spavined, rump-sprung creatures I've ever seen!"

"And what would 'ee expect for five pounds, I'd like ter know?" Jem replied indignantly, much stung by the criticism.

"You never had any judgment about horseflesh, Jem. . . . Oh, well, I should have known."

"Well, I must say, fine thanks that be, and me nearly going all t' way into t' next county to find it!"

"I'm sorry, Jem," said the young man repentantly. "How ungrateful of me. I know you did your best and I do thank you."

"Welcome, I'm sure," said Jem, only slightly mollified.

"Well, we're wasting time. I'll be off now. Just give me a lift up, please."

Jem obligingly clasped his hands together, and the young man placed an extremely small, booted foot in them and sprang into the saddle. Jem snickered.

" 'Ee'll hardly be fit to walk by morning, Miss Pippa."

Grandly ignoring the unmannerly laugh and the remark, the rider dug his heels into the horse's flanks. The only response to this prod was a shudder; then, as though gathering all its forces, the horse slowly put one foot forward, then tentatively another.

Jem clapped the horse on the rump, and it shambled forward in an awkward run. The rider turned to wave, and warned, "Not a word now, Jem. You haven't seen me since this afternoon."

"You be careful, Miss Pippa, and watch yer purse," he called softly as he watched his young mistress ride away into the night.

For this was Miss Philippa Cranville, heiress to a considerable fortune and the family manor and estate of Ayleforth Hall, riding away on the scruffy, swaybacked horse, dressed in the costume of a young gentleman.

The costume had been collected over the past month from gentlemen's emporiums in several neighboring towns, and consisted of the clothes she was now wearing plus a change of underclothes and one extra shirt in her saddlebag.

The costume, the horse, and the flight had all come about when Miss Cranville, who would not ordinarily dream of reading another's mail, had accidentally picked up a letter dropped from her Aunt Emma's workbasket. As she was about to replace it, Pippa's eye was caught by a line ". . . a fine young gentleman, worth at least fifty thousand pounds a year, with whom I feel a most worthy alliance could be made for Miss Philippa."

Now, of course, no mortal could possibly resist reading from the beginning a letter with such a sentence, containing not only one's own name, but plans for the arrangement of one's own future. Pippa, being as mortal as most, read the entire letter.

It was from her guardian, Sir James Seymour-Croft, to her aunt, Miss Emma Cranville; and after presenting his compliments, Sir James informed Miss Cranville that he would be arriving at Ayleforth Hall in one month's time to visit his ward and would be bringing with him a Mr. Robert Danston, whom he felt would make an unexceptionable husband for Miss Philippa.

The letter fell from Pippa's nerveless fingers back to its original resting place on the floor as she stood, paralyzed with shock, trying to assimilate this horrible news. Finally she let out all her pent-up breath in a great whooshing gasp. How *dare* he, she thought, feeling the color mount up her throat as her rage worked its way out. *Never a visit for the past five years, and I was only twelve at the time, and now suddenly he thinks himself capable of picking out a husband for me! Without consulting me, as though I were simply a shipment of goods to be marketed! Besides, I don't* want *a husband, and if I did, I'm sure I wouldn't need to consult* him *about it!*

Fuming and gritting her teeth in rage, she stumped up the stairs to her room, slammed the door as resoundingly as she was able, and turned the key so that Aunt Emma, as she was wont to do, could not come bursting in unannounced.

Throwing herself into the window seat and propping her elbows on the windowsill, she glared out over the peaceful sunlit acres stretched out in her view, to contemplate her life.

It was an uneventful life, to be sure. Pippa, an orphan since her second year, was in the charge of her father's sister, Emma Cranville, a spinster of unbending disposition and tremendous self-importance. The child and the aunt had lived all these fifteen years together in singularly lonely splendor in Sir Jonathan Cranville's family home of Aylesforth, supported by Sir Jonathan's more-than-adequate legacy. His fortune, as well as his daughter, he had left under the guardianship of his old friend, Sir James Seymour-Croft.

Until now Pippa and Sir James had got along perfectly well together, due to the fact that he lived far away in London and had seen Pippa only three times in her entire life. But relations between Pippa and her aunt, Emma Cranville, were another matter altogether.

Emma Cranville's character was a compendium of rigidity and pretension, both qualities bound to conflict with Pippa's hoydenish ways and unruly temper. Their life together, as a result, had been a series of battles. Aunt Emma fought head-on, as implacable as an ironclad, while Pippa's war was more one of retreat and elusiveness.

Since Aunt Emma considered her station in life far above that of most of the families of the surrounding countryside, Pippa had never been allowed to mingle with any of the young people who might have provided companionship suitable for her. So while her aunt was satisfied to confine her social activities to entertaining her three cronies, the two misses Burmond and the vicar, to a weekly dinner and game of whist, Pippa ran wild over the estate in the company of Jem, the gatekeeper's son.

Jem, whose round face and slow speech had changed little over the years, was two years younger than Pippa and completely her slave, following her blindly and loyally through every childhood scrape Pippa could dream up, and accepting without complaint the punishment that nearly always ensued.

It was only natural, therefore, that when Pippa, after brooding for several days, came to him with her plans for escaping from the connivings of her guardian and her aunt, Jem set about to help her in every way she commanded.

With five pounds from her savings he had set out to find her a horse, with strict instructions not to buy it from anyone he knew. She had had to explain very patiently to him why such precautions were necessary.

"Because they will be sure to inquire, Jem, you clunch, and of course the first thing they will do is check our own stables for a missing horse! Please use your head for a change!" So much for patience.

Meanwhile, using her own horse, she had made visits to neighboring towns in quest of gentlemen's attire. She entertained the clerks with highly colorful accounts of a visiting cousin who had been shipwrecked and left without his trunks. She received some dubious looks but was served without question, and finally managed to find a ready-made coat, pantaloons, and boots, plus the necessary linen.

She was slim and tall for her age and, trying on the clothes behind the locked door of her room, felt she made a fine figure of a man, the coat, a trifle large, hiding all the betraying curves of her girlish figure.

She contemplated the long auburn hair streaming down her back, glinting with gold lights and seeming to crackle with life. What on earth was she to do about all her hair? she wondered with dismay. There was far too much to stuff under her hat, and even if she could do so, she would then never be able to remove the hat. It would have to be cut, she decided, with very little compunction, for she thought her hair very ugly. Jem had called her Ginger to tease her when they were children. Her hair had been much lighter in color then, and her face covered with freckles. But these had faded, and her hair had darkened in the past year, leaving an unexceptionably delicate, white complexion surrounded by dark auburn hair. Her eyes, which in her thin, little-girl's face had seemed overlarge, now seemed perfect for her heart-shaped face, and their sherry color matched her hair perfectly.

She would ask the housekeeper for her sharpest pair of scissors and after dinner on the night she planned to leave she would lop it off to her shoulders and club it back with a narrow black ribbon. It would look, no doubt, less than modish, but since she would not be dressed as a Tulip of the ton in any case, it would have to pass. Fortunately her voice had always been huskier than was feminine, according to Aunt Emma, and she was no giggler at any time, so would not be in danger of betraying herself in that way.

All of these plans created for Pippa more excitement than was her usual lot, so that quite quickly the days before the proposed visit of Sir James were nearly past. Pippa had managed to avoid any encounters with her aunt, other than the absolutely necessary meetings over meals. There her short replies to any queries from her aunt earned her several of Aunt Emma's raised eyebrow stares, but little else since Aunt Emma was more than used to her niece's pouts, as she called them. Aunt Emma was so serene in her feelings of her own worthiness that she was rarely given to take notice of another's ill nature. She felt it was beneath her dignity to deign acknowledgment of bad manners. When one of the more pushy neighbors attempted to develop a conversation with her, she expertly depressed all their pretensions, being a lady of such quelling aspect that one look from her was usually enough to make them wish they had kept their civilities to themselves.

The last supper, as Pippa irreverently termed it, was no different than most, aside from the facts that Pippa was hardly able to force the food down her throat, so high was her excitement, and that her cheeks were flushed.

"I hope you are entirely well, Philippa," remarked Aunt Emma blandly, with a long stare of inquiry.

"Perfectly, thank you," answered Pippa, without bothering to look up.

"Your color is rather high, and I notice you do not enjoy your usual hearty appetite. But perhaps you are only overtired and a good night's sleep will take care of it. And I wish you would not push your food about on your plate in that way. If you cannot eat the food served to you, please put down your knife and fork and sit quietly. I have told you before about this, Philippa, and I think at seventeen you should not have to be reminded further that it is very bad manners to make others at the table with you uncomfortable by a display of nerves."

Pippa had placed her utensils quietly on her plate and contented herself with bestowing a smoldering look upon her aunt, who chose to ignore this challenge and quietly continue with her meal.

Pippa despised this tendency in her aunt to refuse to engage in argument. When Aunt Emma saw that Pippa was furious, she simply ignored her. When she had her own point to make, she pronounced slowly and heavily her opinion of the misdeed in question and then withdrew her attention. If a spark of rebellion raised its head in the form of impertinent answers from Pippa, she was sent to her room for whatever length of time Aunt Emma deemed a worthy punishment, ranging from an hour to the record of three days. Pippa always endured these confinements stoically, being too proud to protest or try to escape. That was the principal reason for her silence on the last night at the table, for it would never have done to have said something that would bring down her aunt's displeasure and the possibility of being sent to her room for the whole of the next day. She would have felt honor bound to stay and thus have ruined her plans for escape.

All her plans had until then been successful. Jem had found a horse for her and had it hidden until needed in a small woods on the estate. The gentlemen's wardrobe had been assembled and hidden in the window seat, amongst her discarded toys, where the maids never looked anymore.

After excusing herself from her aunt's company after the last dinner, Pippa had made her way to the kitchen to beg a picnic lunch from the cook, telling her she was going out riding to see the dawn the next morning and would not be back until after lunch.

The cook had obligingly set about slicing ham and buttering bread, setting out the picnic basket and all the dainty accoutrements that fitted into it. But Pippa had said she could not ride about on a horse carrying a picnic basket, and persuaded her to wrap the ham and bread with some fruit in a napkin and leave it on the counter. She had then escaped to her room to wait for the household to go to bed. When she heard her aunt's ponderous tread up the stairs and the door of her room close, she had jumped from her bed, lit her candle, and begun to change her clothes. She had no fear of further interruption, since she knew her aunt's habit of never leaving her room after her door closed for the night. She also knew Aunt Emma fell asleep at once, and heavily, as soon as her candle was blown out.

Pippa carried her candle to the mirror, picked up the scissors, and prepared to cut her hair. Pulling half over each shoulder where she could see it, she took a deep breath and without further hesitation hacked off first one side and then the other. She brushed it back, tied it in place with the ribbon, and looked at herself. Definitely a bit old-fashioned, but it would do. She also realized she was an extremely delicate-looking young boy, but felt perfectly capable of carrying off the masquerade. She clapped the high-crowned beaver hat on, blew out the candle, and cracked her door open.

As she knew, there was no one stirring, so she slipped down the backstairs, picked up her packed lunch, and made her way to the front door.

* * *

Now, as she rode along the dark road, lit only by faint starlight, her heart was high with excitement. She had no fear of being alone, having spent so much of her life alone anyway, and she had no fear of losing her way in the darkness, being perfectly familiar with every road for miles around. She was prepared to ride most of the night in order to put as much distance as possible between herself and Ayleforth before daylight. She was then going to sleep for exactly two hours behind a hedge, have her picnic, and continue on her way before the household behind her would even be awake, or at least her aunt would not be, for she never rose before ten.

The only discomfort she had not reckoned with was the one of riding astride a horse. It had not occurred to her that this would present a problem, though she was now aware that perhaps some thought should have been spared for it. However she was sure that very soon she would get the hang of it and be perfectly comfortable. Meanwhile, though the horse was much less than she had hoped for, it was moving along nicely and she was started on her adventure, happy in the knowledge that she had outwitted all who would try to dictate her life.

CHAPTER 2

Sir Anthony Seymour-Croft stared out the window of his carriage, his heavy black eyebrows drawn together irritably. He had left London the day before to travel down to Ayleforth Hall, and after a wearying day of jouncing about had found the inn where he put up for the night not at all up to his expectations. He was, normally, an even-tempered gentleman, but a night on the board-hard mattress of the inn's best room and a less-than-appetizing breakfast had only exacerbated his already low spirits.

This trip to Ayleforth Hall was a duty that he was not looking forward to, but one he could not possibly avoid. His father's plans for his ward had been divulged to his son before the letter had been written. Two days after it had been posted, Sir James died quite suddenly of a stroke, and several days after that Sir Anthony had written to inform the Cranvilles of his father's death. He had reassured them that since he had inherited the guardianship of Miss Cranville, he would make the proposed trip in his father's place as soon as he could straighten out his father's affairs, which appeared to be in something of a muddle.

This muddle had taken the better part of the past three weeks to work through, to reveal in the end that his father had invested not only the best part of his own fortune, but that of the Cranville legacy entrusted to him, in an ill-advised adventure whose disastrous outcome had resulted in Sir James's stroke and ultimate death.

Sir Anthony had refused to invest his own substantial inheritance from his maternal grandparents in his father's venture, and rashly, according to his father, put the whole sum into a West Indies sugar plantation. Sir Anthony had returned from the West Indies with a tidy fortune with which he now, without hesitation, made complete restitution to the Cranville legacy.

He had worked swiftly and with as much secrecy as possible, with the Cranville attorneys' and accountants' cooperation, to save his father's good name, but had emerged at the end of three weeks with only a few thousand pounds left of his own fortune. However, he could only thank God that he had had the money to make the repayment, for he loved his father and knew him to be a good man, if unwise in the handling of money.

As soon as the disagreeable task of confession to the Cranvilles was out of the way, Sir Anthony planned to return to the West Indies and start again to rebuild his fortune. Visiting the Cranvilles was the last thing in the world he wanted to be doing, but he felt honor bound to see them. He shrugged his shoulders impatiently now at the thought of facing a "formidable dragon," by his father's account, and a silly chit of a schoolgirl. However, in two days it would be over and he could be quit of the whole sorry mess and attend to his own affairs.

Some hours later the carriage slowed to a stop, a gatekeeper hurried out to sweep back the gates, and the carriage arrived shortly in front of the house.

Sir Anthony stepped out wearily and stood looking up at the most imposing pillared facade. *Good God,* he thought, *there must be more than twenty rooms!* The graveled drive and the grounds, as far as the eye could see, were in perfect order. Such perfection bespoke a large staff of outdoor servants, as the size of the mansion presupposed an equally large indoor staff. Great heavens, what could two lone women want with so large a place, so far from any sizable town? What could they do for amusement in such a place?

The front door opened and the butler came down the steps to greet him, followed by several footmen to take Sir Anthony's bags.

"Welcome to Ayleforth Hall, sir. My name is Grigson. Will you come in?"

Sir Anthony obediently followed him into the house and, refusing the offer to be shown directly to his room, requested that he be presented to Miss Emma Cranville at once, if it was convenient. Grigson bowed and led him to the drawing room.

Tony advanced toward the lady seated on the sofa, and bowed over the hand extended to him.

"Miss Cranville?"

"Sir Anthony. Please accept my condolences for your sad loss. This must be a most trying time for you," said Aunt Emma, her glacial expression belying the sympathy she expressed. "Please—will you be seated."

He seated himself, squared his shoulders, and plunged into his story. Emma Cranville's expression never changed through the whole account. When he reached the end with the assurance that complete restitution had been made by him from his own money, she simply nodded her head with a sort of regal complacency.

He wondered if it were possible that she had not understood what he had been telling her. Or, perhaps, having always been lavishly provided for, first by her father and then by her brother, it would never occur to her to concern herself with such mundane considerations: someone would always provide her with what she felt was only her due.

He studied her curiously for a moment. She was not as old as he had pictured her. Her hair had obviously been a most amazing auburn color, though now showing traces of gray, but her skin was still smooth and of the amazing whiteness seen only in redheads. No doubt the lack of wrinkles could be attributed to the fact that she never unbent to smile. If her expression were not so frozen, her eyes not so withdrawn and cold, she would be an exceedingly handsome woman, he thought.

Realizing that he was staring rudely, he withdrew his gaze in some confusion and cast about wildly for another topic of conversation, which she obviously expected him to provide.

"Ayleforth Hall is a very lovely country seat," he said desperately.

"We have always felt it to be so."

"However, it does seem to me to be rather remote." She raised an amazed eyebrow at him, and he hastily added, "I mean to say, I saw few other mansions nearby, which must make it rather lonely for you."

"I have never found it to be so, Sir Anthony," she replied coldly.

"I am happy to hear it. I suppose there *are* young people enough about to provide Miss Philippa with companionship."

"There are no families in the immediate vicinity of consequence enough to associate with a Cranville, sir."

"But then—well—what does she do?"

"*Do*, Sir Anthony? I'm not sure I take your meaning. She is a quiet child, only just out of the schoolroom, and until this year, has been occupied with her studies and with childish games. There has been no occasion for her to *do* anything."

"But now, I imagine, you are thinking of presenting her to society. Will you take her to London for the Season?"

"We are perfectly content here, sir. I see no reason for a removal of any sort. And I detest London."

He decided that it would be less than tactful to pursue this subject further until he was better acquainted with his ward. Never having seen Philippa Cranville, it was impossible to make a judgment on whether she herself was perfectly content with her situation. It was entirely possible the girl was a complete antidote, or even something worse, mental perhaps, or backward for her age. He contented himself, therefore, with a nod of acknowledgment of her statement and again changed the subject.

"I should like very much to meet my ward, Miss Cranville, if you wouldn't mind asking her to attend us."

"She is presently unavailable, Sir Anthony."

"Unavailable? She is away, madam?"

"No." Now for the first time Emma Cranville hesitated, even seemed uneasy for an instant. Her eyes shifted away from him indecisively, flitted about the room without finding a resting place, and finally dropped to her hands, clasped in her lap. "She did not appear for breakfast this morning. I sent to inquire if she were ill, since last night at dinner I remarked a feverish look about her. I was told that she had requested a picnic lunch for today, as she planned to go out riding very early this morning."

"Oh, I see. Well, then I will look forward to meeting her later in the day. Now, if you will excuse me, I will go up to my room and change out of these traveling clothes and walk about the gardens. Or, if I may be so bold, I'll stroll along to the stable and see if they can mount me. A ride in the country air would be very welcome."

"Certainly, Sir Anthony, please feel free to do just as you like."

He bowed himself out on this amicable note, and presently, refreshed and changed, he made his way out of the house, without further encounters with Miss Cranville. *Thank the Lord*, he thought gratefully, *for a more unbending, rigid lady I have never met before.*

He met none of the many gardeners he would have expected to see pottering about the grounds, and when he reached the stables, they too seemed deserted. He called out, and presently a boy emerged from the interior.

"Good afternoon. I thought I'd have a ride, if you would be good enough to saddle a horse for me," said Tony.

"Yes, sir," the boy said and turned back to the stables, Tony strolling along after him.

"Er, about this here mare, sir, she should carry you a treat."

"Fine. Wonderful-looking animal. You keep things in good shape here. How big a staff is there for the stables?"

"Five, sir, counting me."

"Five! Seems very quiet here now. Have they all skipped out and left you alone, then?"

"They're out lookin' for the young miss, sir."

"For the young miss? Oh, you mean Miss Philippa? Why should they do that? I understood from Miss Cranville that she had gone out riding."

"Well, she may have done, sir, but if she did, I don't know what she's a-ridin', since her horse is here and none of t' others is missin'."

"Does Miss Cranville know of this?" Tony asked sharply.

"Well, o' course she does. 'Twas her as sent t' others a-searching."

Tony stood for a moment, trying to make something of this information, while the boy continued saddling the horse. Then, turning on his heel, he set off rapidly back to the house.

"Don't 'ee want yer ride, then, sir?" called the boy.

Tony only waved dismissively and kept going. *So the old lady knew all along that something was amiss, and telling me only that the niece was "unavailable" as cool as you please! But wait, not so cool, for hadn't she looked uneasy for an instant there when I asked to meet the girl? Now, what's afoot here, I wonder?* He made his way straight back to the drawing room, where he found Miss Cranville, calmly stitching away at her embroidery frame.

"Miss Cranville, I have just been informed by a boy in the stables that Miss Philippa is missing. Could you tell me, in more detail, if you please, what this is all about?"

"I do not care for your tone, Sir Anthony. I think you forget yourself, to come bursting in here unannounced, making demands."

"I beg your pardon, madam, if I have offended you, but I think I am within my rights in asking for infomation concerning the disappearance of my ward. I am responsible for her."

"I cannot know what sort of story you may have got listening to the gossip of stablehands, Sir Anthony. I assure you there is nothing you need concern yourself with. My niece has gone off for a picnic by herself, not an unusual thing for her to do, and will be back in time for dinner, I make no doubt."

"Then I wonder why, if you are so sanguine, the entire outdoor staff is out searching for her?" he asked with exquisite politeness.

Again Tony noticed the uneasy glance darting about the room, as Miss Cranville hesitated for a moment.

"Is my ward in the habit of disappearing in this fashion?"

"Certainly not! She has never done so before. Naturally I felt somewhat uneasy when I was informed that though she had announced she would be going out riding this morning, her horse was still here. In fact no horse is missing from our stables. When she did not appear for luncheon, I asked the men to take a look about for her."

"But you are not worried? You told me that you were sure I would meet her later in the day."

"No, sir, I did not. You told *me* that."

"But you did not correct me," he reminded her.

"Because I did not feel it necessary. I think I may be allowed to know my niece better than you can, Sir Anthony. She will no doubt return by dinnertime, if she has not been found before then by one of the men. Now, if you will excuse me, I think I will have my usual afternoon rest. We will meet at dinner."

She set her embroidery frame aside, rose slowly and deliberately, and walked out of the room, showing plainly that it was in no way a retreat. He stared after her helplessly, then turned himself and left the room.

He made his way back to the stables, muttering irritably to himself about old ladies and silly girls. Encountering the stableboy, just returned to the yard after unsaddling the mare and returning her to her stall, Tony requested that the horse be made ready for him again.

The boy turned back resignedly, rolling his eyes heavenward at the changeability of quality.

When Tony came down to dinner, it was to find Miss Cranville in solitary splendor at the table, with no sign of her niece.

Tony bowed politely. "Will Miss Philippa be joining us presently?"

"I'm afraid she will not be, Sir Anthony. She has still not returned," replied Miss Cranville coolly.

"And you still feel no alarm about it?" he inquired.

"I feel rather an irritation of the nerves. I think it is most inconsiderate of Philippa to behave in this way. I shall certainly have a great deal to say to her when she returns."

"Miss Cranville, I'm afraid I cannot take this as calmly as you seem to. In fact I cannot understand your attitude at all. The child has now been missing since early morning, so far as we know. You saw her last at dinner yesterday evening, so it is possible she left during the night for all you know, and yet you speak complacently of giving her a setdown when she returns. What if she doesn't return?"

"Well, of course she will return. Where else could she go?"

"You say she has never done such a thing before; can you think of any reason for her to do so now?"

"I do not take your meaning, Sir Anthony."

"Had there been a quarrel, some misunderstanding, perhaps, between you," he replied as patiently as possible.

"I do not 'quarrel,' sir," she said, giving him her most quelling look.

But Tony refused to be intimidated. "Miss Cranville, there must be some reason for such unusual behavior. I have wondered at the coincidence of her disappearance just as I arrive. Do you think it possible she did not want to meet me?"

"I do not see how that could be, since she did not know you were arriving."

"Well, perhaps not that *I* was arriving, but that my father would be. If I remember rightly, this *was* the day he planned to be here."

"I did not find it necessary to inform her of either visit, sir."

"But—but—well, surely when you knew my father was planning to bring with him a young man he considered a suitable *parti* for her, you would have prepared her for the visit in some way."

"I saw no reason to inform her of that. It would only have succeeded in overexciting her, or perhaps inflating what I deem to be an already overweening sense of self-importance in her."

Unable to think of any suitable reply in the face of such blind, selfish complacency, Tony could only stare at her speechlessly for a moment. Then the anger he had been suppressing since his first encounter with her surged in him.

"Madam, I find your attitude totally incomprehensible. Have you no feelings for your niece? Has it not occurred to you that something quite horrible might have happened to her? That she might even now be lying injured in some way and needing help, or even, God forbid, have been kidnapped? Do you propose simply to go to bed tonight without rousing the countryside to search for her?"

"I must inform you, sir, that I find your manners deplorable. I cannot imagine what company you can have been keeping to have inculcated such behavior in you. I will now retire to my room. I can only hope that a night's repose may give *you* a less exaggerated and excited outlook on the situation." She gave him a nod, barely within the bounds of civility, and sailed from the room.

He was left grinding his teeth in impotent rage. *Unspeakable old baggage,* he thought angrily, *how dare you speak to me in such a way!*

He went out onto the terrace to pace up and down and work off some of his anger. And also to try to think what it would be best to do. Emma Cranville was obviously so wrapped up in her *own* sense of self-importance, she was oblivious of any needs of her niece. It sounded to him as though there was little, if any, communication between them. Witness the fact that the girl did not tell her aunt she was going out but only informed the servants. Which servant, he wondered? Yes, that would be the way, he thought. There must be one among them in whom she has confided, someone she had grown up with. If he could learn nothing from any of them, he would saddle up and go out himself in search of the girl.

He turned and went back into the house to seek the servants' quarters.

CHAPTER 3

Pippa was wakened from a very sound sleep by the sound of a carriage traveling rapidly, and raised up to peer through the hedge just in time to catch a glimpse of it. Even through her sleep-hazed eyes it appeared a very smart carriage indeed, though the face staring out the window, while handsome, had a cross-grained expression that caused her to draw back. There was no possibility that he could have seen her, but it was well to take no chances.

Suddenly recollecting, she swung about to check on the whereabouts of her horse, and then sighed with relief. The ground here slanted down to a small stream, and the horse was halfway down the slope and impossible to see from the road.

She had found her way here a few hours earlier in the predawn darkness, drawn by the thickness of the hedge and the sound of that stream. She and the horse had found their way to the water, and then, tying the horse to a sapling, she had made her way back to a tree directly behind the hedge. Mostly by feel she had located a hollow between the roots of the tree and, wrapping herself in her cloak, had snuggled down to sleep with no trouble at all. Now she reckoned by the very early slant of the sun that it could not be more than seven o'clock, and wondered who could have been the early traveler she had just seen.

If she had been aware that it was Sir Anthony passing on his way to Ayleforth Hall, it was possible she might have turned back, or she would have if she had known the circumstances of his coming. For Pippa, though sometimes quick-tempered, was in every other way a levelheaded girl and would never have have felt that running away was an answer to any ordinary problem. However, in this instance, she had felt the combination of her Aunt Emma and Sir James Seymour-Croft was more than she could deal with. There had never been any question of her being allowed to make a decision for herself so far in her life, being always told what she must do by her aunt or her guardian, so that in the case of a proposed marriage she could only suppose that she would be forced to do as they bade her. The only recourse she felt she had was simply to disappear for a short while. She was sure that Mr. Robert Danston would not be willing to cool his heels for very long, waiting for her reappearance. Any young man in command of fifty thousand pounds a year had no need to wait about for anyone. After a few days Pippa had every intention of returning to her home and accepting meekly whatever punishment Aunt Emma meted out, no doubt a protracted stay in her room.

Sir James, for his part, would never have dreamed of forcing his ward into a marriage, but had only felt, since it would have been such a very good marriage for her, that it would do no harm to introduce the young people. Sir Anthony had been very much against the plan, being a modern young man of an independent turn of mind and feeling it was for all intents and purposes an arranged marriage in the making and, as such, entirely against his principles.

But Pippa, knowing nothing of Sir Anthony's principles, much less of his father's death and the change in her guardianship, was content, at this moment, to be where she was. She cuddled back into the hollow that had made such a comfortable bed and stared up through the leaves of the tree spread above her and at the clear, pale blue of the morning sky. She slowly became aware of a pair of beady eyes staring down at her, and then, curiosity overcoming caution, a squirrel came warily halfway down the tree trunk to get a closer look. She laughed, causing the squirrel to scamper back up to the safety of a high branch, where he turned and began to scold her.

He's right, she thought, *I am a slugabed, and it's time I was on my way.* With that she rose, shook out her cloak, and hung it over a bush. Then she went to the stream to wash. Certain muscles, never used before, made their painful presence felt, but she had decided the night before that this was going to be so and would go away with practice. Therefore she would just ignore it as much as possible. After drying her face and hands on her handkerchief, she led the horse down to the water for a drink, and then got to the business of saddling him again. She had removed it before sleeping, and though she had never saddled a horse before in her life, she had watched it being done often enough to feel confident about being able to accomplish it herself.

When it was done, she fetched her breakfast from the saddlebag and settled under the tree to eat it. She scattered some of the bread crumbs at arm's length, and presently the squirrel came down to join her for breakfast, picking up each crumb daintily with both paws and sitting up properly to nibble at it. Pippa was enchanted, and thought that never before had she experienced such perfect contentment. Finally, however, every crumb having been demolished between the two of them, the squirrel chattered something that she decided was thank you and scurried back up the tree, and she rose, put on her hat, and climbed back into the saddle.

An hour later she was jogging along, munching on the apple from her breakfast, wishing she was mounted on a more prepossessing animal. But the summer morning was so glorious, she was ready to forgive anything. Riding past a huge lilac bush she saw a country lane leading away from the road and not a hundred yards down the lane a crumpled heap of blue velvet and a horse, reins trailing, peacefully cropping the grass at the side of the road.

Pippa pulled up her horse, jumped down, and went running down the lane to investigate. The blue-velvet heap became, as she had suspected, a rider who had obviously taken a toss. Pippa knelt down and lifted the charming confection of a hat, in matching blue velvet with a trailing white plume, which had fallen forward over the face, and found a very young girl. For several anxious seconds Pippa feared she might be dead, so white and still was the face, but, feeling at her throat, she found the girl's pulse beating firmly and breathed a sigh of relief. She pulled off her own hat and began fanning the girl's face, then put it down in the road to chaff her wrists and pat her cheeks. Presently the eyelids fluttered and then slowly opened to reveal extremely blue, but very dazed, eyes. Pippa thought she was the prettiest girl she had ever seen and envied her tumbled, flaxen curls.

The girl, staring mistily, saw a young man of delicate beauty, whose hair, lit from behind by the morning sun, seemed to send out golden sparks. She smiled tentatively at this angelic vision, and the angel smiled back encouragingly.

"It's all right," said Pippa, "you've taken a spill is all. You'll feel better in a moment."

Presently the color began to return to the girl's cheeks.

"Who—are you, sir?"

"My name is—er—Philip—er—Ayleforth," said Pippa, wondering how she could have been so remiss as not to have thought out a name for herself beforehand.

"If you could assist me, Mister Ayleforth, I think I should like to sit up now."

Pippa raised the girl into a sitting position. "Do you live far from here?"

"Not too far. You can just see the house through the trees, if you look carefully."

"Have you no attendant?"

"Mama lets me ride alone in the park."

"I see. Well, I think we should try to get you home now, if you think you are able."

With Pippa's help the girl got to her feet and stood, swaying for a moment, clinging tightly to Pippa's arm.

She laughed shakily. "Well, nothing seems to be broken, though I suspect I will have a few bruises to show for this misadventure. Thank you, Mister Ayleforth, you are so kind. I don't know what I should have done if you hadn't come along."

"My pleasure, I'm sure, Miss—ah—"

"Oh, how stupid of me. My senses are so completely disordered. I am Melissa Barstowe."

Pippa bowed politely, but feeling uncomfortable under the girl's openly admiring gaze, went to fetch her horse. Her own had joined the girl's at the roadside, and she hoped Miss Barstowe wouldn't think her a complete gapeseed when she saw the swaybacked creature.

Melissa, however, was blind to all faults in her rescuer. She thought he was the handsomest young man she had ever seen, and could only thank the Fates that had brought him to her, even by this painful route. A few bruises were small enough price to pay, she felt.

Lady Barstowe, when they finally reached the house, had a clearer head. She had an eye for a pretty young man, as did Melissa, but it was not so clouded that she could not see the ill-fitting coat and the disreputable horse. But her gratitude for his assistance to her daughter was wholehearted, and she charmingly insisted that he come in and take breakfast with them.

Lady Barstowe, at thirty-two, was an older version of her daughter, with the same cornflower-blue eyes, the same blond, dimpled prettiness. She teased and flirted with the handsome youth across the table from her and had no trouble extracting all the information she wanted from him: that he was on his way from his family home to visit an aunt in London. All of this fictitious information Pippa had rapidly invented on the way to the house, so that under Lady Barstowe's questioning it slipped easily off her tongue.

When Lady Barstowe invited Pippa to delay her journey for a few days and allow them to entertain her by way of repayment for her kindness to Melissa, Pippa accepted immediately. She felt quite safe here, so many miles from her own home, and thought it would be just as well to keep off the roads in any case.

"I warn you, we are very quiet here, Mister Ayleforth. Most of our acquaintance go to Brighton or Bath after the Season, but I find there is no rest in that for me, only more of the same. So Melissa and I come here, though I'm afraid she finds it too quiet after a few weeks. I vow you will be doing me a great service by staying to help me keep her in spirits," Lady Barstowe declared with so much warmth in her smile that Pippa blushed.

Lady Barstowe thought this charming. In spite of the coat and the horse, he was obviously a young man of breeding, and though she could bring to mind no family of her acquaintance by his name, she felt content that he was a gentleman, and quality, though perhaps from a family in rather straitened circumstances. However, he would do admirably to entertain Melissa for a few days until the house party Lady Barstowe had planned was assembled. Melissa was prone to fretfulness after too much time alone, just as her mother was, hence the house party. The young man was a happy stroke of fortune—so long as Melissa did not become too seriously involved. Here Lady Barstowe stopped in her musing to study her daughter's face. Still somewhat pale, but with a light in her eye that bespoke her interest in this very beautiful young man. *Well, and who could blame her*! thought Lady Barstowe. *The boy had the face of an angel, and the amber-colored hair and eyes! Most unusual coloring. Best keep a careful eye on them and not leave them alone together at all. I'll have a word with Chitty, she'll stick to them like glue.*

Feeling it safe to leave them chatting over the breakfast table at this early stage, Lady Barstowe excused herself and went away to find Miss Chittern, Melissa's governess.

Presently Pippa found herself ensconced on the terrace with Melissa, listening to Miss Chittern read aloud from "Childe Harold's Pilgrimage," so comfortable in the warm summer air that it was all she could do not to doze off.

This terrace was reached from a small, informal sitting room at the back of the house, obviously the place where Lady Barstowe spent much of her time. Here were her embroidery frame and workbasket, her desk, an easel with a half-finished watercolor painting resting on it, and books and sheets of music everywhere. Large French windows opened directly onto the terrace, which led by wide, shallow steps down to an enclosed garden. Pippa felt that a more comfortable, tranquil spot could hardly be imagined and wished very much there could be such a retreat as this at Ayleforth Hall to escape from the cold formality of its drawing rooms.

Melissa had disappeared immediately after breakfast for a short while and came down some time later, golden curls freshly brushed and arranged, her dress a modish white-muslin round gown with blue silk ribbon. Pippa, whose gowns at home were always of the finest fabrics, now became aware that their cut and style left something to be desired. Aunt Emma's seamstress, though willing and capable, was not completely up on the latest styles for young girls. Pippa wished it were possible to ask Melissa to show her her wardrobe, but she doubted that it was a thing a young man would do. She would simply have to study everything Melissa wore as closely as possible whenever that young lady was not looking.

This was more easily said than done, however, for whenever Pippa looked up, it was to find Melissa's eyes fixed upon her. Then Melissa would blush or smile and look flustered at having been caught, though it was obvious she intended to be. She made no bones at all about her interest in this young man who had chanced her way and flirted with him prodigiously, to Pippa's acute discomfort.

This was the only tiny cloud on a day of pure contentment, however. Lady Barstowe did not fuss about her daughter, but she did insist that Melissa spend the day quietly and retire to her bed after an early dinner. Pippa, in a daze of sleepiness, was most grateful for this and excused herself at the same time.

She found that Lady Barstowe had sent a nightshirt, no doubt one that had belonged to her now deceased husband, and Pippa undressed and put it on. The former Lord Barstowe must have been a large gentleman, for the gown trailed along the floor and the sleeves hung well below her hands. But it would not interfere with sleep, Pippa thought, as she climbed into the bed. And she was right, for she fell asleep in the midst of congratulating herself on the success of her masquerade.

If she had known of the conversation taking place at that very moment between Sir Anthony Seymour-Croft and Jem, it might have kept her awake—for at least a few minutes. Not from fear that all would be revealed, however, for she knew her Jem and knew that a more close-mouthed creature didn't exist when he made up his mind to it. And Jem would never tell on her—his loyalty went too deep.

And in that she was entirely right, for Tony got only "Nope" and "Dunno" from Jem and finally gave up, thinking the boy wanting somewhat in his wits, and wondering if Miss Cranville was aware that, according to the servants, her niece spent most of her time with him. More than likely she did not, and that was another black mark in Tony's book against Miss Cranville.

CHAPTER 4

Pippa, wakened by a stream of sunshine directly in her eyes, rolled over and stretched luxuriously. She was wide awake and felt fully recovered from her lack of sleep the previous night. Since the curtains were opened, she knew the maid had come in earlier to open them, and with that thought she sat up in alarm. She had loosened her hair from its ribbon the night before and hoped very much that the girl had not taken too close a look at her while she slept.

She jumped up and ran to the mirror over the dressing table. Her hair, freed of its former weight, stood out around her head in great loose waves and curls, making her look, if anything, more feminine than when it had hung to her waist. She would have to wet it and pull it back tightly.

She tested the water in the pitcher. It was tepid, so the maid must have brought it more than an hour ago. Oh, well, she thought, stripping off the nightshirt, better than nothing. She washed herself, shivering at the touch of the cool water on her sleep-warm skin. She dressed in the clean undergarments and shirt from her saddlebag, then donned the trousers, vest, and jacket and pulled on her boots. Now the hair. With the brush from the dressing table she wet her hair and dragged it ruthlessly back from her face and tied it behind with the black ribbon and surveyed herself. She still thought she made a fine-appearing young man, and confidently went downstairs to find breakfast.

There was no one down yet, but the young maid laying the table said she'd send in the butler directly. In the kitchen she said he was the prettiest young gentleman she'd ever clapped eyes on. The butler frostily told her to get on about her business and went off to serve Lady Barstowe's guest.

Halfway through her egg Pippa was joined by Lady Barstowe, ravishing in lemon-yellow muslin. Pippa could hardly bear to take her eyes from the gown, with its three-quarter sleeves ending in a ruffle of the same material and the skirt hanging sheer from the bosom to a wide flounce about the hem. Pippa determined immediately to have one exactly like it when she returned home, if she could remember all the details to tell Miss Primsey, Aunt Emma's seamstress. Before she could memorize even part of it, Melissa came in wearing a cherry-striped cotton morning dress that literally took Pippa's breath away. Melissa dimpled demurely and dropped her eyes when she saw Pippa's admiration, and Pippa hastily reapplied herself to her egg.

She devoutly prayed that the Barstowes would not be entertaining any guests for dinner during her stay, for they undoubtedly would be very grand, and it would be too embarrassing to appear before their guests at the dinner table in her riding clothes and boots, the only thing she had to wear.

"Did you sleep well, Philip?" inquired Melissa, with a melting glance at her guest.

Pippa, busy mopping up the last of her egg and not realizing that Philip was the name she must answer to, didn't reply.

Lady Barstowe raised an eyebrow at her daughter at this familiarity. "My dear, have you asked Mister Ayleforth's permission to call him by his first name?"

"Oh, Mama, don't pretend to be such a maggoty creature

that you believe in such nonsense. It's all fustian, and I've heard you say so often."

Lady Barstowe's lips twitched at being so neatly caught out by her daughter, but she turned to Pippa, who was staring at them both, and gravely inquired, "I hope you will not mind, Mister Ayleforth, that my daughter is so wanting in manners."

"Mind?" asked Pippa in bewilderment.

"That my daughter calls you Philip," explained Lady Barstowe patiently, wondering what on earth could be the matter with the boy this morning. He seemed absolutely paper-skulled.

"Oh, certainly not—I mean it does not signify in the least. I like it, you see, much better than always being called Mister Ayleforth. That sounds so stiff."

Pippa was aware that she had behaved like a peagoose, but not only had she been caught out in the matter of her name, she had also been amazed at the easy, lighthearted exchange between mother and daughter. After the cold stiffness of conversation with her Aunt Emma such a relationship came to Pippa as a revelation. Now she envied Melissa's possession of such a relative, as well as her pretty blond looks and beautiful wardrobe.

"Thank you, Philip," Melissa replied to Pippa's assertion that she liked informality. "And you may call me Melissa, please," she requested, with such a blinding smile that Pippa began scraping industriously again at her empty eggshell, while sliding a look from the sides of her eyes to see if Lady Barstowe had noticed her daughter's behavior. She had, and her eyes were brimming with suppressed laughter at Pippa's embarrassment. But taking pity on her guest, Lady Barstowe suggested that if Melissa were quite finished, she might like to change into her riding dress and notify Chitty while she was abovestairs that they were all going riding.

"Oh, Mama, how lovely, you will come with us?"

"Certainly not, you know I detest riding. I meant that you and Mister Ayle—er—Philip and Chitty would go."

"I vow, Mama, I cannot understand you. In the city you used to ride nearly every day."

"Ah, but that was to display my new riding habit, dear child," said Lady Barstowe with a smile. Melissa laughed and went away to change, and Lady Barstowe turned to Pippa. "I'm sure *you* won't mind that I do not come along, Philip."

"Lady Barstowe, no gentleman would willingly give up the pleasure of your company," responded Pippa gallantly, proud of herself that for once she had not behaved like a bumpkin.

Lady Barstowe laughed delightedly, "Oh, and very prettily said, sir. However, I think one chaperone should be enough. Besides, I truly don't enjoy riding in the country. I don't enjoy it that much in the city, truth to tell, but there, at least, one may meet one's friends."

Melissa returned at this moment, though not yet changed. "Mama, Chitty is laid down in her room with the headache. And she says there's not the least need for you to worry, she is confident it will be perfectly proper for me to ride alone in the park with Mister Ayleforth," she reported breathlessly.

"Good heavens, poor dear Chitty. I'll go straight up to her. Do, you two, go along by yourselves. If Chitty says it is all right, we may all rest assured that it is so."

They went off upstairs together, leaving Pippa to finish her coffee and wish that Chitty had not had the headache this morning. Pippa could not look forward to several hours alone with Melissa making eyes at her and wondered if she had been wise after all to agree to spend some days here. She was beginning to feel very guilty at her deception of these very open-hearted people. She only hoped she would be able to leave without them ever becoming aware of the trick she was playing on them. She would like very much for them to remember her with kindness.

But she could not regret being here, not on such a morning as this, and mounted so well on a really superb animal from the Barstowe stables. The park was not as extensive as Alyeforth Hall's, but it was very pleasant, with many lovely rides, which they explored through leafy tunnels of trees and across open meadows. Finally Melissa suggested they dismount and leave the horses and take a walk through a small copse, which surrounded a truly lovely glade. There was a low stone wall surrounding this copse that Pippa, with her longer legs, was able to step up on quite easily and jump down on the other side. Melissa stopped.

"Oh, dear, Philip, I think you must help me, for it is much too high for me to climb over alone."

"Pooh, it's nothing at all. Just put your foot there and then there and then jump."

"Will you not give me your hand?" she asked, with a melting look.

"Oh, for goodness—I mean—of course I will," said Pippa, smothering her impatience and trying to behave like a gentleman. She took Melissa's hand and helped her to the top; then Melissa was fearful of jumping down, though the wall could not have been more than two feet high. Pippa thought Melissa was being excessively silly.

"Have you never visited this copse before?" Pippa asked.

"Well, of course I have, many times."

"Then how did you get over the wall *those* times?"

"Oh, please, Philip, don't be cross with me. I cannot think what has put you into such a temper."

"I'm not in a temper, but I cannot believe . . . oh, well, never mind. Put your hands on my shoulders and I'll lift you down," Pippa said, consenting.

Melissa immediately did so and Pippa put her hands to

the girl's waist and lifted her down while Melissa squealed. But then she did not seem inclined to remove her hands from Pippa's shoulders, but stood there, very close, her laughing face raised as though waiting. Pippa quickly removed Melissa's hands and bowed, to allow the girl to precede her down the path. Great heavens, the girl was absolutely shameless, Pippa thought. If Chitty only knew, she would never allow her out alone with a young man. Pippa couldn't help feeling, rather smugly, that no doubt Chitty had seen at a glance that Pippa was to be trusted.

They explored the glade, Melissa chatting gaily all the while, and taking every opportunity offered to avail herself of Mr. Ayleforth's arm. When they returned to the stone wall, Pippa resignedly climbed over and turned to hold out her hand to Melissa. The performance was repeated, only this time Melissa not only kept her hands on Pippa's shoulders, but closed her eyes and leaned forward, holding up her rosy mouth invitingly.

Pippa, extremely shocked, snatched the hands away from her shoulders and pushed the girl back.

"Melissa, you are being silly, and I insist that you stop immediately."

Melissa stood there for a moment, her mouth open in shock, and then the blood rushed up into her face.

"Oh—oh—you are—*odious*!"

"And you are a goose to behave so. What would your mother think of such behavior, or Chitty?"

"My mother! Why—why—"

"I suppose she will thank me for betraying her hospitality by taking advantage of her daughter."

"Oh, you are hateful. How can you speak to me so. I trusted you. I thought you were a gentleman—and you—and you—" She stamped her foot helplessly, knowing full well that she was in the wrong and that her young man had behaved faultlessly.

"Now *don't* fly up into the boughs," pleaded Pippa.

"You were just practicing your flirtations for next Season, and well you know it." That Pippa had scored a palpable hit was obvious in the way the stormy blue eyes widened in surprise and then dropped to the ground uncomfortably. "Furthermore I think if you hadn't thought I was a green 'un you could handle with no problems, you wouldn't have tried this at all. If I'd been some City smart you wouldn't have dared try such tricks. Now, am I not right?"

Pippa peered under the brim of the blue velvet riding hat and tried to make Melissa look at her. Melissa didn't, but Pippa was reassured by the sight of a dimple appearing in one pink cheek, in spite of Melissa's efforts to check it.

"Come now, do admit I'm right," Pippa teased.

Melissa finally began to giggle and looked up. "Oh, very well—but I still think you are an odious boy."

"Then you should be grateful that I am just the sort of odious boy that I am," said Pippa enigmatically. "Are we friends?"

"Oh, very well. But I'll tell you this much—you are a regular clunch with girls. A little town bronze wouldn't come amiss for you." Having had the last word, Melissa flounced over, stepped easily up onto the wall, and mounted her horse. Pippa hurriedly followed suit.

"I'd like to see what you would have done if I had been one of those smarmy fellows, forever reciting pretty speeches and trying to take advantage of you the moment your chaperon's back was turned," said Pippa, catching her up.

"Oh, I think I could handle . . ." Melissa began airily.

"Hah!" replied Pippa derisively, "you'd run screaming more like. Now listen to me, Melissa, I'm speaking to you like a sis—er—brother. No sixteen-year-old chit straight out of the schoolroom should be behaving in such a way when alone with a man—any man. You'll have a very bad reputation before you know it."

"There's no need for you to take that superior tone with me, Philip Ayleforth. You can't be much above sixteen yourself."

"Seventeen—nearly eighteen actually. Old enough to know what is right, which you obviously don't."

"Pooh! Seventeen—what is that?"

And arguing amiably, they proceeded homeward.

Lady Barstowe, armed with her special eau de cologne, quietly opened the door of Miss Chittern's room and peeked around the edge.

"Do come in, Lady Barstowe," called Miss Chittern.

"I've just come to see if you are feeling any better, and I've brought my eau de cologne to rub into your temples. I'm sure it will help."

"You are very kind. However"—Miss Chittern sat up in bed—"I'm feeling ever so much better. Perhaps you wouldn't mind opening the curtains. I won't mind the light now."

Lady Barstowe obliged, then lingered at the window for a moment. "Oh, here come the children. I do hope, Chitty, that you were right about letting them go off unattended like that."

"Madam, you may be completely easy in your mind on that score," responded Chitty.

"Well, I suppose you are right, he is a very nice-seeming young man, perfectly reliable, I'm sure."

"Oh, yes, Lady Barstowe, I assure you that as far as *that* young man is concerned, Melissa is entirely safe," responded Chitty with the very faintest emphasis on "that," and a distinct twinkle in her calm, gray eyes. For Miss Chittern had spent a great many years in the company of young girls, and there was very little about them she had yet to learn. Others might think what they liked about Mr. Philip Ayleforth, but Chitty was perfectly sure in her own mind about the true state of affairs. There were no flies on Miss Chittern! She had already decided that before the day was out, she would have the whole truth about young "Master" Ayleforth!

CHAPTER 5

Blissfully unaware of Nemesis being at hand, Pippa gallantly offered her arm to a fully recovered Miss Chittern after luncheon, when that lady expressed a wish to take the air by a stroll in the shrubbery. Melissa and her mother were closeted in the sewing room with the seamstress, and though Pippa would have been very interested in the whole business of fabric and cut, she had adopted a manly, bored attitude and retired to the back drawing-room terrace, where Miss Chittern found her.

As they strolled along Chitty questioned Pippa gently about her home, her parents, and her aunt in London, while Pippa, carefully avoiding Chitty's eyes, told her fictitious story, fingers tightly crossed behind her back. Finally Chitty fell silent and they walked on quietly to the far end of the garden where a carved bench stood under an oak tree. Chitty suggested that they sit for a time, since the weather was so fine.

"Now, my dear, suppose you tell me all about it," suggested Chitty, with a smile.

"I beg your pardon, Miss Chittern?"

"My dear young lady, I am asking that you tell me your story. I promise I will not act upon it without your express permission. But do let us discuss it."

During this speech, Pippa, her blood seeming to turn to ice water in her veins, had slowly turned to stare at the governess, her eyes wide with horror.

"If I have upset you, I hope you will forgive me. But I thought it best to bring it all out in the open and talk about it. Won't you confide in me? Perhaps I can help you in some way." She looked at Pippa with so much sweet warmth in her eyes that Pippa felt her throat tighten with tears and could not answer for the moment.

"Have you had a quarrel with your parents, dear child, and run away to punish them?"

Pippa shook her head dumbly.

"I hope you are not just kicking up some lark, for that would be a dreadful thing. Not only for the worry you will have caused your dear mama and papa, but for the deception you have practiced for no good reason on Lady Barstowe and her daughter."

"Oh, but I do feel dreadful about that!" Pippa burst out, for that was the one thing that bothered her about this whole business more than any other.

"Of course you do. I was sure you were just the sort of well-brought-up young lady who would feel just as she ought in such a situation." She took Pippa's hands and pressed them warmly in her own. "Now, just tell me the whole, and we'll see what must be done."

Pippa unhesitatingly poured out the entire story, from the moment she had read her guardian's letter (and here she blushed with embarrassment at having to confess such a thing) to her meeting with Melissa on the road. Miss Chittern was much too wise to interrupt with questions, but listened quietly, and with interest and sympathy clear in her expression. She was shocked to discover that a girl in this day and age could be so totally ignorant of her rights that she would believe she could be forced into marriage without her consent. What sort of woman was this Aunt Emma, to have allowed her to believe such a thing? There was a coldness in the girl's voice when she spoke of her aunt that was evidence of a lack of love, on the girl's part in any case.

"Dear Miss Cranville," said Chitty when the recital was finished, "do you not think your aunt will be in a dreadful state of anxiety by this time?"

"Oh, no, I shouldn't think so at all," replied Pippa calmly.

"But surely she must be! She is responsible for you and will be required to answer to your guardian should anything happen to you. Besides, she is your aunt and is bound to care for you and be concerned for your safety."

"Aunt Emma has never cared for me, nor worried about me so long as I did as she said and kept quiet. Oh, I don't mean that she mistreated me in any way, but she is just not a caring sort of person."

Chitty was shocked speechless by this answer, not only by its content, but by the tone of voice, which clearly portrayed a woman of monstrous selfishness. It was also obvious that, never having known any other state of affairs, the girl accepted the situation as being perfectly normal. *Oh, how I should love to give that woman a sharp setdown,* fumed Chitty silently. *But that is not the answer to the immediate problem of what to advise the girl to do.*

"Tell me, child, what had you in mind for the future?"

"Well, I shall go back in a few days. Sir James will have gone away and taken the young man with him. Aunt Emma will be exceedingly cross and make me spend some days in my room, and then it will all have blown over."

"I see. And will you tell the Barstowes of your real identity before you go?"

"Oh, Miss Chittern, I do hope you will not feel it is necessary for me to do so. I would be ashamed to face them after so many lies, and I have not harmed them in any way, truly. If you are worried about Melissa you can set your mind at rest, I assure you. I admit she was behaving in a stupid way, but I straightened all that out this morning."

Miss Chittern studied the young woman next to her for a moment, then a twinkle appeared in her eyes.

"I would like very much to have heard *that*," she declared. "Now, my dear, do not worry, I have no intention of saying a word to the Barstowes without your permission. But I do think you must either go back or communicate your whereabouts to your aunt immediately. It will not do for a young woman to be traipsing alone about the countryside—however safely disguised she may feel."

"Oh, I will, truly, in just a few days. Just long enough to be sure Mister Danston has tired of waiting about for me to appear."

"That's another thing I must discuss with you. There is absolutely no way, in this day and age, that you can be forced into marriage without your consent. I don't know where you can have come by such an unusual idea, but this is not the Middle Ages. I think you have been reading romances."

"No, I'm ashamed to admit that I read very little. But you don't know my aunt Emma! She never seems to even hear me when I disagree with her, and somehow things always come about the way she has decided they should."

"Well, I assure you that this is one area where she must have your consent. In fact I am well acquainted with Sir James Seymour-Croft, and he is a most good-natured gentleman who would never dream of forcing you to do anything you did not wish."

"Perhaps he and Aunt Emma have decided that no one will offer for me, and that is why he is bringing Mister Danston," offered Pippa, avoiding Miss Chittern's eyes and speaking in a feigned tone of indifference that even someone not so perspicacious as Miss Chittern would have recognized as a deep, and previously unexpressed, fear.

Miss Chittern could only stare at her in astonishment for a moment. Was it possible that the child was totally unaware of her own beauty? Even with the hair dragged back severely from her face, there was no disguising the delicate beauty of her complexion, and such a style only revealed more clearly the cameo perfection of her profile. However, if no one had ever told the girl how lovely she was, Miss Chittern had to admit that it was possible she did not know.

"Miss Cranville, will you take my word for it that you would have but to appear in society to have more proposals than you would know what to do with," Chitty assured her, somewhat dryly. "However, there is plenty of time to think of that, since you are not exactly moldering on the shelf yet. Shall we agree between us on the day after tomorrow as the time of your departure, Miss Cranville?"

"Yes, of course, Miss Chittern, and I do thank you for your kindness to me. I will never forget it, I assure you. But you will remember to call me Mister Ayleforth, won't you?" she asked anxiously.

Chitty did not forget through a long, lovely family evening or at breakfast the next morning. Pippa, keeping to their agreement, announced over her eggs that she would be leaving the next morning. Both Melissa and Lady Barstowe protested that Philip could not desert them so quickly, that surely his aunt would not be upset if he stayed on just a few more days. However, Pippa stuck to her resolution that she must be going on her way and finally they ceased pleading with her. She was, naturally, tremendously gratified to know that they had found her pleasant enough to bring forth this urgent invitation. This visit with the Barstowes constituted her first foray into "company," and she congratulated herself that she had acquitted herself fairly well, even if in the guise of a boy.

However, in the middle of the lazy afternoon on the terrace, a guest was announced whose name caused Pippa's heart to stop completely for a moment. She remained frozen to her chair as Lady Barstowe and Melissa, exclaiming with pleasure, rose quickly to greet Sir Anthony Seymour-Croft!

"Tony, my dear! What a delightful surprise this is! How come you to be in this part of the country? Will you be able to make a visit with us? Do say that you will," bubbled Lady Barstowe, going over to take his hands in greeting.

Tony laughed, "Well, Maria, I can only surmise from this excessively warm welcome that the country has begun to pall. You know perfectly well that you go through this every year."

"Ah, you know me too well, provoking creature. But still, I am happy to see you. And here is my darling Melissa, waiting to say hello. Do sit down and I'll ring for some refreshments and we can have a nice coze. I hope you know all the latest *on dits*."

"Melissa, dear child, how you have grown. You must be ready for your first Season, and here am I thinking you still in the schoolroom. Maria, I must congratulate you on your daughter."

Melissa blushed happily at this attention, and managed with no subtlety at all to seat herself beside him on the couch.

"Have you just come down from town, Sir Anthony? Do tell us all that is happening," she said in her most grown-up voice.

"Well, truthfully I know very little, I'm afraid. For the past three weeks I've had no time to go about at all. It is quite unpleasantly warm there, however, so I suspect all your friends have gone into the country."

While all this conversation was going forward, Pippa had remained in her chair, desperately hoping the moment of revelation could be put off just a few more moments until she had had time to think what she should do. Here was her guardian's son, by the wildest coincidence a close friend of the Barstowes, and sent by an unkind Fate at the very time when it was least convenient to herself. She had heard of Sir Anthony, of course, though she had never met him, and all that she had heard of his business acumen made it impossible for her to entertain any hopes that upon being introduced to a Philip Ayleforth, he would not become suspicious. Why, oh why, had she been so stupid as to use a name like that? Why hadn't she said Philip Smith —or—or—anything else other than Ayleforth? At any moment now Lady Barstowe would remember her other guest and call her in. *Well,* she thought, *I must just try to brazen it out. It is always possible that he has not been anywhere near Ayleforth Hall and will not know that I am missing.*

"And what have you been so busy with these past three weeks? Business as usual, I make no doubt," said Lady Barstowe.

"Well, no, Maria, actually it is my father's estate I have been settling."

"Your father's . . . good God, Tony, did your . . . oh, my dear, I didn't know of it."

"I've had no time to write anyone, though I put an announcement in the paper."

Lady Barstowe and Melissa expressed their sympathy, while Pippa sat, her mind in a turmoil at the unexpected turn of events, wondering what it could mean for her. She was not moved to sorrow over Sir James's demise, having no basis for any feelings about him one way or the other. Their three encounters had consisted of her curtsying to him and his patting her on the head and asking if she was attending to her lessons. But if he had died three weeks ago, he would not have visited Ayleforth Hall three days ago with Mr. Danston. Her whole adventure had been unnecessary, though of course she was not to know. She wondered if it were possible that Aunt Emma had known and not thought it necessary to inform her. *If so, and she is now upset about my disappearance, it serves her right*, thought Pippa angrily. But now her ears pricked up at the sound of her name.

". . . my father's ward, Philippa Cranville of Ayleforth Hall, now *my* ward. However, when I arrived, it was to find the child gone and the aunt without a clue as to her whereabouts. And I must say, she is the coldest, most self-engrossed woman it has ever been my misfortune to encounter."

Lady Barstowe, the word Ayleforth prodding her memory, turned to the terrace in dismay. "Oh, good heavens, how disgraceful of me. I've forgotten all about Philip." She came to the French door, "Philip, do forgive me, I have neglected you shamefully. You must put it down to my muddled head and the surprise I've had at seeing Tony here. Do come and be introduced."

There was no help for it, so Pippa rose manfully and came forward.

"Tony, allow me to introduce to you our young guest, Mister Philip Ayleforth," said Lady Barstowe, leading Pippa forward. "Philip—Sir Anthony Seymour-Croft."

Tony, midway out of his chair to acknowledge the introduction, paused fractionally, then rose up to stare at the young man before him with one eyebrow raised in surprise. Pippa bowed and murmured, "Servant, sir."

"Well, well, how very surprising, to be sure, Mister Ayleforth," said Tony. "Here am I just come from Ayleforth Hall. Are you connected to the Cranvilles?"

"Er—it seems possible, Sir Anthony. I'm afraid I never pay much attention to that sort of thing," replied Pippa gruffly. "Leave those intricate family connections to the women, don't you know."

"Oh, how exciting this is," exclaimed Melissa. "Why to think, Philip, you might be related to Miss Philippa Cranville. She is a great heiress, you know. It might be worth going there and trying to fix your interest with her," she continued teasingly.

Pippa flushed, "Stuff, Melissa, you are always carrying on about the most foolish things."

The company reseated themselves and Pippa took the opportunity to sit down at some distance from the rest, hoping they would go ahead with their conversation and forget her presence. They did continue, as Lady Barstowe pursued her quest for gossip about her friends in London, but every time Pippa dared to let her eyes stray toward Sir Anthony, she found him staring at her quizzically.

She saw no hostility in his regard, but there was a distinct feeling that he was studying her intently and was seeing more than she would have him see. His nearly black eyes held a gleam of discovery, and one dark eyebrow was raised ever so slightly, as though in amusement. She squirmed uncomfortably and wished she were anywhere but sitting opposite him, even though she found him exceedingly handsome to look upon, with his black curls and sun-browned complexion.

After a nearly unbearable hour Lady Barstowe, having secured Sir Anthony's promise to stay for dinner, declared that she and Melissa must go change and would leave the gentlemen to entertain each other until the meal was served.

Pippa's heart sank at this announcement, though it rose somewhat when Sir Anthony declared that he would be leaving immediately after dinner to continue his search for his missing ward. He said that he was happy for the early dinner hour in the country as this would give him several more hours of daylight. Pippa thought that if she could just maintain her pose for three more hours, at most, he would be gone. In the morning she would ride as fast as she could get that dreadful horse to go back to Ayleforth Hall. It was perfectly possible that she would get back before Sir Anthony did, and with her hair down and in her best gown he would surely never recognize her.

The ladies withdrew, and Pippa was uncomfortably aware that she now had Sir Anthony's undivided attention. He studied her in silence for a few moments.

"Tell me, Mister Ayleforth, where did you say you were from?"

"Why—Sudbury, sir," said Pippa, naming a town some thirty miles west of Ayleforth Hall.

"Strange that you should not know of the Cranvilles, isn't it? I should have thought, living that close, you would have been aware of your relatives in the vicinity."

"Oh, well, sir, who's to say they are relatives? I mean there might be some distant connection, of course, but the whole thing was lost sight of long ago."

"Possibly. What was your mother's maiden name, if I may ask?"

"Ah—Carlton—yes, Carlton," answered Pippa, throwing out the first name to enter her mind.

"Carlton? Hmm, now I wonder if that could be the same Carltons I am acquainted with from Sussex?"

"No, I hardly think so. My mother's family was from Wessex."

"Do you say so? I don't believe I've ever heard of any Carltons in Wessex. And the Ayleforths? Have they always been situated in Sudbury?"

"Oh, yes, my father is the vicar there, and his father before him."

This devilish interrogation continued for another half hour before the ladies rejoined them and dinner was announced. Pippa wondered for a wild moment if she could claim to be feeling ill and request a tray in her room. However, she thought this might rouse Sir Anthony's suspicions even further. She could not deny to herself that he was certainly suspicious about something. However, in spite of the fact that Miss Chittern had penetrated her disguise so easily, she could not feel Sir Anthony could have done so. After all both Melissa and Lady Barstowe had not only accepted her as a boy, but had flirted with her, each in her own way.

Tony, while continuing to entertain the Barstowes with stories of London, studied the young man across the table from him. The more he looked the more convinced he became in his mind that this young man was in reality Philippa Cranville. Even more convincing than the coincidence of the names, there was that extraordinary coloring! Why, Emma Cranville must have looked just so as a young girl. Even now the resemblance was marked, except that the eyes in the young face across from him were still alive and accepting of the world. They were hiding something, true, but they were filled with animation and expectancy just the same.

He must take the first opportunity after dinner to have a few words alone with Maria Barstowe. How the woman could have been so chuckleheaded as not to have spotted the true state of affairs, he could not imagine.

Pippa breathed a sigh of relief when, the meal finished, Lady Barstowe declared the party too small to stand on ceremony, so they would not leave the men to their wine. They all trooped together into the small back drawing room where, the evening being so fine, the terrace doors were standing wide open to the late afternoon sun. Pippa gallantly offered her arm to Melissa, which she gigglingly accepted, invited her to stroll in the garden, and made her escape.

CHAPTER 6

Tony declined Lady Barstowe's offer to play for him while he had his wine and asked her to please sit down as he had something he would like to discuss with her.

"Provoking man," pouted Lady Barstowe, "you know it's my only talent. However"—she gave him her most ravishing smile—"I am also known for my conversation. What would you like to talk about?"

"That young man. Where do you know him from?"

"Well, he is a new acquaintance actually."

"How new?"

"Let me think. . . . It must be three days."

"Three days! And who introduced him to you?"

"As a matter of fact," Lady Barstowe replied with a laugh, "Melissa did. She had taken a toss, you see, down at the end of the lane where it joins the road, and Philip happened to be passing and picked her up, dusted her off, and brought her home."

"I see. And he's been here ever since?"

"I vow, Tony, you are the most suspicious man. What is the matter? One has only to look at the boy to see he's exceedingly well brought up. Why, I would trust him completely."

"Maria, have you looked at that *young man*? Really looked at him."

"Well, of course I—"

"No. I don't believe you have really. You and Melissa were here, getting bored for company, and along comes an attractive male, and you saw what you wanted to see."

"Well, really, Tony, you are putting me out of all patience! First you bore on and on about this perfectly unexceptionable boy, then you insult me. I am not so desperate for male company that I would take just anyone into the house! I—"

"I beg your pardon. That was a discourteous thing for me to say, I know. But I was presuming on our long friendship to be perfectly open with you. Will you forgive me?"

"Oh—odious creature—you can always get around me," said Lady Barstowe, who was much too good-natured to be angry for more than a moment.

"Thank you. Now let me get on with it. I think you are too intelligent a woman not to admit there is some truth in what I say. But now that you think about it, what is your main impression of the boy?"

"Well, gently bred, rather—ah—delicate for a boy, perhaps too pretty, but no doubt a few years will change—"

"Think of him as a girl in disguise," suggested Tony softly.

Lady Barstowe visibly started, her head jerking around to stare at him and, as she comprehended his meaning, her eyes grew wider and wider.

"Good God! Is it possible? But no, Tony, surely you are jesting. Why should—"

"Exactly. Why should she be going about in boys' clothes?"

"I really cannot believe. . . . Tony, why are you starting this hare? What made you think of such a thing?"

"Don't be such a peagoose, Maria," pleaded Tony, "here am I scouring the countryside for a missing girl, and the first thing to greet my eyes when I come here is an extremely girlish young man, who, to my eyes was obviously *not* a young man at all."

"Well, I think it perfectly possible that *you* could be guilty of seeing what you wanted to see, as you accused me earlier! But I know how to settle this in a moment.

Melissa and I may be influenced by a pretty young man, as you say, but there is one person who would not be. I'm going to call Chitty down here. She'll settle the problem once and for all." And so saying, Lady Barstowe marched to the door and sent a footman to fetch Miss Chittern.

They waited in silence for the lady to come, both very busy with their own thoughts. Miss Chittern came in a moment and stood quietly inside the door.

"You wanted to see me, Lady Barstowe?"

"Dear Chitty, thank you for coming down. Sir Anthony and I want to ask you something," said Lady Barstowe, then paused and looked uncertainly at Tony, wondering how to put her question.

Tony obligingly took over. "Miss Chittern, it has occurred to me that Mister Ayleforth is not all he seems. What is your opinion?"

"I'm not sure I take your meaning, Sir Anthony," replied Miss Chittern evasively, quite sure that she *did* take his meaning and that the game was up for Miss Cranville, but unwilling to give anything away, since she had promised the young woman that she would say nothing.

"I mean, Miss Chittern, that I think Mister Ayleforth is a young girl in disguise."

"Oh—I see—how interesting."

"Yes, very interesting, Miss Chittern. The question we are asking you is do you think this is possible."

"Well, I suppose it is possible, Sir Anthony."

"Do you think it is probable," he asked, holding her eyes with his own. Miss Chittern did not attempt to look away, but gazed back at him steadily.

"That is a more difficult question, Sir Anthony."

"I think the difficulty is someplace else, Miss Chittern. I think it's probable that you have already penetrated the girl's disguise and—this is only my guess—perhaps promised her not to speak if she will return home."

Miss Chittern looked at him respectfully, thinking that

here was a gentleman as smart as he could stare and wondering if it were only an inspired guess that just happened to hit the nail so squarely on the head.

When she didn't answer immediately, Lady Barstowe suspected that Tony must be right, for it was not like Chitty to equivocate in this way.

"Chitty, for God's sake—this want of openness is unlike you. If you know anything of this havey-cavey business, please speak."

"Yes, I think I must, since I am so fairly caught out," replied Chitty slowly. Chitty did not take her promises lightly, but she also owed a responsibility to her employer and would not want to put her in an uncomfortable position. Besides, it seemed that the truth was out already in any case. "The young lady confided all to me when I confronted her with it, and promised to go back to her home tomorrow morning in return for my promise not to reveal any of it. She left her home for what she considered a very good reason. I think I have convinced her that she had nothing to fear by staying there to face it. The child is very unsophisticated, has never been out in the world, and has no one to talk to. She had only meant to be absent a few days in any case."

"But who is she, for heaven's sake?" asked Lady Barstowe.

"If you will forgive me, madam, I would prefer not to tell you. I have told you, so far, only what you have guessed yourselves. I think you must ask the girl for any further information."

"She is right, Maria," said Tony, as Lady Barstowe made an impatient gesture. "She gave her word to the girl and it wouldn't be fair to ask her to break it. I think, Miss Chittern, that the girl is Philippa Cranville, my ward. The coincidence of the names Philip and Philippa, Ayleforth and Ayleforth Hall made me suspicious immediately, and so I looked at her more carefully than Lady Barstowe or Melissa—with an unbiased eye, if you will." Tony bowed slightly to Lady Barstowe, in further apology for the rather harsh remarks he had made at the start of their conversation.

Lady Barstowe smiled forgivingly upon him and wished, not for the first time, that he was not a full ten years younger than herself. She speculated for a moment on the possibility of him as a *parti* for Melissa—but dismissed the thought. Melissa had not had even one Season yet and considered men of five and twenty to be tottering on the brink of senility.

"Well, then, let us have him—er—her in and get her answer," said Lady Barstowe, and rising, she went to the terrace to call the young people in.

Melissa came flying at her mother's call, but it was obvious that the young man was not all that eager. He followed Melissa reluctantly and stood in the doorway, as though prepared to fly away, eyes darting from one to another of the group in quest of information and finding every gaze but Melissa's fixed upon him, Lady Barstowe's bewildered, Miss Chittern's gently reassuring, and Lord Anthony's slightly amused, but impossible to look away from.

Tony went directly up to Pippa, who was still holding her eyes with his. Then seeing the fright in hers, he put out his hand to her arm.

"Please don't be afraid, Miss Cranville."

Pippa started violently and made to pull away, but he tightened his hold on her arm.

"It is Miss Cranville, isn't it?" he asked quietly.

Pippa drew herself up and raised her chin. "I'm afraid I don't understand you, sir."

"Mama, what on earth . . ." began Melissa, but her mother hushed her quickly.

"I think you do. It is my belief that you are Philippa Cranville, and therefore my ward. I think you ran away from Ayleforth Hall three days ago for some reason known only to yourself and Miss Chittern here."

Pippa turned accusing eyes upon the governess, "Oh, Miss Chittern, did you . . . ?"

"No, child, I told him nothing he did not know or guess. I think you must own up, my dear."

Pippa's shoulders slumped in defeat for a moment and she studied the floor. Then she raised her head and, staring Lord Anthony in the eye, answered him.

"Very well. Yes, I am Philippa Cranville." She gave him a smoldering look. "And if you have brought Mister Danston with you to Ayleforth Hall, you might just as well send him packing."

Melissa gasped and turned to her mother. Lord Anthony released his hold on Pippa and walked away.

"Lady Barstowe, I wonder if you would be so good as to leave Miss Cranville alone with me for a few minutes."

"Well, of course, Tony. Come Melissa, Chitty, we'll go into the front drawing room and have some music. No, Melissa," she said to her daughter, sensing a protest, "not now. Just come along, if you please."

And they left, closing the door softly behind them. Lord Anthony seated himself.

"Won't you please sit down, Miss Cranville."

"No, thank you."

"Now you are being childish. There is no purpose to be served by standing there, but as you will. Will you tell me why you ran away from your home, Miss Cranville?"

"Because I was not willing to step up onto the block and be sold to the highest bidder."

"Please do not enact any Cheltingham tragedies, child. You know very well that this is an exaggeration. My father thought only to introduce you to an eligible young man and—"

"Yes, and if Aunt Emma decided it was what she wanted, I would have been married to him before I had time to blink."

"Your consent would have been necessary, Miss Cranville, before any—"

"Everyone keeps saying that! Or at least Miss Chittern did and now you. I can only say that Aunt Emma has never considered my consent necessary so far in my life when she wanted me to do something. Even if my nurse or later my governess interceded for me, she paid no attention at all. I remember when I longed to be sent away to school and Miss Greer, my governess, said that she thought it would be a very good idea even though it meant losing her post to say so, Aunt Emma simply said no and that was the end of it. There is never any appeal when Aunt Emma makes up her mind."

"But if you had appealed to my father, he would—"

"Your father! And where would I find him, pray? I didn't know his direction to send him a letter, and Aunt Emma would not tell me—she said there was no need for me to write him a letter. He only came to the Hall three times in my life and the last time I was but twelve years old, and he stayed but three quarters of an hour and I was never allowed to speak while I was in the room. Not that it would have mattered if I had. If I had said I should like to go away to school, Aunt Emma would have said, 'Nonsense,' and sent me away and that would have been the end of it. Your father would have taken her word for everything, and well you know it!"

Tony was amazed to note that throughout this impassioned speech there was never a trace of self-pity. Anger, yes, but obviously she was stating her case with a very clear-eyed view based on past experiences that had taught her the uselessness of whining about the state of affairs. He admired her in spite of his preconceived notion that he was dealing with a spoiled, self-willed child. Also he felt his own position regarding his father was shaky, in view of Sir James's mismanagement of the Cranville money and her own statement that he had visited her but three times in her life. At the thought of what her life must have been like in the care of Emma Cranville for fifteen years, he could hardly suppress a shudder.

"Miss Cranville"—he held up both hands and smiled engagingly—"please allow me to finish a sentence. I can see that there is certainly much to be said for your believing as you do. It is useless to assure you now that my father would never have allowed to take place a marriage that he thought was not agreeable to you in every way. The fact is you had no reason to know any such thing, and based on your previous experience with your aunt, I am forced to admit that disappearing for a few days was not such a far-fetched notion of how to deal with the situation."

She was standing at gaze, completely astonished that, for the first time in her life, someone who was in charge of her was acknowledging that her point of view might have some validity. Suddenly realizing that she was still standing defiantly in the middle of the room, and feeling rather foolish, she walked over and sat down.

"Thank you, Sir Anthony," she said humbly. "I suppose you will think me completely rag-mannered for not having said a word about your father's death. I am truly sorry to hear of it."

"Thank you, my dear. He was not a bad sort of person, you know, or rather you don't know, I suppose. However, he wasn't really, though I can see where you might think differently."

"Oh, Miss Chittern spoke very kindly of your father. I'm sure it was only that he had a great many other things to think of than myself, and no doubt felt confident that I was safely taken care of by my aunt and he had no need to worry."

"Yes. Well, now we must decide what it is best to do.

I think, with your permission, I will take you back to Ayleforth Hall tomorrow morning. After that we will talk together about how we shall go on."

"Very well. Will you—will you be staying there for a few days?"

"I will be staying there for as long as it is necessary, have no fear. I suppose you have no other clothes with you?"

She laughed, "Only an extra shirt. I didn't think a young man would be traveling about with women's gowns in his saddlebags."

"Could have raised an eyebrow or two, I admit. Well, then, we will travel back as two young men until we reach Ayleforth Hall. I suppose you must be tired after all this excitement," he said, noticing her suppressing a yawn.

"A bit I admit—and I still have to face Melissa and about four hundred questions before she'll allow me to sleep," she said with a rueful smile.

"More like a thousand, I would say. I'll say good night then." He rose and held out his hand, and she stood up also and shyly put out her own hand. He stood for a moment, holding her hand and looking down at her, and thought what a nice child she was after all. Then he walked her to the door and bowed as she went out.

Presently he heard Melissa's excited questions as the two girls went upstairs together, and then Lady Barstowe joined him.

"Well, Tony, so you have found your ward. Melissa is nearly beside herself with excitement. I think it is all rather romantic, like a story somehow."

"You would not be so enchanted if you knew what she must go back to."

"Is the aunt really so wicked, then?"

"Oh, not wicked I think. Much less romantic than that. Do you know that she admitted to me that she would not let the child associate with any of the neighbors—they are not good enough for a Cranville is her explanation. If you ask me, it was only that she did not want to be bothered. The child has never been in company, even to take a cup of tea. She has never been to a dinner party, or a ball, or had a female friend her own age."

"Now, Tony, surely the child is exaggerating the case somewhat."

"The child didn't tell me any of this. I learned most of it from the servants, and when I asked Miss Cranville if she would be presenting the child soon in London, she said that she saw no reason for it and that she detested London."

"But she must prepare the child to take her proper place in society in some way. After all, from all that I have heard, she is a considerable heiress."

"I think Emma Cranville thinks of the money as her own by now, and that as long as she provides a home for the child, she is fulfilling her obligation."

"But that is—is—unconscionable! You must do something!"

"Yes, I am aware of that. But I'm blowed if I can think what to do. If I had a single female relative who could take charge of the child, I would set them up in London. But as it is. . . ."

"What of your father's sister, is she not still alive?"

"Just barely, and certainly not going about anymore at all. No, there is no one. I have been thinking about this since my last encounter with Miss Emma Cranville. Well, never mind; no doubt something will occur to me eventually."

"She could come stay with us when we go back in October, but that is some months from now."

"Bless you, Maria, that was just such a good-hearted offer as I would expect from you. And who knows, I may take you up on it yet."

CHAPTER 7

Tony was bent over, leaning against the balustrade, laughing helplessly. Every time he stood up and tried to stop, he had only to glance once more at Pippa's horse to begin all over again. In spite of her first indignation, Pippa began to giggle also, for the faults in the animal were all the more glaring as it stood, drooping and swaybacked, beside Tony's glossy mare.

Lady Barstowe and Melissa were already holding on to each other in paroxysms of mirth set off by Tony's first shout of disbelieving laughter. Miss Chittern herself, usually so calm, was moved to join in, so infectious was the general hilarity.

"I cannot—oh, dear—" And again Tony began to laugh. "Now—forgive me, Miss Cranville"—he took out his handkerchief and wiped his eyes—"where on earth did you come by that unlikely-looking animal?"

"I bought it, or rather, Jem bought it for me."

"Jem, eh? And how much"—he whooped again, and then tried to pull himself together—"er—how much did he pay for it?"

"Five pounds."

"He was cheated! Well, Miss Cranville, I refuse to be seen riding the public roads beside such an animal. Maria, have you a horse for Miss Cranville? I'll send it back with a groom tomorrow."

"Of course, Tony. Wilkens, take this poor thing away

and bring up Star. I think she should be just right for you, Pippa."

Miss Cranville had become Pippa to Melissa only a few moments after Pippa's bedroom door had closed the night before. Melissa had followed her in and extracted the whole story from her with many gasps, exclamations of horror, tears, and sympathy. She had hugged Pippa fiercely and kissed her cheeks and vowed eternal friendship. Pippa was enchanted—here at last was a friend, a confidante. They decided that they would be best friends forever and write faithfully once a week and that Pippa would come for a long visit to the Barstowe home in London during the winter.

Lady Barstowe, at breakfast, had adjusted to the diminutive of Pippa without a blink, and now, though they were all parting, they felt so close that there was no question in any of their minds that they would see each other often in the future.

Tony's reaction to the sight of Pippa's horse had further eased the parting, so that when Star was brought around and Pippa and Tony mounted, the farewells were lighthearted, and they trotted off down the drive, waving and calling promises of letters and meetings to come.

The ride back to Ayleforth Hall was uneventful, and much faster than Pippa's ride away from it. Tony bent his every effort toward making his ward feel at ease and confiding in him. She was a bit stiff at first, but he put that down mostly to shyness. He realized that it was all made easier for him by the fact that she had talked with Melissa first. Pippa admitted to him that Melissa was the first person she had ever really talked to in her life.

"Of course, there was Jem, but it was not the same thing. He's younger than I," she said loftily of her two-year seniority, "and he's a boy, so there was lots I couldn't talk to him about. He wouldn't have wanted me to anyway; he'd have thought I was soft or something. We used to have some wonderful adventures together though—you know, pirates and soldiers and things. The last two years though I haven't seen so much of him, since he had to work and hadn't so much time, and I guess I sort of lost interest in such childish games anyway."

"When you went out riding so much by yourself, did you ever visit any of your neighbors?"

"Aunt Emma rarely let me leave the park. If I did and she got to hear of it, she would make me stay in my room to punish me. Oh, I got out of the park many times and rode all over, but it would have been useless to try to make friends. Aunt Emma wouldn't allow me to invite them to the house and wouldn't give me permission to visit them. She said I had a position to maintain as a Cranville and must keep up the standards of my family, and all such nonsense as that. I think the Cranvilles must always have been fearful snobs."

"Your mother and father were not, in any event, for I knew them fairly well, though I was only a boy. Your father and mine were very close friends and our families were much together, and I can assure you they were warm, friendly, gracious people."

Pippa felt the tears start to her eyes at this speech, for this was more knowledge of her dead parents than she had ever known. Aunt Emma never spoke of them except to use them as examples of exemplary behavior; ". . . your mother would never have done such a thing" or ". . . your father would turn in his grave if he knew of your conduct" were oft-repeated phrases.

Now Pippa begged him to tell her more of her parents, and he obliged her with every memory that he could dredge up from his mind. He told her of visits he had made to Ayleforth Hall as a little boy with his parents; how Sir Jonathan, Pippa's father, had given him his first pony; of return visits by the Cranvilles; and of many small details about her mother that Pippa never knew. She had studied the painting of her mother in the drawing room for hours at a time but had never known anything of her character or personality. Aunt Emma had replied to all such questions with short answers about her impeccable family background and the spectacular dowry she brought with her.

Now Tony told her of her mother's wit and sparkling gaiety, and of her beauty.

Pippa began to feel that her parents were real people, who had loved her and been proud of her, and felt also, for the first time in her life, grief for their deaths. The tears came in earnest, though silently, and she let them come.

Tony held out his handkerchief wordlessly, and she took it gratefully.

"Thank you, I'm sor—"

"If you dare to apologize, I'll take away my handkerchief," he threatened without looking at her.

She laughed with a little hiccuping sound and wiped her face, feeling much better. When she handed back the now sodden handkerchief, he surveyed her face and laughed.

"Well, now, you look very much as you did when I first saw you."

"When you first saw me! I didn't know you—I mean—when was that?"

"When you were two days old. I was a strapping lad of eight at the time and thought you were the sorriest thing I'd ever seen and was much disgusted with your mother when she asked me did I not think you were beautiful. I told her I was sorry to tell her that I did not and that I was also very sorry she could not produce just such a child as myself, since *my* mother told me often that I was a handsome boy."

Pippa was laughing delightedly by this time and protested, "Oh, surely you could not have said such a thing."

"Well, I don't actually *remember* doing so, but it was repeated to me as a direct quote many times by my proud parents. I fear I was quite dreadfully spoiled by them, and by your parents for my first eight years."

"And then I came along to take some of the shine off you. Did you hate me for it?"

"Very probably. Our families still saw a great deal of each other those first two years after you were born. But then your father became ill with pneumonia and your mother nursed him night and day until he died, and then was so weakened by exhaustion that she contracted the same disease and had no strength to fight it. After that I never saw you again, for not too long after my own mother became ill, and though she lived as an invalid for many years, there was no more visiting. When my father came here—and I agree it was not often enough—he came alone, for I was in school and then a young man in London, living my own life. I must plead guilty to not having given you more than a passing thought in all these years until I inherited your guardianship. But I promise that I will try to make up for it. Have you given any thought to what you might like to do?"

"Do?" she asked with a startled glance. "What do you mean, Sir Anthony?"

"Well, it is too late to send you off to school, so we must consider your education finished. But you must want some other life for yourself than the one you have."

"I don't think there is any way in the world that Aunt Emma would allow—"

"Let us not concern ourselves with what Aunt Emma would or would not allow," said Tony somewhat grimly. "Just for now let's only consider your own wishes."

"Well, I would like to live where there are more people," said Pippa wistfully, "and I should like to be near Melissa and Lady Barstowe. They are the most wonderful people I have ever met!"

"You have a house in London, you know, and if I remember rightly, it is not too far away from the Barstowes' London house."

"I have! *I* have a house? Where did I get it?"

"Miss Cranville, you must surely be aware that the Cranvilles were an extremely wealthy family. Ayleforth Hall alone should tell you that, for it is as grand an estate as I've ever seen. Naturally there is a family mansion in London as well."

"And my father left it to me, the London house?"

"Well, of course he did. Who else should have inherited it?"

"I suppose I—I never thought about it."

"Pippa, you are naturally your father's heiress. Everything he had has come to you. Surely you *must* know this."

"So that is what Melissa meant! I have been so puzzled. I know I must seem stupid to you," she said, too ashamed to look at him, "but I thought it was all Aunt Emma's. She is always telling me how ungrateful I am, so I thought that she only kept me because there was no one else who would do so."

Tony was unable to answer for a moment, he was so shocked. His mouth tightened into a grim line of outrage. He could hardly wait now, to get back to Ayleforth Hall and say a few of the things that were in his mind to Emma Cranville.

They made such good time that this came about very soon. By the time the late afternoon sun was slanting across the road, they were approaching the gates. Tony rang the bell, and Jem came out to open the gates, his jaw dropping in astonishment at the sight of Pippa.

"Hello, Jem, I'm back, you see," Pippa called out.

Jem recovered his aplomb quickly. "Well, o' course I see. Where did you get that there horse?"

"Oh, I borrowed it from some friends," she said casually."

Jem looked from her to the gentleman and recognized the man who had questioned him so closely about his mistress's whereabouts.

"I didn't tell 'im nothin', Miss Pippa. He didn't find 'ee through anythin' he got from me," he said defensively.

"No, indeed, I certainly didn't," affirmed Tony. "If I'd waited for you to tell me, I never would have found her."

Pippa smiled and held out her hand to Jem. "Thank you, Jem, I knew I could trust you not to let me down."

Jem took the proffered hand, but then turned beet-red and jerked his own away. "Best watch t' old lady, Miss Pippa. She's ready to tear a few strips off'n yer."

Pippa only laughed gaily at this, and she and Sir Anthony proceeded on their way up the drive. As they were stiffly dismounting, the front door opened and Grigson came hurrying down.

"Miss Philippa, thank God you're safe."

"Safe as can be, Grigson. How are you?"

"Very worried about you, miss. All right now you're back."

"Where is Miss Emma Cranville?" interrupted Tony.

"She is in the drawing room sir. She's just come down for dinner."

"Good. Announce me please, Grigson. Miss Cranville, I'm sure you will want to go up and—er—change. Grigson, will you send Miss Cranville's maid up to her."

"Her maid, sir?"

"Yes. Her abigail, or whatever you call her."

Pippa laughed. "I don't have an abigail, Sir Anthony. Where did you get such an idea?"

"I thought all young ladies . . . well, never mind. Go along and change, and then come down to dinner. Grigson, you will also inform the cook that we will delay until Miss Philippa comes down, and send one of the maids up to help her change," ordered Tony in a tone of voice that made it clear he expected them to do exactly as he asked. They did so with alacrity.

Tony followed Grigson, waited to hear his name announced, and then strode in quickly.

"Madam," he said, bowing slightly, "I have found my ward and brought her back."

"Then I will have Grigson bring her to me immediately. If you will excuse me, Sir Anthony."

"Miss Cranville is in her room changing from her journey. She will be down for dinner."

"I don't believe I can allow that, Sir Anthony. After such childish behavior as she has exhibited these past few days, I think it will be better for her to keep to her room."

"No, she will not," said Tony very firmly. "She will be down when she has changed. I've told Grigson to inform the cook to hold back dinner until she arrives."

"You have done *what*! Why, how dare you, sir, to come in here and start ordering my servants about," replied the old woman indignantly.

"Miss Cranville's servants, madam, Miss Philippa Cranville, whose house this is and whose servants' wages are paid from her own money," said Tony quietly, determined not to lose his temper for as long as possible.

"I will remind you that I am in charge here, Sir Anthony, at the express wish of my dear brother."

"I will not quarrel with you on that point, but I would own myself astonished to learn that he ever, at any time, meant that his daughter was never to be consulted about her own wishes."

"There is no question of my finding it unnecessary to consult a child on the proper managing of a household," she said icily.

"Nor, evidently, of even informing her of her status in that household."

"I don't know what you mean, sir."

"I mean that it is Miss Cranville's impression that she

lives here on your charity. How do you explain the fact that she is apparently totally unaware that this is *her* home, not yours?"

"I don't believe that it is necessary for me to explain anything to you, sir."

"Yes, I think it is, Miss Cranville. Your dear brother also made other stipulations in his will. He left this estate, his town house, his property in Scotland, and all of his money to his daughter, and a home here for you for the rest of your life, in return for which you were to live here and raise the child. But the direction of all Philippa Cranville's affairs, including the right to make all decisions regarding her welfare, he left to my father as her guardian. I have inherited that position and I intend to be very much more particular in the carrying out of my duties than my poor father was, I assure you."

"No doubt you think you have snared an heiress for yourself, Sir Anthony," she sneered.

Tony was so completely taken aback by this remark that he could not speak. He felt as though someone had punched him in the stomach, and then, catching his breath, he felt such rage as he had never experienced in his life. But he would not give her the satisfaction of letting her see it.

"I assure you I have no need to be on the lookout for an heiress, madam. I will not honor such a discourteous remark by replying further on the subject. I will now go and make myself ready for dinner. When I have made my plans regarding Miss Philippa's future, I will inform you."

He bowed slowly and very deliberately turned his back and strolled out of the room, leaving her to stare after him, greatly affronted at such treatment.

CHAPTER 8

Dinner that night at Ayleforth Hall was a less than festive occasion. Each of the three people around the table were silent except for the merest conversational trivialities. Aside from the natural taboo of speaking of what was really in their minds in front of the servants, they were all so much preoccupied with their own thoughts, they had difficulty attending to the meal being placed before them.

The servants, aware of the change in the atmosphere, as servants generally are, were practically tiptoeing about, presenting the dishes and refilling the wineglasses.

Miss Emma sat in frozen outrage, answering with the merest nod any comment directed to her by Tony. She would have preferred to express her displeasure by refusing to sit down at the table with him, but this would have been admission of defeat. Her dignity and sense of unassailable right would not allow her to withdraw from the battlefield. So she sat there stonily. Silence had always been her answer to presumptuousness; she never quarreled. Pippa, being under the ban of her displeasure, she would not even look at.

Pippa was very grateful for this. Given the choice, she would not have minded missing this meal entirely, so uncomfortable did she feel. She had not really had time yet to absorb all that she had learned from her guardian. She could not prevent herself from gazing at each article of furnishing, indeed the very rooms themselves, with the new eyes of ownership. *My father left this house to me, and that epergne, and that picture, and this table!* In her thoughts she was not yet able to encompass the whole of her inheritance, but only an individual piece at a time.

She was also suffering from an excess of shyness before her guardian, whose eyes had widened in surprise when she had entered the dining room, and continued to express admiration each time he glanced at her. She felt gauche and awkward and pleased, all at the same time. *Even Melissa at sixteen has more polish than I,* she thought ruefully.

Tony's thoughts were even more confused, and since most of the burden for carrying on some attempt at polite conversation fell upon him, he had even less time to deal with them.

He had been almost too startled to speak when Pippa had come down for dinner. Her dark red hair, which he had previously seen skinned back from her face, was now a tumble of ringlets and waves, threaded through with a pale green satin ribbon to match her gown. This gown, though far from modish, being of extreme simplicity, became her slim figure very well. The girl was an out and out stunner, he thought, rather breathlessly.

This recognition only made things more difficult for him. He had felt himself perfectly capable of handling a young girl, practically a schoolgirl he had thought, but this was a young woman, and an excessively beautiful one at that! *Add to that the size of her fortune, and her first appearance in society will cause a sensation,* he thought. *I will receive more offers for her hand than I will have time to handle, and every time I turn one down, I will be accused of saving her for myself. Ah, yes, there is the very crux of the problem, and I didn't even have to leave Ayleforth Hall to hear it for the first time. That horrible old woman only said what most people will be thinking as soon as they set eyes on the child. Child! If only it were so, and by the time she reached her majority I would have been safely married with a wife to protect me from wagging tongues.*

And what shall I do about Aunt Emma? One can't simply show her the door. This is her home, she was born here and has lived here all her life—really no great wonder that she thinks of it as belonging more to her than to her niece. Strange that I have no memory of her being here when I came to visit as a child. Where could she have been? Perhaps there is another relative that I know nothing of, and when Sir Jonathan brought home his bride, Aunt Emma left the family home. I must make inquiries about that.

If she will not take the girl to London for the next Season and present her, who will do so? Perhaps Maria Barstowe would be willing to do it, and she has already invited Miss Philippa for a visit. But it really is asking a lot on such short acquaintance to present a girl so strikingly beautiful at the same time you are introducing your own marriageable daughter.

But there is the question of what I should do with the girl in the meantime. She should be prepared so that she will know how to conduct herself in society. She will have to learn how to deal with all those scarce-breeched sprigs who will be swooning about her as well as all the doddering, penniless nobility on the lookout for an heiress to bolster up the family estates.

I suppose I could take her around the neighborhood and introduce her myself, but that will be a daunting experience, to say the least. A complete stranger coming to call with the mysterious and so far invisible Miss Cranville of Ayleforth Hall in tow. And after all these years of being snubbed by this dreadful, stiff-necked dragon, they will no doubt be delighted for the chance to get a bit of their own back by snubbing Miss Cranville.

The dragon interrupted these musings by pushing back

her chair and rising. She directed an imperative glance at her niece, obviously indicating that she should follow her out of the dining room and leave the gentleman to his wine. Pippa gave Sir Anthony a wild look, and he promptly responded to her message by rising.

"I see no reason to sit here alone. Perhaps, Miss Cranville, you would honor us with some music?"

He held out his arm for her, which she took with a grateful smile, though she did not respond to his request. They followed Aunt Emma's stiff back out of the dining room and down the hall to the drawing room.

However, Aunt Emma did not turn into the room, but went to the stairs.

"I'll bid you goodnight," she said with a rigid nod of her head and stumped up the stairs. They stood watching her for a moment, then proceeded into the drawing room.

Tony settled himself into a corner of the sofa, but Pippa stood uncertainly in the middle of the room. She looked at the piano and then back to him.

"Do you play, Miss Cranville?"

"Oh, indifferently well, I fear. But I do love music above anything."

"Then will you play for me?"

"I don't think Aunt Emma . . . well, you see, she is used to going to bed immediately after dinner always, and she says the piano keeps her awake, so I never play in the evenings."

"Not play in the evenings? Just because—"

"No, please. If you will forgive me, I think it would be better." Pippa paused, searching for words to express this strange new feeling she was experiencing about her aunt. "You see, she cannot change—and somehow it seems spiteful in me to do what I know she will not like, just because you are here to give me permission."

The words, that this was her home and her piano, were ready to spring to his lips but were stilled, and he began to feel that he had been behaving in a churlish fashion. Here was this nice child showing him how to be compassionate to a beaten enemy. The girl was right, the old lady would never change, but also her reign was finished and she must be aware of it. There could be no honor in it for him to rub her nose in her defeat. *I will take a lesson from my ward, and try to be more understanding,* he resolved.

The following week tried his patience sorely, however, and put his new resolve to the test so frequently that he became quite exhausted by it. Aunt Emma seemed determined to challenge him at every possible opportunity and in the process made herself as disagreeable as possible.

He escaped with Pippa on the slightest excuse that offered itself, morning rides, afternoon rambles, visits to the nearest villages on made-up errands.

Aunt Emma found reasons to send Pippa back to her room to change her costume, to insist, whenever she intercepted them, that someone must attend her niece on every occasion, and then complained mightily about the necessity.

He found his nerves becoming more and more irritated with this continual sparring and wondered if after all he was doing the right thing. What had he really accomplished by it? He had not helped the child to make a single new friend, nor had he been able to come up with a solution to the problem of what to do with her. He was determined, however, not to leave until he had resolved something for her.

On the plus side though there was much to congratulate himself upon. His ward was gaining confidence with each day that passed. Not that she had been a shy, giggling girl when he met her, but she had been so under the shadow of her aunt and under the burden of the obligation she thought she owed her that her personality had been dimmed. Now, with the weight of her inheritance behind her, she seemed to stand taller, her eyes, those unusual sherry-colored eyes, sparkled and glowed. She carried her head more proudly, as though to say to the world, "I am not a charity child who must submit my will or be sent away. I am Miss Cranville of Ayleforth Hall, whose parents loved me and saw that I would be beforehand with the world."

In spite of this, however, Tony was feeling irritable with the situation and beginning to worry not a little about himself. Always before, though he had had his share of flirtations from time to time, he had been much too busy to follow them up, finding the feminine charmers less interesting than the excitement of investing in ship's cargoes or real estate in the West Indies. He had never, till now, been thrown so continuously into female company, and was finding that he was as susceptible as any healthy, young gentleman to a beautiful companion, especially when that beauty was unaccompanied by the usual silliness he found in girls of her age.

It would be much better for his peace of mind and his concept of what a guardian should be if he could find a solution to the problem of what to do with her as speedily as possible.

When a stableboy rode in one morning with a letter from the Barstowes, Tony found that his immediate prayer had been answered.

Lady Barstowe wrote to say that the Shelbournes, whose entire family was to make up a house party for the Barstowes' entertainment for the next month, were now unable to come. The youngest daughter, still in the nursery, had developed a case of measles, and Lady Shelbourne would not leave her and the rest of the family felt they could not desert her at such a time. Therefore they would have to regretfully cancel their visit.

Lady Barstowe and Melissa, unable to face the prospect of the rest of the summer alone, had decided to take a house in Bath and proposed that Pippa should come to them there.

Tony wasted not a moment in sitting down to write an acceptance for his ward, knowing that he would have no need to consult her about it. He wrote that rather than Miss Cranville being their guest, he insisted that they be hers. He himself would engage a house in Bath and hire the servants and have all ready for them within a week.

By the time Pippa came down for breakfast, he had sent another letter off to a house agent in Bath telling him just the house he wanted there, if it was still available, and requesting him to contact an agency there and hire the required number of servants to begin preparing the house for their imminent arrival.

Pippa was wild with excitement, dancing around the table in an exhibit of sheer happiness, asking questions, exclaiming over the joy of being with the Barstowes, wondering what clothes would be suitable. She halted in mid-spin as Aunt Emma entered.

"Might I inquire the occasion for this unseemly behavior?" she asked coldly.

"We are to go to Bath!" exclaimed Pippa, too overcome with the joy of it to feel the need for further explanations.

"Bath!" replied Aunt Emma in tones implying that something unmentionable in polite society had been said in her presence.

"You do not approve of Bath, madam?" Tony asked, unable to keep a hopeful note out of his voice.

"Certainly not! A paltry place where every jumped-up merchant goes to find a title for his daughter. One is forced to meet all sorts of people there whom one would never dream of speaking to in the ordinary way. Bath! Never!"

"Miss Cranville is taking a house there for a month. I am sorry, of course, that you will not be joining her there," said Tony after exchanging a speaking glance with Pippa.

"Taking a house? I forbid my niece to go to such a place!"

"I have decided that it will be the best possible experience for her. I have therefore hired a house and invited Lady Barstowe and her daughter to come and stay with Miss Cranville. It is as well that I have done so, since you feel so strongly that you will not go," replied Tony smoothly.

Aunt Emma glared at him for a moment, then turned and marched out of the room, every line of her body expressing disapproval and outrage.

Pippa turned to Tony with such a smile of unalloyed happiness that he instinctively held out his hands to her. She ran to take them, and together they danced silently and gleefully all the way around the dining room table.

When they came to a halt, breathless and laughing, he looked down at her flushed, happy face and his heart seemed to fling itself upward in a funny little lurch. He attributed it to the pure spontaneity of the moment and to the fact that he, a worldly man of affairs, could so forget his dignity and enter into the spirit of the moment. He could remember such moments as a child, but that was a long time ago, and now this strange girl-woman had caused him to experience again that freedom to express joy that adults usually put away with their childish toys.

CHAPTER 9

Pippa, with entire unselfconsciousness, was hanging half out her bedroom window, eyes sparkling with avid curiosity and excitement as she watched the traffic passing below on Great Putney Street. The carriages bowling along, frothing with ladies in pale summer gowns and plumed bonnets; the cavaliers, in pairs or singly, carocoling on their glossy horses; the family parties strolling past on their way to Sydney Gardens; even the merchants' drays were a feast to her eyes.

She was delighted that her bedroom faced the front of the house and all this delightful bustle, and on this, the first day in the house in Bath, she had spent every spare moment kneeling on the window seat, arms resting on the windowsill, enjoying the feeling of being part of such a large community. She could not understand how her Aunt Emma could speak of Bath with such loathing when it was so filled with life and interest. And the people are so friendly, she thought, waving gaily to two ladies passing in a carriage at that moment and smiling up at her.

"Pippa! I vow you're a complete gapeseed! How *can* you be so shameless—hanging out the window like a serving maid," exclaimed Melissa, entering just in time to catch the wave. She pulled Pippa out of the window and back onto the window seat.

"Oh, Melissa, is it not wonderful in Bath? I vow I could live here all my life and never tire of it."

"Oh, pooh, it is really a pokey place compared to London," retorted Melissa with devastating superiority.

"For you perhaps, but for a country girl like me who's never been anyplace it is exciting. I can hardly wait to get out into the town and explore."

"Mama sent me to tell you that we shall go out after luncheon. She wants the time till then to attend to the servants and give them directions."

The Barstowes had arrived in the very early morning at the house on Laura Place, taken for Pippa by Sir Anthony, and were waiting to welcome Pippa when she and Tony arrived. The servants he had requested had arrived the day before to put the house in order.

Everything had gone extremely smoothly from the time Tony had announced that he would take Pippa to Bath and invite the Barstowes to stay there with her. He had informed Aunt Emma of each step of the plan as it occurred, but she had only eyed him haughtily and disdained to comment in any way, as though, the authority having been taken from her, she refused to take any interest in or responsibility for her niece from that moment on.

Pippa, worried about her wardrobe, had been forced to apply to Sir Anthony for his opinion. But he had laughingly told her that anything she required could be purchased in Bath and that nothing could give Maria Barstowe more pleasure than having the opportunity of dressing a young girl. He had assured Pippa that she could rely with every confidence on that lady's taste, and Pippa had fervently agreed, having already been enchanted by the gowns of the Barstowe ladies.

His only other advice in that department had been that no doubt she would require light clothing as Bath could be very warm. She had pulled out all her summer gowns and with dismay had noticed how unsophisticated they seemed, not to say downright dowdy. However even that had not sufficed to dampen her wild excitement.

Tony had heard from the house agents that the house he preferred was available and had therefore planned that they would set out for Bath in three days. He had planned to drive her there in his own carriage, which he said he would leave in Bath for her use during her stay.

"But, what do you mean—leave it there? Where will you be? Will you not be staying at Laura Place also?" she asked, her voice filled with apprehension.

"Dear child, certainly not! Whatever can have put such an idea in your head? It would not do at all. No, I shall put up at the White Hart whenever I am in Bath."

"But—but—" She didn't know how to explain her feelings, hardly recognizing them herself. Here was the first adult in her life who was entirely dependable and understanding, and now he was talking of abandoning her.

Tony himself had been chagrined to find that she thought of him as so ancient that he could with propriety stay in the same house with three young, unrelated ladies and not become the object of wagging tongues and spiteful gossip.

"You will be quite safe with Lady Barstowe, I assure you. Surely you don't think that I would make such an arrangement otherwise? Besides, I have my own affairs to consider and must get back to London as soon as possible," he added somewhat coldly.

"Oh, of course, I see," she answered in a chastened voice. For she realized that she was behaving childishly, and that of course he must have a great many more interesting things to do with his time than take her around Bath.

However, aside from this one small disappointment, all went smoothly. He had requested of Aunt Emma that one of the maids be released from her duties to make the trip as a chaperon for Miss Cranville and been told to do as she liked. The girl was in raptures at this assignment, never having been further away than the nearest village. She and

Pippa had spent the entire trip pointing out the sights to each other, and on arrival in Bath the maid had timidly requested that she be allowed to stay and was even now below, pressing out the creases in Pippa's best muslins.

After showing the Barstowes and Pippa through the house and assuring himself that all was as he had ordered it to be, Tony had taken himself off to bespeak a room at the White Hart, Lady Barstowe had settled herself in the drawing room to interview the servants, and Melissa and Pippa had inspected their rooms and unpacked. At every chance Pippa had returned, as she had now, to her window.

"Oh, Melissa, do look at that bonnet!" she exclaimed, leaning forward to get a closer look at a towering confection of plumes, flowers, and ribbons nodding past in an open carriage.

"It is beyond anything!" gasped Melissa in an awe-filled voice.

"I wonder where she got it? Do you think it would suit me?"

Melissa turned to her with such a look of horror that her mouth hung open, while Pippa gazed back wistfully.

"You—you—cannot be serious, Pippa, surely you cannot want—"

Pippa collapsed into a fit of giggling. "Oh, Melissa—your face—I was only funning, you silly. I may be a country girl, but I hope I am not such a clunch as that!"

Lady Barstowe walked in at this moment to find the two girls laughing and clutching at one another helplessly.

"If I didn't know better, I would think you were both bosky," she said meditatively. This only caused them to start again.

"Well, I suppose I shall just have to go down and tell Tony that you are unable to receive him now," Lady Barstowe said threateningly.

Pippa sat up instantly. "Sir Anthony? But I thought we

were not to see him before dinner. He is below? To see me?"

"Yes, and I should think beginning to be impatient by now, so you'd best tidy your hair and go down."

Pippa jumped up and snatched up her hairbrush. Her mind also began to jump about, and as usual with the human mind, it leaped first to the conclusion that something must be amiss—Aunt Emma had found a way to make her come back—Sir Anthony had changed his mind and would *take* her back. . . . She hurried down to the drawing room as fast as possible, her heart beating painfully.

Sir Anthony turned away from the front window and came to the table in the center of the room as she entered.

"Ah, there you are," he said pleasantly, wondering why the child was searching his face so fearfully. "When I began unpacking, I realized there was one bit of business I had not completed, so I came straight back to be sure to catch you before you went out shopping. Knowing Maria Barstowe, I made sure that she would make straight for the silk warehouses and mantua makers the moment she had unpacked her cases. I've something here for you that might help her in making her choices for you."

With that he began opening several flat, leather cases lying on the table. When she didn't move, but still remained at the door, staring at him, he motioned her impatiently forward, and finally, with a start, she came hesitantly across the room.

"These were your mother's. Not all of them are here of course. Some I didn't consider suitable for a young girl. I hope Maria will agree with my taste."

Pippa looked down, and there sparkling and flashing in the morning sunshine streaming through the window were jewels and more jewels—more than she had ever seen. There were sapphires, shaped into cornflowers with tiny diamond centers, making a necklace and matching bracelet; golden amethysts; and a double strand of the most beautiful pearls she had ever beheld, creamy pink in color.

"These—were my mother's?" she whispered, stretching out tentative fingers to caress the lustrous pearls.

"Yes, and there is much more besides, most of it Cranville family jewelry that came to her on her marriage. Also a number of pieces that were gifts from your father. But these, I believe, were her own, given to her by her own family when she was a young girl. I hope Maria will not think them hopelessly old-fashioned."

"Oh, no, they are beautiful," she gasped, and then added defensively, fiercely, "and I would not care if they *were* old-fashioned, I should wear them anyway!"

"Gently, child, gently. Of course you shall," he said soothingly.

She picked up the sapphire necklace and held it up in the sunshine. "Where did you—I mean—have you kept them for me all this time, or did your father?"

"Neither of us. They were in Ayleforth Hall in the keeping of your aunt."

"And she never mentioned them to me," she said, making it a statement rather than a question. She felt the tears well up, blurring her eyes as she looked at the necklace, causing the glittering flashes to shimmer. "It would have meant so much to me to have seen them, to have known they were something of my mother's that belonged to me."

He could think of no reply, and could only look away helplessly, wondering why he must be so tongue-tied, first by his sympathy for her and then by his rage against an insensitive old woman who, as he well knew by now, had no thought to spare for anyone but herself.

"Well," she said with a small laugh, "why am I standing here sniveling? I have them now, and I am so grateful to you for thinking to ask her for them for me. You are very good to me, Sir Anthony."

"Nonsense! I'm only doing my duty as your guardian.

You must not refine too much upon it," he protested with embarrassment. "Now, I've some things to attend to and must be off. I will see you at dinner, to which Maria has very kindly invited me."

He left abruptly, leaving her still standing in the middle of the room, holding her mother's sapphire necklace and wondering if it were possible that such a sophisticated man of the world as Sir Anthony had blushed.

Tenderly she laid the various pieces back in their cases, then gathered them up and went off up to Lady Barstowe, the pride of ownership glowing in her eyes.

"Lord, what a want-wit I am," said Lady Barstowe as she opened the boxes, "it had completely flown out of my mind that you must of course have something to wear with your gowns of an evening."

"Are they—do you—do you think they will do?"

"*Do*? Dear child, they are just the thing! How can you ask?"

Pippa, in her relief, wanted to throw her arms around Lady Barstowe's neck, but was much too unused to demonstrations of affections to follow such an impulse. But she was greatly pleased that her mother's taste had found favor in Lady Barstowe's eye, as her taste was impeccable.

Luncheon was accompanied by a lively chatter as the three ladies discussed all the possibilities for fabric and cut offered by the sudden acquisition of the jewelry. Since the girls were much too excited to eat in any case, the party set off very shortly for Milsom Street, home of all the best shops, according to Lady Barstowe.

Pippa's head was switching back and forth so ceaselessly as they drove along that Melissa declared she was sure to have a stiff neck in the morning. Pippa couldn't be bothered to reply, so busy was she craning about to see the beautiful buildings and the even more beautiful people strolling along or passing by in their carriages.

"Oh, I do wish we were walking so I could see everything better," she cried.

"Sight-seeing, my dear child, your guardian will have to be responsible for. I will take you to the assembly rooms and to parties, but I abhor walking about just to look at buildings!"

"Oh, well, I don't know. . . ." Pippa's voiçe trailed away uncomfortably.

"Don't know what, my dear?" asked Lady Barstowe kindly.

"Well, I shouldn't like to bother him with trifles after all he's done for me already."

"Not trifles, at all, Pippa dear. After all, we are here so that you can see Bath, and I'm sure he will be delighted to make sure that you are entertained."

After Sir Anthony's tart reminder to her that he had his own business to attend to, Pippa was not quite so sanguine on this subject as Lady Barstowe seemed to be, but she decided it would be best not to pursue the matter. Perhaps, if she didn't pester her with her longings to see the sights, Lady Barstowe would forget all about it and would not mention it to Sir Anthony at all. Pippa would much rather that she did not, feeling that Sir Anthony would soon lose all patience with his ward if he felt her to be a millstone about his neck, continually clamoring for his time and attention. She wanted him to think of her as a reasonable adult who could be responsible for herself and her own entertainment.

With this thought she pulled her head back from the carriage window and sat back demurely in her seat, hands folded quietly in her lap, and assumed an expression of what she felt to be sophisticated boredom.

"Good heavens, Pippa, what a queer way you're holding your eyebrows," exclaimed the irrepressible Melissa. "Whatever is the matter? Do you have a stomachache?"

CHAPTER 10

Tony, with Pippa on one arm and Melissa on the other, strolled along, trying to maintain a dignified demeanor between the two chattering girls. Pippa was so brimming with excitement, she was fairly dancing.

Sir Anthony was escorting the girls to the Pump Room for Pippa's first venture into the society of Bath, and her first taste of the waters. Lady Barstowe was closeted with a seamstress and yards and yards of silks and muslins and dimities, fruits of the shopping expeditions of the past two days. She laughingly declined the honor of taking the girls on this first visit to the Pump Room.

"Let Tony take you, my dears. I find the place boring beyond words, all filled with such maggoty creatures as you never saw. I shall own myself astonished if you want to stay beyond a quarter of an hour."

Pippa was not discouraged in any way by this speech and, when Sir Anthony agreed to take them, begged him to allow them to walk there.

"I vow if I don't get some exercise soon, I'll lose the use of my limbs! Besides, I want to go along slowly and see everything!"

Sir Anthony agreed, since the Pump Room was no great distance at all from Laura Place, being just across the Pulteney Bridge. So they were now walking along, having the sights pointed out to them and whispering excitedly about some of the ladies' costumes.

The Pump Room itself was mobbed with people, walking up and down, sipping the waters. Sir Anthony took them to sign their names in the book and checked through to see if there were any acquaintances of his own in Bath.

"Good heavens, Strangeways is here! That is above everything great!" he exclaimed, turning around to survey the room eagerly.

"A friend of yours from London?" asked Pippa.

"From the West Indies actually. Oh, you will like him exceedingly, I assure you. He's a fine fellow!"

"Is he married, Sir Anthony?" inquired Melissa with an air of casual interest.

"No, you baggage, he is not, nor would he interest you in that way, being old enough to be your father," answered Tony, laughing.

"Oh" was Melissa's disinterested reply as she turned back to the book in search of names she knew.

"Come along, come along. I must take a look about for Strangeways. Haven't seen him since I returned to England. In fact I didn't know he had come back himself."

They pushed their way through the crowds without seeing any acquaintance, were given glasses of the mineral water to drink, and all agreed that it was nasty and therefore probably very healthful. After only a sip, all three discreetly disposed of their glasses.

"Well, Tony, is it really you?" said a voice behind them. Tony spun around, and there followed a most enthusiastic reunion between old friends, accompanied by much handshaking and backslapping. Finally Tony remembered the girls and turned with a grin of happiness to introduce his friend.

"Miss Cranville and the Honorable Melissa Barstowe—Mister Peregrine Strangeways."

The girls dropped their curtsies and shyly offered hands. The gentleman was most imposing: tall, slim, and with a thick mane of silvery white hair. Since his face was quite tanned, the effect was striking in the extreme.

"I can see that you have been much in the sun, sir. Did you come straight to Bath from the West Indies?" asked Pippa, smiling up into his eyes.

"Yes, I found it much too warm in London and—so few. . . ." His voice trailed away as he stared down at her. His face went quite still and he seemed to be far away.

Pippa became uneasy under his look, although he didn't really seem to see her. She turned to Sir Anthony questioningly.

"Strangeways? Is there anything wrong?" asked Tony, putting his hand on his friend's arm.

"Eh? What's that?" said Mr. Strangeways, turning slowly to Tony, his eyes rather dazed-looking.

"My dear fellow! What is it? Is there anything wrong?" asked Tony anxiously.

"No, no. Please, I do assure you that I am quite all right. Say no more about it. Now, young ladies, you must tell me of your impressions of Bath. Are you enjoying yourselves? Is this fellow taking you around? I hereby tender my services as an escort to anyplace you would like to go."

Naturally Pippa and Melissa were greatly intrigued by this gentleman. The contrast between his present cheerful animation and the inward-looking stillness of a moment ago could not have been greater. It had been as though he were listening to another voice from another place. However, they could not inquire about something he so obviously did not want to discuss.

Now he gallantly offered his arm to Pippa and said they must walk around and see if they could meet some of his or Sir Anthony's acquaintances to be introduced to. The crowds by this time had become even more pressing, and Pippa had to admit that Lady Barstowe was right: there were a great many elderly people in attendance, but there seemed to be a fair scattering of young people also, pushing their infirm relatives about in wheelchairs or supporting them on their arms.

They presently met the old Duchess of Haverford and her granddaughter, Lady Fanny, a pert, tomboyish young lady who promptly deserted her grandmother and, joining arms with Melissa, went off on a walk of exploration.

The duchess pulled Mr. Strangeways down beside her and began making inquiries of common friends, while Tony and Pippa stood before them, Tony making a contribution to the conversation from time to time, while Pippa became engrossed with watching the people passing by.

An extremely stout lady in a most unsuitably ruffled walking costume and a hat sporting several towering plumes suddenly espied the duchess and came bustling up, all smiles.

"Your Grace, how very fortunate. My son accompanies me today—now, where can he have got himself." She looked about worriedly. "Ah, well, he met a friend, no doubt, and will catch me up presently. How *are* you today, my dear madam? I hope you are finding the waters salubrious."

Throughout this speech the duchess had stared at the lady in astonishment, making it obvious to the rest of the party that she had no idea of who this woman could be. But being a gentle and well-bred lady, she pulled herself together and attempted to find out.

"I fear I am at a loss, madam—at my age one has these little lapses and must be forgiven. Perhaps if you could just refresh my—ah—"

"But we met only last night, Your Grace," cried the stout lady in disbelief, "at Lady Hereford's ridotto, and had such an interesting conversation about your granddaughter, Lady Fanny."

"Oh—oh, yes. Now I remember, you're the lady with

the son. Yes—Mrs.—ah. . . ." The duchess paused encouragingly for the name to be supplied.

"Mrs. Otway, Your Grace. Ah, you are naughty to have forgotten me so soon." She laughed heartily, if rather falsely. "I think you are but teasing me. I shall own myself astonished to learn that you have *really* forgotten our plans."

"Plans? I cannot recall any—oh, yes, I do remember your saying something about introducing your son to Fanny."

"There, you see! I knew you could not have truly forgotten," exclaimed the lady triumphantly.

"My dear Mrs.—er—Otway, please allow me to introduce my friends to you. Miss Philippa Cranville. Mister Peregrine Strangeways. Sir Anthony Seymour-Croft."

Mrs. Otway acknowledged these introductions with a speculative eye to Miss Cranville and coyly flirtatious smiles for the gentlemen. Then, with no hesitation, plumped herself down beside the duchess in the seat Mr. Strangeways had vacated upon her approach, saying that now she and the duchess could have a nice coze. The duchess threw a wild, pleading sort of look at Mr. Strangeways, who smiled reassuringly to let her know her friends would not abandon her to the mercies of this rapacious lady, who immediately bent toward the duchess and began murmuring rapidly in her ear several *on dit*s she had picked up during her morning stroll through the Pump Room. Since these were obviously not meant for the ears of the rest of the party, they hastily began talking together.

"Tony, dear fellow, I was very sorry to hear the news of your father's death. How fortunate that you had arrived back in England."

"A sad thing, but not a lingering illness fortunately."

"Will you be going back soon, or do you plan to make a long stay in England? I suppose, since you did so well on that last venture, you really have no need to go again soon."

"Oh, well, as to that I fear it will be much sooner than I had originally planned." He glanced nervously at Pippa, but was reassured to see that she was not attending closely to their words, being too engrossed in looking around. "We will talk of this later, Strangeways. I would like to ask your advice on certain subjects, if I may?"

"Anytime, dear fellow, anytime. Only too happy, as you must know. Could we have supper tonight and discuss it?"

"Delighted. You'll take supper with me at the White Hart. They do you very well there."

Pippa, meanwhile, had caught the eye of an engagingly handsome young man standing with a group of other men in conversation. She had looked away quickly but could not prevent her eyes from sliding around toward him again and again to find him staring at her. She dropped her eyes but was aware that he was now excusing himself from his friends and making his way toward her.

He was not above medium height, but so trimly built, he seemed taller than he was. His hair was a light brown, curling down over his forehead, and his eyes were brown and smiling. With his fine complexion and strong profile he was altogether a most prepossessing young man.

"Mama," he exclaimed as he neared them, "I see you have found some friends. I'm sorry that we became separated, but see now how easily I have found you at last."

"Naughty boy, I don't think you have been looking for me at all," said Mrs. Otway, reaching out for his hand and pulling him possessively to her. "Dear Duchess, you will allow me to present my son, Mister Sidney Otway, to you."

Mr. Otway disengaged his hand from his mother's and stepped forward to bow gallantly to the duchess.

"Mister Otway," the duchess acknowledged pleasantly, "I've heard many good things of you from your mother."

"Mothers tend to exaggerate, Your Grace, as I'm sure you know. I hope she has not been boring on forever about me. If she has, you must forgive her. I am her only child, and she must needs pour out an excess of maternal feelings on my own undeserving self."

This charming disclaimer could not help but make a good impression on the company, who all looked now with more interest upon the young man, forgiving him for having such a dreadful, pushing mother.

"There now, dear Duchess, did I not tell you that I had a most exceptional son? Now, please do not wander away again, Sidney. I want you to meet the duchess's granddaughter, Lady Fanny. Such a charming creature."

The duchess made Mr. Otway acquainted with the rest of the party, but before she could enter into a general chat with them, her attention was again claimed by Mrs. Otway, whispering urgently into her ear, no doubt listing all the marvelous qualities of her son.

He turned to the two gentlemen and spoke a few words to each and then turned to Pippa.

"Is this your first visit to the Pump Room, Miss Cranville?"

"Indeed, it is my first visit to Bath, sir. I like it exceedingly, do not you?"

"Most certainly, and more now than at any time previously," he replied meaningfully, and adroitly managed to edge her slightly away from the rest of the party and quite casually turn his back to them. This maneuver was watched with amusement by Mr. Strangeways and with irritation by Sir Anthony.

"Oh, you have been here many times then? How very fortunate for you," exclaimed Pippa, completely missing his compliment, which she was not experienced enough to recognize.

"Yes, we come every year for a few weeks, but it has never been so—interesting—as it is now," replied Mr.

Otway, looking directly into her eyes in an effort to make sure she took his meaning.

Pippa responded to this sally with an open, candid smile and replied, "I am so happy to hear you say so, sir, for I would hate my first visit to Bath to be during an uninteresting time."

Mr. Otway realized ruefully that his flirtation was not having its usual effect, but he was more titillated by this knowledge than discouraged. The girl might not be up to the way the game was played, but she was a stunner, and after all, it was rather refreshing to meet such an innocent, he thought. *Yes, by gad, much more interesting than the usual girls one meets. A real challenge! I must think of a whole new plan of action.*

However, before he could carry out any new campaign, Lady Fanny and Melissa returned and Mrs. Otway called her son to her side. Everyone watching the encounter was aware that Mrs. Otway was doing her best to promote the interests of her son with the duchess and Lady Fanny, and all felt embarrassed for him.

Lady Fanny responded to the introduction carelessly, but not ungraciously. She was but sixteen, but had been much in the company of the great and the near-great, and so had more poise than usual for a girl of her age. Melissa was obviously enchanted with her, and Pippa could not help liking her and envying her self-possession. She also experienced another pang, which she did not recognize as jealousy. She only felt, regretfully, that Mr. Otway could surely have no further interest in herself after meeting this fashionably dressed, attractive young granddaughter of a duchess.

CHAPTER 11

Lady Barstowe sat at the pianoforte idly playing the melody of a new piece of music she had received that day from a friend in London. Melissa and Pippa sat before the fire with their embroidery frames, though neither could be said to have set more than a few stitches in the hour since dinner. Since Sir Anthony was engaged to dine with Mr. Strangeways, the three ladies had spent an uneventful, but contented, evening together.

Melissa was chattering away happily about their visit to the Pump Room and the people they had met there, especially her new friend, Lady Fanny.

"I know you will like her as much as I do when you know her better, Pippa. She is beyond anything great!"

"I'm sure I shall," agreed Pippa absently, staring into the flames.

"We have agreed to meet again tomorrow at the Pump Room and you must talk with her then. I'm afraid I rather monopolized her today."

Pippa merely glanced up fleetingly to smile, and then her eyes were drawn back to the fire. Melissa stared at her friend for a moment, then a glint of mischief appeared in her eyes.

"Or perhaps you will not have the time," she suggested teasingly.

"Not have the time? Whatever do you mean, Melissa?" asked Pippa.

"Perhaps *your* new friend will keep you so occupied, you'll have no time to spare for Lady Fanny."

"My new friend?"

"Yes. Now what was his name? I met him so briefly—Mr. Otway was it?"

Pippa felt her face turn pink in spite of herself, though she had not been thinking of him at all at that moment. She had thought of him pleasurably when she had first sat down, and wondered—hoped—she would see him the next day again, for she thought she had never seen so handsome a young man, and with such a charming, open way about him. And then she had thought of Mr. Strangeways and wondered again about the disturbing way he had stared at her. From that her thoughts had wandered to the dinner he was having with Sir Anthony tonight, and then to the kindness of Sir Anthony from the very beginning of their acquaintance. How understanding he had been with her, and how patient. These thoughts led to ones of Aunt Emma. For some reason she could not fathom, she felt less than tranquil in her mind about Aunt Emma. In spite of the years of coldness and neglect, Pippa's own happiness now made her think more kindly of her aunt. *How terrible for her, all alone in that great house*, she thought, *while I am here in delightful company, going about and meeting new people and being lavished with attention. Perhaps she would welcome a note from me. In fact it is surely my duty to write her and at least inform her of our safe arrival. I will write to her tonight before I go to bed.* She had just reached this resolution when Melissa interrupted her thoughts with her teasing suggestion.

"Really, Melissa, I can't think what you mean by referring to him as '*my* new friend,'" she protested. "I did but meet him briefly. We spoke a very few casual words about Bath and then you came up with Lady Fanny."

"Well, he seemed to me most particular in his attentions to you," declared Melissa.

"Pooh, nonsense, nothing of the kind."

"And do not tell me you were not most pleasantly impressed, for I saw you blushing and casting down your eyes shyly when he took your hand to say good-bye."

"How ridiculous you are! But there, you are still a child and one must not expect too much. But you really should strive for a little more conduct, Melissa," said Pippa loftily.

"A child! I suppose your one year—"

"Nearly two!"

"—makes you so much more an adult? Besides, in experience I am certainly the senior."

"Indeed!" Lady Barstowe said, rising from the pianoforte and coming forward, "I should be most interested to know what that experience might be."

"Oh—well, I only meant, Mama, that I had been about more in company than Pippa and—"

"And—do go on, dear child," encouraged Lady Barstowe interestedly.

"Well—that I had—had—more experience in *observing*," Melissa replied, somewhat triumphantly at having been inspired with just the right word to avoid the awful pitfall she saw waiting just ahead. There *had* been that rather unsuitable young man last winter whose outrageous flirtation she had encouraged though she knew her mother would have forbidden it had she known.

Lady Barstowe's lips twitched, but her only comment was "Hmm."

Pippa was less restrained. "You may have been about more, but since you're always chattering, I doubt very much that your powers of observation have had much practice!" she answered tartly.

"Ah, me, you grow more like sisters every day," sighed Lady Barstowe. "Now, let us take ourselves to our beds.

We need an early night, for the dressmaker comes here for you immediately after breakfast, Pippa, and then I'm sure you'll both want to be jauntering about Bath all day."

"I think I will just stay down for a few more moments and write a line or two to Aunt Emma," said Pippa.

"What? Great heavens, Pippa, I thought you could not bear the woman and—"

"Melissa," said Lady Barstowe with a quelling glance, "Pippa is doing just as she ought. Just because it is difficult, one should not shirk one's duty. Pippa owes it to her aunt to write to her from time to time. Now come along up with me and leave her to herself so that she can order her thoughts. I'm sure no one could concentrate with you here talking all the while."

Pippa went to the morning room, where there was a desk and stationery, and, after many false starts and scratchings out and crumpled sheets, produced a letter.

Dear Aunt Emma,

We are settled in Bath, after a pleasant journey, in a very grand house on Laura Place, with three drawing rooms and a very fine view of the countryside. I find Bath a beautiful city, though as yet I have seen very little of it. We went today to the Pump Room, where people stroll about and drink the waters (very nasty!). Sir Anthony introduced us to his special friend, Mr. Strangeways, who in turn introduced us to friends of his, the Duchess of Haverford and her granddaughter, Lady Fanny, and through them we met a Mrs. Otway and her son, Mr. Sidney Otway. So though we came with no acquaintance at all, we have now met five people, all very pleasant (except for Mrs. Otway, who didn't seem to me to be so very nice, though I know it is wrong to judge her on such very short acquaintance). That is all I can think to tell you now, but I will be sure to write again soon and tell you of all we are doing.

Sincerely,
Your niece,
Philippa Cranville

Tony and Mr. Strangeways sat comfortably relaxed over the remains of their dinner in a small private room at the White Hart. There was a small fire to take away the chill of the evening, and Tony, idly twisting the stem of his wineglass, had been staring into it silently for some time. Mr. Strangeways glanced at him from time to time, but was content to wait for his friend to be ready to speak of whatever it was that troubled him.

Finally Tony looked up and smiled apologetically. "I fear I am being less than entertaining as a host, sir."

"Not at all, my boy, not at all. I am most comfortable. A fine meal, a good fire, and good company. I like a friend I can be quiet with as well as talk with."

"Very kind. By the way, I meant to ask you before, are you quite recovered?"

"Recovered? I don't know what—"

"I refer to this afternoon, sir. I was fearful for a moment that you had become ill. You turned quite pale, you know."

"Oh, that was nothing at all. The girl struck me as—oh—familiar, I suppose you could say, though I'm sure I've never met her before."

"No, you could not have, for she has never been away from her home before. She was my father's ward, and I have inherited the responsibility, and therein lies much of my problem."

"Take your time, my boy, the night is young," said Mr. Strangeways, reaching out to refill both their glasses.

So Tony began, hesitantly at first, to tell of the terrible state of affairs prevailing now after his father's death and of what steps he had taken to amend the situation, including the restitution of the Cranville legacy from his own newly made fortune.

"My dear fellow, how very dreadful," was Mr. Strangeways's restrained comment.

"Yes. Well, there it is, the whole sorry tale, and now I must decide what I must do."

"I'm sure you know how privileged I would feel to help you, Tony. I've more than I'll ever need in my lifetime, and no one to spend it on."

"Good God, sir, say no more, I beg of you. I would never dream—please say no more on that subject. I've a few pounds left to make a new start. I thought perhaps you would know if there were any ships going out."

"Then you're going back to the islands?"

"No, no, but I could invest what I have in a cargo going out and when it's sold there invest in sugar coming back. A few of those would see me able to come about again. It would, of course, be better for me to go out there myself, but I wouldn't like to go away for that length of time and leave Miss Cranville."

"Ah, I see. Well, of course I think my man of business in London could put you on to something. Shall I write to him?"

"No need. I will go up to London myself in a week. And that is where you can help me. I promise it won't be too unpleasant a task."

"Anything at all, dear boy, only name it."

"If you could take my place with my ward, keep your eye on her, and keep me informed of everything. You see, she is so innocent, and such an heiress, apart from being exceedingly pretty, that I fear every fortune hunter in town will be dangling after her in a matter of days. That young whelp Otway wasted no time today."

"True. But I don't think we need worry too much about him. His mother wants a title with the fortune he marries.

She's a social climber. I've met her a number of times these past few years and seen her at work."

"Yes, but Miss Cranville won't know that and might fall in love with someone like that, an accomplished flirt if I ever saw one, and get her heart broken."

"But see here, Tony, if you are worried, there is surely no need for you to take yourself away to London. We could contrive to do the whole thing by post, through my man in London and a draft on your bank."

"No, there is another problem. If I am here, I'll have all these fortune hunters applying to me for permission to pay their addresses, and if I refuse, what will they say? That I'm saving her and her fortune for myself. That damned aunt of hers has already said it. If my pockets were not to let right now, I'd ignore that kind of talk, but since I've hardly a shilling to bless myself with—well, you can see—"

"Yes, a pretty predicament indeed. Well, well, calm yourself. You know that I will be more than happy to act as your agent, if Miss Cranville will have me. The aunt sounds a sticky problem, I must say."

"Indeed she is," said Tony feelingly, "you would hardly credit such a situation, Strangeways. There they were, rattling about together in that enormous house, rarely speaking to each other, never going out, no friends. It was an intolerable situation for the poor child. The aunt has simply detached herself from life entirely, from what I can see. She cares for no one and refuses to have anything to do with the problem of preparing her niece to take her proper place in society. My father neglected his duty there shamefully, though I hate to admit it of him. I feel I must make it up to her now. She is a most—engaging—child."

"Yes, she is that," replied Mr. Strangeways with a carefully veiled scrutiny of the eager, young face before him. *Ah-ha*, he thought, *now I do begin to wonder what is here.*

"Well, there it all is. I cannot tell you how much better I feel about things for having spilled it all out to you. I've had no one I could really tell the whole thing to, especially about my father. He was a good man, you know, but somewhat misguided in money matters."

"Probably just took some bad advice. Not to worry, dear Tony, you'll come about, I'm sure of it, and meantime I shall make myself available to the adorable Miss Cranville with all the pleasure in the world. If I had had a daughter, I should have liked her to be just such a girl."

The very next morning Tony presented himself at Laura Place with Mr. Strangeways in tow. They found the ladies still at the breakfast table and, at Lady Barstowe's urging, seated themselves and accepted coffee.

"My dear Lady Barstowe, I believe I was acquainted with your husband, though I never had the pleasure of meeting you."

"That must have been some time ago, sir. He has been dead for five years now."

"And how is it that such a beautiful, young widow has not been snapped up long ago?" he quizzed gently.

"Oh, la, sir, I am not so eager to enter the married state again. I enjoy myself very much as I am, as I make no doubt you do yourself."

Mr. Strangeways laughed at this tart rejoinder. "Touché, madam. Though I must admit I would have liked to marry, had it been my good fortune to meet a young lady who would have had me."

"Pooh. I should own myself astonished to learn that there were less than a dozen brokenhearted ladies at present in England who had flung themselves at your head and been rejected. I fear you have been too nice in your tastes, Mister Strangeways."

"Perhaps you are right, Lady Barstowe. Or perhaps the women are prettier now, for I vow if I were but a few years younger, I should waste no time trying to attach your affections."

Lady Barstowe smiled prettily in acknowledgment of this compliment and wondered for a brief moment just what his age would be. But, no—she stopped herself—it would never do.

Tony informed the girls that they had come to escort them to the Pump Room this morning, and both girls jumped up immediately, saying they must change.

"Now, now, Pippa, have you forgotten? The seamstress will be here any moment. You must give her an hour or you'll never have any dresses to go out in the evening."

Pippa's face fell with disappointment, and Tony hastily assured her that they would wait for her. She wanted to throw her arms about him in gratitude, but she only smiled with her whole heart and hoped he'd know how grateful she was.

CHAPTER 12

Daily attendance at the Pump Room did indeed improve Pippa's acquaintance with Lady Fanny, and Pippa grew to like her very much, but Fanny was quite obviously much more in tune with Melissa. The two girls greeted each other rapturously each morning and were to be seen for the next hour marching about the rooms arm in arm, whispering and giggling together. Pippa spent more of her time with Sir Anthony and Mr. Strangeways and was introduced to many people who treated her very kindly.

She could not prevent herself from searching the rooms for sight of Mr. Otway as soon as she was inside, and more often than not he was present. He always came straight to her side and spent most of his visit with her, under the watchful eyes of Tony and Mr. Strangeways.

During the afternoons they were taken on various expeditions about the city: to see the Abbey Church just across from the Pump Room and the beautiful carving on the West Front of the angels and saints going up and down the ladder to heaven. They visited the labyrinth at Sydney Gardens, took tea with the duchess, shopped for slippers and gloves and ribbons, and had fittings for new gowns.

But the peak of the first week was when Lady Barstowe announced that, the first gown being finished, they would attend the assembly in the upper rooms that evening. Excitement reached a fever pitch.

Pippa's gown, of palest yellow gauze over silk, had tiny

puffed sleeves and a daringly low-cut corsage. It was laid out now across her bed as she sat in her chemise, with a towel about her shoulders, having her hair arranged by a woman Lady Barstowe had hired.

Cassie, the maid from Ayleforth Hall, had been elevated to abigail for both girls and was standing beside the dressing table, lower lip caught in her teeth as she concentrated on the ministrations of the hairdresser. She was determined to learn to do the misses' hair herself in future.

After vigorously wielding the hairbrush, causing Pippa's hair to crackle with electricity, the hairdresser sighed with pleasure.

"Such wonderful hair, miss. You should congratulate yourself on possessing such hair. So thick it is, the likes I've never seen, and curly withal. Ah, there's nothing we can't do with such hair."

"I was wondering. I saw a young woman today—ever so stylish she looked. Her hair was cut short, close to her head, all little tight curls—"

"*À la Titus!* Surely you would not be asking me to cut off this hair. Why, I would refuse to do it!"

"Oh—well, I only thought—"

"Now just you leave yourself to me, miss. I know just what would be best. Of course, nothing could be so beautiful as to wear it just as it is, falling straight down your back, but of course that would never do. No, I think *à la Grecque* would be perfect."

As she talked the woman began expertly arranging the hair up and back and into a knot, from which spilled a foam of hair that she curled into ringlets with the curling tongs. When all was set in place, she took a long pale yellow satin ribbon and wound it around and around Pippa's head. She finished and stepped back to survey her work, then gave a satisfied nod.

"There you are, miss, suits you a treat if I do say. Now I'd best be off to the other miss and Lady Barstowe. Mind you step into that gown and not try pulling it over your head."

Trembling with excitement, Cassie, the abigail, lifted the delicate gown and held it for Pippa to step into, then buttoned it up the back. Dainty satin slippers to match were tied by their ribbons around Pippa's ankles, and then Cassie reached for the necklace.

This was the amethyst and pearl necklace left to Pippa by her mother, and the silk and gauze of the gown had been chosen especially for it. The matching bracelet was fastened about her wrist, and Cassie led her to the full-length mirror.

Pippa gasped with pleasure at this first sight of herself. Never had she looked so fine, she thought, and wondered if Sir Anthony would approve. Then she whirled away from the mirror and headed for the door.

"Miss, watch how you go! Don't get yourself all in a lather or muss your gown!" warned Cassie.

"I'll be careful—but I must show Melissa and Lady Barstowe. Do you think they will like me?"

"Oh, miss—and you like an angel!"

Pippa laughed happily and ran down the hall to Melissa's room.

After being exclaimed over by Melissa, herself fetching in blue, and approved complacently by Lady Barstowe, Pippa was sent to put on her long white kid gloves and find her fan before going down to greet Tony and Mr. Strangeways, who had just arrived to escort the ladies to the ball.

She felt quite shy as she entered the drawing room and the two gentlemen turned from their contemplation of the fire to greet her.

They both stood stock-still for a moment, staring at her in a most gratifying way. *Surely this must be pleased surprise they are expressing*, she thought. *Yes, yes, now they are both smiling—I can see they approve.*

Tony came forward and took both her hands in his, and stood so, smiling into her eyes.

"Well, my dear," he said finally, "you look charming."

"Come now, Tony, is that the best you can do," said Mr. Strangeways, coming forward. "I can say it much better. Miss Cranville, you are beautiful—no less a word will do for such an enchanting picture as you present. I shall claim the privilege of my great age to kiss you." And he did so.

"You shall turn my head completely, sir, with such gallantries," said Pippa happily.

"Young, beautiful women should have their heads turned," he declared.

"Before you use your privilege any further, I shall exercise my own and ask the honor of the first dance with my own ward," laughed Tony.

Pippa dropped him a curtsy. "With pleasure, sir."

"And I shall claim the second, for if I wait till we arrive, I shall find myself out of fortune, as you will have no free dances five minutes after your appearance, I'm sure," said Mr. Strangeways.

"Mister Strangeways, I hope I am not so poor spirited as to say I would not find that most gratifying, but I fear it cannot be so. Among so many I will hardly be noticed."

She said this with a small tone of regret and with nothing at all in her voice to convey an angling for further compliments.

Mr. Strangeways thought he had never met such a young woman. She had no coyness about her, no shyness or giggling, but looked you straight in the eye when she spoke to you and said just what she thought. He also thought that these admirable qualities would very shortly vanish and be replaced by the others when she learned that was not the way young ladies were supposed to behave in society—most unfortunately.

* * *

Their entrance into the assembly rooms caused all the sensation that could have been wished for. Lady Barstowe, resplendent in pale green and diamonds, led the way on Mr. Strangeways's arm, and the girls came behind, one on either side of Sir Anthony. Lady Barstowe seemed to know everyone in the room, and they were soon surrounded by her friends, and by an eager swarm of young men, clamoring for an introduction to the young ladies. Soon they had both promised more dances than they could remember.

Pippa had searched in vain for sight of Sidney Otway and felt a rush of disappointment that he was not there to witness her popularity. It had never entered her mind that he would not be there, but now she realized how foolish she had been. There was really no reason in the world to suppose that he would come tonight. It had not been mentioned between them at any of their meetings in the Pump Room, but Pippa had felt sure that *everyone* must attend the assemblies.

Melissa, looking around at that moment as they made their way to a sofa at the side of the room, said casually, "I don't see Mister Otway here tonight, Pippa. But perhaps he will come later."

Yes, of course, thought Pippa with a welling happiness, *he is bound to come before the evening is over.*

"My dear Miss Cranville," Tony said at the end of the dance, "I must own myself surprised. I had not expected to find you such an accomplished dancer, since I know this is your first ball."

"Aunt Emma provided a good dancing master. Though I have wondered why, since she obviously had no plans in mind for me to put my skills to use."

"No doubt she felt that providing you with the teachers was the extent of her responsibility. Ah, I see your next partner approaching."

"My dance, I believe, Miss Cranville," Mr. Strangeways

said, holding out his arm to her. "You will excuse us, Tony?" He led her to the floor, where sets were being made up for a lively country dance. As they skipped together to the end of the floor she dropped him a curtsy, looking up with her sparkling amber eyes, her cheeks flushed from the exercise, lips parted in their happiest smile.

As he smiled down at her he again felt a strange sensation of having seen her just this way before. He was in better control of himself now than he had been that first day in the Pump Room and managed to laughingly pull her arm through his own and lead her back to Lady Barstowe, where her next dancing partner awaited her.

He watched her dancing and tried again to recapture the feeling he had just experienced. But the mind is capricious, and the feeling would not come at his bidding, the curtain would not part again. He would simply have to wait for it. But his heart was beating rather uncomfortably, and it was not the dancing that had caused it to do so. He could only hope that at last, after so many empty years— He would not allow himself to finish the thought.

Pippa was enjoying her first ball enormously, in spite of her disappointment that Mr. Otway had not arrived. Her partners, one after the other, were all pleasant company and paid her outrageous compliments, which she managed to accept unblushing, since she thought this was the way young men were supposed to speak to young women in society.

During one set, which she had begged her partner to sit out with her, saying that her feet must be given a rest, she noticed that Sir Anthony was dancing with Lady Barstowe. Lady Barstowe's gay laugh trilled out at some remark of his, and then he also began to laugh, and it was clear that they were enjoying themselves enormously. For some reason this realization caused a slight darkening of the brilliance of Pippa's evening. She suddenly felt extremely weary and slightly chilled. *I wonder if they—but, no—she is much too old for him; she must be quite thirty-eight at least and should really not be flirting with him in that way for everyone to see.* But then she pulled herself up sharply. How could she be thinking of dearest Lady Barstowe in such a coldly critical way after all her kindness? *I hope I am not grown so selfish that I would begrudge anyone else having some happiness, and after all, she is beautiful and it is no wonder he finds her attractive. It is perfectly possible he has been in love with her these many years and now that she is free to wed again, he has hopes of attaching her affections.* This thought did nothing to raise Pippa's spirits, though why she should be so cast into the glooms, she could not fathom.

She looked away from the sight of them and turned to her partner with such a blinding smile that that young gentleman felt encouraged to ask if she would allow him to call for her in his carriage the next day and take her for a drive. Before she could answer, she heard someone say her name and turned to find Mr. Otway smiling down at her.

"Why, Mister Otway, how pleasant to see you here," she said, her heart jumping with gladness. "I had thought you would not attend this evening."

"My mother had one of her boring dinner parties and I was unable to break away till this moment. I hope you will give me the pleasure of a dance. In fact several dances."

"Well, I will—" And then she stopped, looking up at him with dismay, for it was not until this moment that she realized she had promised every dance. Why, oh, why, had she not realized that she should have held at least one open for later in the evening in the possibility that he might appear? She had just assumed that of course she would dance with him if he came, not realizing in the joy of being sought after that she was giving away any opportunity.

"Good heavens, Miss Cranville, what can I have said to have caused such a look on your face?" he teased. "Have I gravy spots on my cravat?"

"Oh, no, no—you see, I'm very much afraid I have no dances unpromised, Mister Otway. Oh, dear, I am also being rude. Mister Jameson, have you met Mister Otway?" she asked, turning with confusion to her partner, who had been patiently waiting.

The gentlemen acknowledged each other's presence courteously, if unenthusiastically, Mr. Jameson obviously desiring this intruder to take himself off as quickly as possible, and Mr. Otway just as obviously determined not to oblige him.

"Ahem—as we were saying, Miss Cranville," said Mr. Jameson, leaning close and speaking softly to indicate that it was a private conversation, "I should be delighted if you would accept." He cast a glance up at the blandly smiling Mr. Otway, a slight frown appearing on his brow.

"Er—I fear tomorrow will not be—I am so sorry," intervened Pippa hastily, "perhaps another day in the week."

"Certainly. I shall call around if I may, and we can settle on a time."

"That would be very nice," Pippa said with more eagerness in her voice than she would have used ordinarily, but she felt guilty about his unhappiness at Mr. Otway's interruption of their *tête-à-tête*. His face now brightened and he stared at her in a bemused sort of way.

Before he could pull himself together and take advantage of having her complete attention at last, there was a further interruption, as the set finished and Pippa's next dancing partner appeared to claim her.

Mr. Otway did not come to her side for the next several dances, but she was always very much aware of where in the room he was and was decidedly depressed when she saw him leading a giggling, but entrancing looking, Lady Fanny to the floor.

Several sets later she was sitting with Lady Barstowe, Mr. Strangeways, and Sir Anthony when her next partner approached. This young man was obviously making a debut appearance in society himself, being half a head shorter than Pippa, with rather protruding ears and a distressing habit of blushing every time he spoke. When he had, with great difficulty, managed to stutter out a request for a dance with her, Pippa had instantly assured him that she would be delighted. She felt sorry for the young man, and now, as he stood before her, the blood flooding his cheeks as he tried to maintain his poise and speak coherently, she nodded and smiled at him encouragingly. Lady Barstowe twitted him gently upon the elegance of his cravat and both the older men contributed pleasantries in an effort to put the young man at ease.

Just as the fiddlers began tuning for the next dance, Mr. Otway appeared.

"Well, Miss Cranville, I declare that it is now my turn, whether or no. You must dance with me."

"I would most happily, Mister Otway, had I not promised this one to Mister Watkins."

"Oh, Watkins won't mind, greatest fellow in the world, always most accommodating, aren't you, Watkins? We are old friends; I've known him since he was in leading strings." And so saying, he began leading Pippa away.

"But—I—Mister Otway—" Pippa protested in great confusion, for she wanted with all her heart to dance with him but knew what they were doing was not right. She cast an apologetic smile back at the stunned-looking Mr. Watkins and caught also expressions varying from disapproval to outrage on the faces of the older people.

But a waltz was being played and she was very young. It was her first waltz, and she was more than a little infatuated with the very handsome Mr. Otway, and she allowed herself to be swept away into the joy of it all without dwelling on anything else. His hand at her waist sent small electric tingles through her skin, the room spun deliciously, and she was aware only of blissful happiness.

CHAPTER 13

Though Lady Barstowe greeted Pippa when they met at the breakfast table the next morning, there was such gravity in her manner that it was perfectly clear to Pippa that she had come under the lady's displeasure.

After enduring for several moments the silence that followed the greeting, Pippa burst out, "I am indeed sorry that I behaved in such a way to make you unhappy, Lady Barstowe!"

"I felt quite sure you were aware of what was wrong in your conduct last evening, dear child, and would regret it very much when you gave it more thought."

"Yes, it was ill done in me, and I did regret it very much when I came to reflect," Pippa said humbly. However, even though she knew she had cause to feel shame, she could not admit that she had only given the matter thought this morning. After her waltz with Mr. Otway, the rest of the previous evening became a blur for her. She knew that she had danced all the dances, spoken with each partner, been driven home in the carriage with Melissa by Mr. Strangeways, Lady Barstowe following with Sir Anthony, but there were no distinct images of these events in her mind. She had gone straight up to her bed and fallen into a heavy sleep, in which the face of Mr. Otway had figured prominently in her dreams.

But the clear light of morning had brought more sobering thoughts, and she was able to remember very definitely the look in Sir Anthony's eyes as he bid her goodnight. It was very much like the one facing her across the breakfast table now.

"Yes, it was ill done, but it can be excused by the stress of the moment, by your youth and inexperience, even by the fact that Mister Otway is ever so much more desirable as a dancing partner than Mister Watkins. But for *him* to behave so was reprehensible! To take advantage of Mister Watkins's youth and lack of social polish in such a way was the outside of enough! I fear I shall have trouble being civil to Mister Otway when next we meet."

"Oh, please, Lady Barstowe, do not say so! I'm sure he meant no harm, and I am the one who was responsible, after all. He has always been everything that is courteous with me. I don't think he quite realized—"

"I think he realized very well what he was doing, Pippa. He knew you were not free to stand up with him and he waited until he saw a man younger and greener than himself who would not know how to prevent his taking you away. Oh, yes, say what you will, I am sure of it."

Pippa felt her eyes filling with tears during this speech, but she could not think of how to defend Mr. Otway's conduct. She could not help but feel that there was some truth in what Lady Barstowe was saying, and she wished, now, that he had not done it, but she also could not help excusing him since he had done it in order to dance with her. Any young girl, or even an old one, would have had to respond with gladness to the compliment implied, or at least she must if that very dance was what she also desired with all her heart.

Lady Barstowe was unable to withstand the stricken look on Pippa's face.

"There, there, my dear. We'll say no more about it. Perhaps you will be very kind to Mister Watkins when next you see him. Now, what are your plans for today?"

"I don't know—I hadn't—" began Pippa, swallowing in an effort to stop her tears.

"Well, there are a number of cards here offering all sorts of entertainment in the days to come. When Melissa gets up, we must go through them together and decide which ones you will like to attend. And I would imagine, after your success of last night, there will be morning callers, so you had best finish up your breakfast."

But this last kindly spoken speech served to break down Pippa's last defense, and she rose and fled the breakfast room, calling back in a choked voice, "Excuse me, dear Lady Barstowe, I must—"

She managed to gain the privacy of her room, where she flung herself across her bed and sobbed brokenheartedly, berating herself for an ill-mannered, ungrateful wretch, overgrown in conceit of herself under all the compliments and gallantries she had received this past week, who deserved no better than to be sent back to the country and abandoned. This brought on a fresh outburst of tears, for the thought brought the stern, disapproving face of Sir Anthony into her mind, and she knew she could not hope to escape his censure so easily as she had Lady Barstowe's.

She felt she would never be able to redeem herself in his eyes, he must surely despise her now and wish he had not expended so much kindness upon her. A pall of black despair descended upon her, for she knew that it was *his* esteem that was most important to her, more than Lady Barstowe's or Mr. Strangeways's. How could she have displayed such a lamentable want of conduct before someone whose good opinion of herself she wanted so desperately? How could she ever face him again? He would surely call around this morning . . . ! This realization brought her sitting up straight, the sobbing stilled to hiccups.

Good heavens! If I don't stop crying, my eyes will be so red and swollen, I won't be able to leave my room all day. She rose wearily and went to the washstand in the corner to pour some cold water into the basin.

Although she was honestly ashamed of herself for what she had done, it must also be reported that the release of emotions she had just experienced was not an altogether unpleasant one. Never having indulged in crying fits as a child, she had never allowed herself unrestrained surrender to her sensibilities and was unfamiliar with the cleansing properties of such an indulgence. She felt drained now, almost languorous, but better. She was unaware that a young girl in the throes of her first love affair needed the outlet of tears.

She was still bathing her swollen eyes when Cassie came to tell her that there were gentlemen below and Lady Barstowe would like her to come down.

Cassie helped her to rearrange her hair into some semblance of order, and a survey of her somewhat puffy face showed her that the signs of her tears were still apparent, but she decided that if she smiled and behaved in a gay and easy manner, perhaps it would not be noticed.

But it was very hard to follow such a program when she entered the drawing room to be confronted by Sir Anthony and a shyly smiling Mr. Watkins!

"Good morning, Miss Cranville," said Sir Anthony. "I found Mister Watkins camped on your doorstep when I arrived and brought him in with me." He divided a smile between her and the young man and stood back, clearly indicating that he left further conversation to her.

In spite of her dismay at being faced so immediately with what she had been dreading only a few moments before, she didn't hesitate for an instant, but went straight up to Mr. Watkins, hand extended.

"This is too kind of you, Mister Watkins. I quite feared, after my disgraceful exhibition of bad manners last night, that you would wash your hands of me. I hope you will put it down to the inexperience of a green country girl at her first ball."

Mr. Watkins, blushing scarlet, took her hand reverently in his own. "Not at all, I mean to say—please do not—I would never think—" This confused tangle of sentences halted abruptly as he bent jerkily and planted a kiss on the hand he still held. Then, as though suddenly aware of what he had done, he dropped her hand and blushed even more furiously, then opened his mouth, but could bring forth no sound at all. He looked about at the other people in the room, desperately seeking assistance.

"Very handsome of you, Mister Watkins. I'm sure Philippa is as grateful for your forgiveness as I am," said Lady Barstowe, coming forward and taking his arm. "Won't you sit with us for a while? We've all been longing for callers so that we can discuss the company at the assembly last night." So saying, she lead him to a sofa, where he subsided gratefully.

Lady Barstowe, with practiced ease and great kindness, set about drawing all of them into conversation. In a few moments Melissa came dancing into the room, looking as fresh and rested as though she had slept the clock around, demanding to know what the plans were for the day.

Before the possibilities could be explored, Mr. Strangeways was announced, and Pippa, who had not yet made her peace with Sir Anthony, was faced with another of the people she had offended the night before. When he took her hand in his and smiled down at her so sweetly, so encouragingly, she felt a lump swell in her throat. *I have done nothing to deserve such good friends*, she thought.

The next half hour passed most pleasantly, while plans were bruited about, and it was finally decided that they would all go in a party to further explore the delights of Sydney Gardens and take some refreshment there.

It was decided that Lady Barstowe, Mr. Strangeways,

Melissa, and Mr. Watkins would be driven in Sir Anthony's carriage, while Pippa would be driven by Sir Anthony in the phaeton, which only held two, since he announced that there were several things it was necessary for him to discuss with his ward. Pippa developed small fluttery feelings of fear in her diaphragm at this portentous announcement, but made no comment, feeling that she must face the music some time anyway and it would be best got out of the way.

Mr. Watkins's face fell a trifle, but he was not seriously displeased. Melissa had been teasing him outrageously since she came in, and he responded to it with nothing of his usual stammering and reddening. He said she reminded him of his sister, who treated him the same way, and laughed amiably at whatever she said.

As soon as the carriage was moving along steadily and Pippa felt Sir Anthony was able to take his attention from his horses, she turned resolutely to him.

"Sir Anthony, I know that I behaved very badly last night, and I hope you will be able to forgive me for it."

"Dear child! I forgave you the moment you spoke to Mister Watkins. It was very well done and showed just the proper feelings—as well as courage, for I'm sure it was not easy for you to do."

"Oh, no, it was very easy for me to do, indeed I was most grateful for the opportunity. I feared he would never come near enough again for me to apologize to him. But my greatest fear was that you and Lady Barstowe and Mister Strangeways would be in such disgust with me that you would not be my friends any longer."

"Good friends are not so easily disgusted as that, thank goodness. And we don't need the reproachful looks of our friends when we are already swamped by guilt for our wrongdoings. It is then we need from them the forgiveness we can't give ourselves. Have no fear, your true friends will know how you are feeling at such a time and want to show you they understand and sympathize."

"I—I—thank you very much, sir. You are all so kind to me. I fear I have had little experience with friendships."

"Oh, I make no doubt you'll know your way about in no time at all. You seem to have any number of people already who stand friend to you. But what I really wanted to discuss with you when I asked you to drive with me was the matter of my going away."

"Going away! Oh, why—I mean—that was rude of me, I didn't mean to sound nosy. But *must* you go away?" The distress in her voice was so obvious that it caused him to turn and look at her in surprise.

"Well, yes, I fear I must. Just for a fortnight, perhaps, to begin with, but I think my business will require me to be away the better part of the next two months or so. My problem is that I don't like to leave you with no one to stand in place of guardian and have wondered if you will object to Mister Strangeways filling that role while I am away?"

"Mister Strangeways? But will he not mind? Perhaps he will think it a great bother to have to concern himself with me?"

"You may be easy on that score. I've spoken to him of this and he holds himself delighted with the task. He likes you very much, you know, and says he would like nothing better than to spend as much time in your company as possible."

"That is very kind of him, is it not? I like him very much also. And of course I should hate to feel that I was keeping you from your own concerns."

"Believe me, Pippa, I would give the world not to have to go away now!" he replied, so earnestly that it was her turn to look at him with surprise. They rode on in silence for a few moments, each mulling over the vehemence with which he had spoken.

Tony was more than a little startled by himself. Why on earth had he said such a thing, he wondered? And where had this feeling sprung from so strongly?

For Pippa the very real regret in his voice matched so exactly her own feelings that she needed to be very quiet for a time and wonder over it quite privately. *He truly does not want to go away! And I thought he had grown weary of dragging me about and was merely using his business as an excuse to get away from me for a time.* She was very elated by this thought and promised herself that in the future she would be a better person so that she would deserve his friendship.

"You will come back?" she finally asked, trying to sound casual so that he wouldn't sense how very much she dreaded the thought of his going away.

"Of course I will come back. How can you think I would just abandon you? I hope I will always be there for you to turn to if you are troubled, Pippa. And in the meantime, Mister Strangeways will drop me a note from time to time to tell me how you go on, and play the part of stern parent when I'm not around and you are besieged by new-breeched young whelps who think to take advantage of you."

"Like last night, you mean? I truly don't think he meant to take advantage of me."

"Do you not? I'm not so sure I agree with you there. I cannot quite like young Otway." Then, seeing the distress on her face, he hastily added, "But there, perhaps, I am influenced by his dreadful mother."

Pippa could not help laughing at this. "Yes, she is a fearsome creature, is she not? I must own myself terrified of her. She looks at one as though she—"

"Were pricing your gown? And very likely she is; she has rather that reputation. I think," he said cautiously, "that she would like it very well to be able to call the duchess a relative, if only by marriage."

Pippa turned a puzzled stare upon him while she thought about this. Then his meaning became clear to her. He was warning her of Mrs. Otway's ambitions for her son and Lady Fanny.

Quite suddenly the day seemed less sunny and her spirits plummeted. She sighed wearily. She was not sure that she liked this business of growing up quite so much as she had thought she would. It was like being on the end of a yo-yo, with one's emotions being lifted and dropped so rapidly that it was exhausting.

CHAPTER 14

Dear Aunt Emma,

Our stay here continues to be most pleasant, and as the weather holds fine we are able to go out every day. We go for long rambles about town quite often, and in this way I have managed to see most of it. The shops are above anything wonderful, and I fear I have been extravagant, but I have managed to curb it now that I have sated the need to purchase something in every shop. I have an excessively beautiful ball gown, as well as other nice gowns that Lady Barstowe has had made for me.

I wore the ball gown to the assembly in the upper rooms last week and felt very fine in it. There were plenty of dancing partners, and Melissa and I danced every dance.

Sir Anthony has had to go away to London to attend his business and has left me in the care of Lady Barstowe and his friend, Mr. Strangeways. Mr. Strangeways says that he is a much more suitable type to stand as guardian in any case, because Sir Anthony is too young to know how to go about it. Mr. Strangeways is an older man, but he does not seem so, for though his hair is white, his skin is tanned and he moves most gracefully. I have asked him to call me Pippa, and when I did so, he laughed and said his given name is Peregrine (Is that not a charming name?) but that it had been many years since anyone had called him by it. I replied that I preferred Mr. Strangeways, that it seemed disrespectful to call him otherwise. Do you not think I am right in this?

We go this afternoon to a ridotto alfresco given by the Duchess of Haverford. I have a new gown of white jaconet muslin with *three* flounces at the hem and the most ravishing Lavinia chip bonnet to go with it. I shall be very stylish!

I hope all is going well at Ayleforth Hall, and if you should feel so inclined, perhaps you might write a line or two to me to tell me you are well. With my very best wishes, I remain,

Your niece,
Philippa Cranville

Pippa sat back triumphantly, feeling that this was a quite creditable effort. She had promised herself to write to her aunt once a week, whether her aunt was interested in hearing from her or not, but the effort to find things to say to someone so habitually uncommunicative was difficult. She wondered what her aunt's response to her first letter had been. Had she been glad to receive it in spite of herself? After receiving several letters over the weeks, would she gradually thaw enough to respond? Or would she always remain her implacable, unresponsive self? There had been growing in Pippa, for some time now, the need for some sort of communication from her aunt. Though they had never been close, they had been together for fifteen years and Pippa found it impossible to simply erase the woman from her thoughts. There was also a kind of guilt attached to thoughts of her aunt, for she could not help contrasting her present situation, filled with friends and entertainments, to the barren sterility of her aunt's existence. When she tried to discuss this with Melissa or Lady Barstowe, they pooh-poohed her notions and said her aunt was obviously perfectly content with her life as it was since she made no effort to change it.

I suppose I am being a peagoose, thought Pippa, folding the paper and addressing it. *There now, I feel better, no matter what Melissa says.*

Thus having relieved her mind, she hurried happily up to her room and the entrancing white muslin, which she felt quite certain would cause even such a London smart as Mr. Otway to stand at gaze.

And she was right about that, she noted happily as she was assisted by Mr. Strangeways from the carriage that afternoon. Mr. Otway's eyes widened in appreciation, and with a large smile he strolled across the grass to greet her.

Melissa and Lady Barstowe strolled away to greet the duchess, who was holding court beneath the trees. Mr. Otway paused to raise his hat to them politely, but Lady Barstowe only nodded unsmilingly and passed on, though Melissa could not resist dimpling up at him flirtatiously.

Mr. Otway bowed over Pippa's hand and then smiled at her ruefully. "She still looks upon me as a shockingly loose screw, I fear. What must I do to get back in her good graces?"

"Cultivate a bit more sensitivity and address, sir," answered Mr. Strangeways promptly.

"Oh, afternoon, Strangeways, didn't notice you there," said Mr. Otway carelessly.

"Exactly so," Mr. Strangeways said dryly.

But Mr. Otway was not schooled in such subtleties and so did not take offense at the reproach implied. He was a young man upon whom fortune had smiled so continuously and generously all his life that no effort had ever been required of him. He was favored with good looks, a large fortune, and a lazy sort of charm that was immensely appealing to women. His father had obligingly passed away many years ago, leaving Mrs. Otway to concentrate all her many energies in her son's behalf, and since that time she had made sure that everything in his life was ordered as he would have it. He was, to give him credit, a good-natured enough fellow, but so used was he to thinking only of his own needs that there had never grown in him any sensitivity to the needs of others.

He had not meant to be offensive the night of the ball, but had only desired to have his dance with Pippa and felt Mr. Watkins of too little account to consider. He was truly bewildered that Lady Barstowe should feel differently; after all Watkins was but a scarce-breeched whelp from some obscure country family. *Surely there could be no reason to consider the feelings of such a paltry creature,* thought Mr. Otway. *Why, I should own myself astonished to find that he had any to speak of.*

With such an attitude it is not surprising that he now held out his arm to Pippa and began to walk away with no further thought of Mr. Strangeways. It was Pippa who stopped and turned back to put her arm through that of her surrogate guardian.

Mr. Otway raised his eyebrow at this, but obligingly came back and held out his arm at her other side, thinking what strange creatures women were.

There were many people strolling about the lawns of the duchess's mansion, and presently Mr. Otway was able to detach Pippa from Mr. Strangeways and lead her off apart down a little path through the shrubbery.

"Now, Miss Cranville, I have you alone at last. I vow I spend all my waking moments working out little plans whereby I can steal a few moments to speak to you without dozens of pairs of ears stretched out to overhear."

"I did not realize it, Mister Otway. If you had but asked me, I should have been happy to speak alone with you."

"Would you now? Yes, I suppose you would. Then I must tell you, Miss Cranville, that it would be most improper in you to contrive at such *tête-à-tête*."

"I should not be improper, sir."

"I know you would not be, but it would be thought so anyway. For you must know young ladies must always be attended when in the company of gentlemen."

"How ridiculous! As though we could not be trusted to know how to conduct ourselves. Why I've gone about for years alone with Jem at home. Though, perhaps he would not count, for he is not a gentleman, in your sense of the word, but only a farmboy."

Mr. Otway gave a shout of delighted laughter at this unsophisticated statement. "Oh, Miss Cranville, what a refreshing creature you are. Never dissembling, never being coy. Ah, delightful girl." He took both her hands in his and pulled her closer so that they were standing face to face. She stood there, trustingly, looking up at him, and he, with no thought of consequences, leaned down and kissed the lips that seemed to be offered to him.

Pippa felt that had he not been holding her hands, she would surely have swooned away, so delicious was his kiss to her.

There was a shocked gasp behind them, and Mr. Otway jerked around. There, standing in the path, her hand over her mouth, was Melissa. She had been sent after them by her mother who had seen Mr. Otway leading Pippa away.

Pippa smiled upon her friend dreamily and said, "Why, Melissa, where have you sprung from?"

"Pippa, my mother—would—like you to come and meet a special friend of hers," lied Melissa, unable to come up with something better, so surprised was she by what she had seen. Young as she was, Melissa had had some experience in dalliance, but never had she gone so far as to allow a young man to kiss her. Why, only suppose one of the other guests had happened to come down the path at that moment? Pippa's reputation would have been ruined! How could Mr. Otway have been so careless of her good name? Her mother was right, he was an odious young man.

Melissa held out her hand to Pippa and sent Mr. Otway

one blistering glance before pulling her away down the path and back to the party.

"How could you do such a thing?" she whispered fiercely when they were out of earshot of Mr. Otway. "Have you so completely lost your senses? And you dared to lecture me on how to behave that time at home when I did but flirt with you a little when you were masquerading as a boy!"

"But you are just a child and should not—"

"I am not so much a child that I would think nothing of kissing a man in front of an entire garden full of people!"

"But we were not in view of anyone."

"That does not make it right. Besides, at any moment someone could have come down the path as I did and discovered you. Your reputation would be in shreds before you were properly out. Really, Pippa, you put me out of all patience."

"But, Melissa, I have discovered that I am in love with Mister Otway, and I am certain he is with me also."

"Fiddle!"

"But even you must be aware of how particular he has been in his attentions to me since we've been here in Bath. Why, from the very first day! Oh, yes, I am convinced it is so."

"Has he told you so?"

"He has not spoken yet, but he said himself he spends all of his time trying to conjure a way to speak alone with me. What else could he mean but that he was but waiting for a chance to tell me."

"Fiddle again!" snapped Melissa crossly, "you really are a complete gapeseed! Why, anyone has but to speak to him to see that he is an accomplished flirt. I make no doubt he has made that same speech to half the young women in Bath by this time! Why, he even flirts with me, for heaven's sake, and I've heard he calls here every day to see Lady Fanny."

During this speech Pippa felt all the sweetness of Mr. Otway's kiss draining out of her, and she had so much wanted to hold on to the feeling until she could be alone and savor it. Why was Melissa telling her these things? *I don't believe her,* she thought angrily. *He could not be such a person as she implies.*

"I cannot believe you," she said now, gathering the tattered rags of her faith, "and I would ask you not to speak of him in that way."

"Very pretty," replied Melissa grimly, "now if your conduct were only as lofty as your loyalty. No, there's no getting past it, Pippa, such things are just not done. If you know no better, I'm sure *he* should, and I know my mother will tell you I'm right."

"Oh, you will make a report to your mother?" asked Pippa cuttingly.

"No," Melissa replied promptly, "for she has not set me to spy upon you, nor would I do so. She but noticed you going apart with Mr. Otway and sent me to join you so that others would not remark upon it. But you must listen to me, Pippa. I know you feel you did nothing wrong, but truly it is simply not the way to go on in society. Women may flirt as much as they like under the eyes of their chaperons, but they cannot go about kissing in corners and expect to be received or invited to parties. You must give me your word that you will not do so again."

"And if I won't?"

"Then I must tell my mother, surely you can see that. For your own sake, dearest Pippa, and for mine too. For my mother would never forgive me if I knew what was going forward and kept it from her. She is responsible for you; she has undertaken to bring you out in society, and her own good name would suffer if she allowed yours to become smirched while you were in her charge." Melissa's eyes filled with tears, so earnestly did she feel about the subject, and Pippa softened immediately.

"Oh, how cold and unfeeling I am grown! *Please* do not cry, Melissa. Of course I will give you my word. I was not thinking clearly. I would never do anything to make you or Lady Barstowe unhappy. You have shown me every kindness and made it possible for me to come here and—oh—everything! I wonder at myself for being so selfish. What can have made me so?" she asked wonderingly.

They threw their arms about each other, overcome by their love for one another and the easy emotions of very young girls.

"Never mind, darling Pippa. It will be all right, I know. It's just that you are not used to being flirted with, and you are so straight and true yourself, you think everyone else must say just what they mean also. But most of the time it's just manners, it's what is accepted as polite behavior. Unless a girl is a complete antidote, a gentleman is *expected* to pay extravagant compliments and pretend he is dying of love. Sometimes, if the girl has enough dowry, it doesn't even matter if she *is* an antidote! But it's not to be taken seriously."

"You may be right, and he was only repeating pretty speeches he's made hundreds of times, but what of me? I feel quite sure of my own heart."

"I think it is only because it is the first," said Melissa wisely. "I felt so the first time too, but a week later I met someone else and discovered I felt the same thing all over again. After that I realized it wasn't real, it was just playing."

"But, what do you mean—playing?" Pippa asked, much bewildered.

"Oh, you know, it was like making up little stories about myself, with myself as the princess and the young man the prince who would carry me away. It would make me feel all giddy and light-headed for a few days and then it would wear away and I'd want to feel that way again, so I'd start all over with the next young man I met."

"I don't think I have ever thought of myself as a princess," said Pippa, rather sadly.

"No, I don't guess you have. And that is probably the problem."

"But you must not be too harsh on Mister Otway, Melissa. I'm the one who behaved in an idiotic way, and you can hardly blame him for thinking I was encouraging him. In fact I *was* doing so. I know really that one must not behave that way with everyone, but I admired him so much and thought, like the green thing I am, that he felt the same and that there could be nothing wrong where one felt honest emotion. But what if I don't change? What if I continue to be in love with him? What then? Do you think it is so impossible for him to be in love with me?"

"Dear Pippa, of course it is not impossible. I'm sure half the young men you've met so far are in love with you. How could they help but be? But I can't help thinking that if he truly loved you, he would not be so careless of your good name as to behave as he has."

With this dampening thought, they joined Lady Barstowe, who pulled Pippa's arm through her own and never left her side for the rest of the afteroon. She was never to know what had just transpired in the shrubbery, for Melissa, true to her word, never told her, but she had more than a suspicion that something had happened, for both girls showed signs of tears. *That young man definitely wants watching,* she thought grimly. *Well, in the future he shall find I have a very sharp eye indeed!*

CHAPTER 15

For the next week every moment was filled with callers, visits, or entertainments of different sorts. Sidney Otway, being extremely popular, was to be seen everywhere, and he always came to speak to Pippa the moment she appeared at any gathering. He seemed completely unaware of having committed any transgression and continued to flirt lazily and charmingly with her.

But they were seldom alone together. Wherever they were standing, Lady Barstowe materialized almost immediately. She managed to do it so unobtrusively that Pippa was unaware of it, but Mr. Otway was not so blind to what was happening. He found it only mildly irritating, but was much too sure of himself to be really annoyed. Ways to circumvent her would present themselves, and meantime the beautiful Miss Cranville was still interested, of that he was certain. And when she wasn't present, or when Lady Barstowe's presence became too stifling, there were many other charming young creatures waiting for his attention.

At one evening musicale Pippa was introduced to a young man she had not met before but whose name was only too familiar to her: Robert Danston! She dropped her fan in confusion, which he recovered and presented to her with great ceremony. Pippa turned quickly to a hovering Lady Barstowe to introduce him to her, and while they exchanged courtesies, tried to regain her poise.

He was the very last person she would have expected to meet, though why it should not occur to her that it was possible, she could not explain. Perhaps he was associated so much in her mind with her life before Bath, that he had been relegated to the past and had dropped from her mind. But here was the very man who had unknowingly precipitated the events that had led to her present happiness. For if he had not been proposed for a visit by her former guardian, she would never have run away and would never have met Lady Barstowe and Melissa and would in all probability not now be so pleasantly ensconced in a comfortable house in Bath. In truth, she owed him a debt of gratitude!

While he spoke to Lady Barstowe, she was able to study him and found him to be a pleasant-looking young man, though not in any way as handsome as Mr. Otway, and certainly with nothing of his presence. She couldn't help wondering how she would have reacted to him if it had all come about as Sir Anthony's father had planned it and they had become acquainted at Ayleforth Hall. Inexperienced and lonely as she had been then, no doubt she would have found him more than acceptable. Why, they might even have been engaged by this time! Terrible thought! For though he was presentable enough certainly, he seemed—young—unpolished in some way.

He turned to her now. "We were so nearly acquaintances, Miss Cranville, that I feel we have already met."

"Ah, really, Mister Danston?" She hoped desperately that she would not blush, but it was very hard for her to equivocate in this way, and of course she could not admit to knowing what he was talking about.

"Yes, my father's friend, Sir James Seymour-Croft, was bringing me along for a visit to your country estate when he passed away quite suddenly and the trip was canceled. I was quite disappointed, you may be sure."

"Well, thank you—at least I mean to say I'm sorry that

you could not come, Mister Danston. Ayleforth Hall is most beautiful."

"Are you new to Bath, Mister Danston?" Lady Barstowe interposed.

"Yes, madame. After my stay with Sir James I went back to Kent to visit my own family. But there is little to do there, they are so remote, so I decided to come here. I'm hoping to find some of my London friends down for visits."

"I make no doubt you will find some, as the town is filled with Londoners."

"I wonder if you know Sidney Otway? He mentioned to me that he might be here about this time."

"You are a particular friend of Mister Otway?" Lady Barstowe asked, her voice noticeably cooler.

"Oh, indeed, Lady Barstowe. He's a very good sort of chap," exclaimed Mr. Danston, "he sort of took me under his wing in London when I first went up—showed me about, introduced me to his friends."

"Very kind of him, I'm sure," commented Lady Barstowe dryly.

"Yes, wasn't it? Meant a great deal to me, I can tell you. And he's up to every sort of new start, really knows how to go on," rattled Mr. Danston with boyish enthusiasm. It was plain to all that he had come to Bath in the wake of his new idol.

Pippa was very happy that this endorsement had been made in Lady Barstowe's hearing and hoped fervently that her opinion of Mr. Otway would be changed by hearing of how kind he had been to a young man from the country. She felt a warm glow in her own heart to know that he was not without kindness as everyone seemed to think.

Sir Anthony was due on the weekend, and he would no doubt meet Mr. Danston and hear about it, and would have a better opinion of Mr. Otway. It was, strangely, most important to her that Sir Anthony approve of him.

She gave Mr. Danston a heart-warmed smile to repay him for his compliments to Mr. Otway, and that gentleman, at that moment entering the room, saw it. He felt the flick of jealousy, a new emotion for him, and made his way rapidly across the room.

"Well, Miss Cranville, I am happy to find you so well entertained," he said smoothly.

"Oh, Mister Otway, how you startled me! I did not see you come in. Here is a great surprise for you, your friend from London, Mister Danston."

"So I see. Danston"—he made a perfunctory bow—"thought I had you all safely stowed away in the country for the summer."

Mr. Danston laughed appreciatively at this supposed witticism. "Well, you see me here, Otway. Come to taste the pleasures of Bath."

"Watch where you do your tasting, sir," was Mr. Otway's reply, and then, holding out his arm, he invited Pippa to stroll around the room with him.

Lady Barstowe's brows creased in a frown at this rudeness, and Mr. Danston's face fell in dismay. He could not imagine why Otway should be snubbing him in this way after their closeness a few weeks ago in London. He had come to feel that Sidney Otway was his best friend.

Before taking Mr. Otway's arm, Pippa held out her hand to Mr. Danston and smiled. "I hope you will call on us at Laura Place, sir, while you are in Bath."

"Oh, thank you—how kind—I should be delighted," spluttered Mr. Danston disjointedly, still trying to fathom the reason for his hero's displeasure.

As they walked away Pippa turned to Mr. Otway with a puzzled look. "Mister Otway, I am surprised you would behave so to your friend."

"Friend! Why I barely know the man."

"But he was just telling us how very kind to him you

had been in London, taking him around and introducing him to your friends."

"Oh, I took him under my wing for a bit, gave me someone to go about with. Rather amusing for a while, but now he's becoming tiresome. Why should he have followed me down here? Expects more of the same, no doubt, but there he'll be disappointed. Does the fellow think I have nothing else to do but entertain him?"

"Oh, I cannot think Mister Danston would expect—"

Mr. Otway stopped and turned to her with raised eyebrows. "Why, what is this, Miss Cranville? Such warm defense of the fellow on your part? You must tell me, of course, if he is an especial *friend* of yours and I will extend myself—"

"No, no—that is, we have just met this moment!" she protested.

"I am glad to hear it. I should hate for you to develop a *tendre* for a fellow with straw in his hair still."

"I think you exaggerate, Mister Otway. There is a lack of polish, certainly, but he is well-mannered for all that." She could not help defending Mr. Danston from this bewildering and unfair attack, though it pained her to disagree with Mr. Otway. There was also pain in having to acknowledge that he was behaving badly.

Seeing her displeasure and realizing that he had said rather more than he had ought, he laughed lightly and raised her hand to his lips. "Bravo, beautiful Portia. How charmingly you leap to the defense of the underdog. You must forgive me, fair one, I fear I am suffering the pangs of jealousy."

"Why, how so?" Her heart flipped impudently at this admission.

"It seemed to me you smiled upon him too warmly. I cannot like to see those smiles bestowed upon someone else," he said, leaning closer to look meaningfully into her eyes.

"Pippa, my dear," came the loud, clear voice of Lady Barstowe, "the music is about to begin, and we must find our seats before Lady Chester becomes nervous. You know how she hates to keep the musicians waiting about."

Drat the woman! thought Sidney Otway. She had an absolute genuis for choosing the wrong moment. Pippa, with an apologetic smile, turned to follow Lady Barstowe into the music room, where she was seated with a Barstowe on each side. Mr. Otway turned away in disgust, decided that this party bored him, and made his way out, brushing by Mr. Danston, who was on his way to the music room, with barely a nod. To say that Mr. Danston was crushed by this treatment would be a sad understatement.

Pippa sat quietly between Lady Barstowe and Melissa, but though the quartet was excellent, she did not really hear them. Her mind was much occupied with Sidney Otway, adding here, subtracting there, trying to rearrange her feelings about him to accommodate the inescapable minuses of his personality. She had been witness, now, to several instances of insensitivity to the feelings of others. His rudeness to young Mr. Watkins was balanced, in her mind, by his flattering eagerness to dance with her. Not that she condoned such behavior. She had tried in every way this past week to be particularly nice to Mr. Watkins to make up for it. He was a regular morning caller at Laura Place now, treated almost as a son of the house by Lady Barstowe and Melissa, and content to gaze bemusedly at Pippa.

Then there was Mr. Otway's rather disrespectful negligence of the courtesy owed to Mr. Strangeways that day at the ridotto alfresco. Search her heart as she would, she could find no excuse for him in that instance.

The incident of the kiss, condemned by Melissa as gross carelessness for her good name, she tended to blame herself for, knowing that she had not discouraged him in any way.

And now this exhibition of rudeness to Mr. Danston. Perhaps he felt that he was being used by the younger man to further his social ambitions—but, no, she could not believe he could look at the open, disingenuous face of Mr. Danston and accuse him of even *having* social ambitions. But then Mr. Otway had admitted that he had been jealous and, unworthy an emotion as she knew this was supposed to be, her heart had been warmed by his admission. Surely that must mean that he cared for her.

On the other hand Sir Anthony had warned her of Mrs. Otway's ambitions for her son, and Melissa had told her that he called every morning upon Lady Fanny. And it must be so, for certainly he had never yet paid a morning visit to Laura Place. She herself had noticed that while he seemed always to come to her side immediately when she entered a room, he did not neglect Lady Fanny if she were there, nor indeed any passably pretty young woman.

She wished she had someone to speak to about all this, someone who could advise her. Lady Barstowe and Melissa had already given their opinions, and Sir Anthony—*no*, she could not speak to him about it! She recoiled inwardly at the thought of such a discussion with him, though why she should feel so she didn't know.

Ah! Mr. Strangeways, with his calm, unprejudiced eye! The very person, she thought. He would surely be the best person of all.

> Dear Aunt Emma,
>
> I hope this letter finds you, as it does me, in good health. I have not received a letter from you. If you have written, I hope it has not gone astray.
>
> We were all invited to a musicale at Lady Chester's last evening, and it was very nice and the musicians excellent. We met a young gentleman there who said

he had been intended to come for a visit to Ayleforth Hall with Sir John before his death. A Mr. Danston. He seemed very pleasant. [*That should give her a start,* Pippa thought rather gleefully.]

Sir Anthony is expected back this weekend, and we are all looking forward to his return very much, though he will only stay a few days.

I had occasion to speak privately with Mr. Strangeways this morning and heard from him the most unusual story. Though I have not told it to the Barstowes, for he said he never speaks of it to anyone for fear people will look upon him as freakish, I'm sure he would not mind my telling you, for I know you will be discreet.

Since I am revealing his secret, I think it only fair to reveal my own and tell you that I asked to consult him about a young man. Mr. Sidney Otway, whom you will remember I mentioned meeting in a previous letter, has been rather particular in his attentions to me, or at least so it seemed, and I cannot deny that I have been pleased to receive them, but there are certain traits of character that puzzle me and I felt a more experienced and less prejudiced eye was needed. When I told Mr. Strangeways of my problem, he said that generally we base our judgment upon past experiences. I told him that I had none, that indeed I almost felt that I had no past, upon which he visibly started and turned quite pale and was silent for a very long time. When I exclaimed upon it, he said that it was so queer to hear me say such a thing, for he always thought of himself in such a light. I asked him to explain, and it was then that he told me this most fascinating story.

It seems he has no memory whatsoever of the first twenty-one years of his life! He was thrown from a horse while visiting right here in Bath some thirty years ago and was ill for a long time, but the worst part of it all was that he has never been able to remember any part of his life before that time. Is that not like a tale of romance by Mr. Southey or Mr. Lewis?

I fear I have crossed my lines so much that this letter will be illegible, so I must close. Lady Barstowe asked me to send her regards, and I would take it kindly if you would convey my own to Jem, Grigson, and Cook. I remain,

Most sincerely,
Pippa

CHAPTER 16

Sir Anthony arrived by the mail coach and went directly to his room at the White Hart to change his rumpled and dusty clothes, before setting out to pay a call on Mr. Strangeways. He was very eager to have his report of the events since he had been away.

He found his friend just going in to his breakfast and was easily persuaded to accompany him.

"I hope things are going well for you in London, Tony."

"Very well, indeed. I cannot thank you enough for directing me to your man of business. He has been very helpful. Wonderful man. But I really don't want to discuss that. I am very eager to learn how things are going with my ward. Has she 'taken,' as they say?"

"Excessively well. She is invited everywhere, and I hear on every side of her beauty and pretty manners. She is a great favorite with everyone."

"And young men in droves, I imagine?"

"Certainly more than her fair share," said Mr. Strangeways, laughing.

"Is young Otway still hanging about?" Tony asked with a very creditable attempt at casualness.

"I must report that he is, but I don't think you need be unduly concerned."

"Ah. Mrs. Otway still pursuing her ambitions, I take it?"

"No doubt she is, but that isn't what I meant. I think the

child will get his measure by herself in a very short time. She's well on the way already. Yes, young Otway is his own worst enemy."

"Do you think she is smitten?"

"Oh, I should imagine she is, but I shouldn't worry if I were you. Look here, I think I had better tell you, though I do betray her confidence. She spoke to me about Otway yesterday, asked my advice about him."

"The devil you say!"

"Yes, extraordinary girl, that. She may be green, but there are no flies on her, just the same. I think she has realized that he's a coxcomb, but just doesn't want to admit it yet. He conceives himself to be so irresistible that he thinks he can behave just as he likes, ride roughshod over people's sensibilities, with no fear of the consequences. But he's due for a comeuppance with our young lady, never you fear."

"But will she be hurt?"

"I think she will be somewhat, but it won't do her any real harm. After all, how can she know what happiness is without experiencing pain. No need to put yourself in a pucker about her, she'll be right as a trivet in next to no time. It's only infatuation, you see, not love."

"And Otway?"

"Oh, he dangles! But then, he dangles after all the pretty girls. He's a collector of hearts, wants every girl he meets to fall in love with him. Needs it for his vanity's sake and to make him feel an exceptional fellow. He goes as far as he's allowed to go with each girl, but never *too* far. Knows just when to draw back before he's trapped."

"Young whelp! I'd like to box his ears for him. Maybe it would knock some sense into him."

Mr. Strangeways laughed. "I doubt it, though I admit I've had the same impulse myself. Now then, if you've finished your breakfast, I'll order my carriage to take you over to Laura Place."

* * *

Pippa had been hanging about the front windows since breakfast on the lookout for Sir Anthony. She had been awake at a very early hour this morning, though she knew the time of the mail's arrival was still hours away. When that hour had come and gone and he had not appeared, she had begun pacing about the house, too restless to sit anywhere for long.

"You don't suppose something has happened, do you?" she asked Lady Barstowe.

"Like what? Are you imagining an accident? Really, child, you must calm down or you will give me an irritation of the nerves."

"An accident! Good heavens, what if . . . ?"

"Pippa! Sit down and calm yourself. You will do yourself no good this way. Of course there has been no accident, but the man travels all the way from London, sitting in a carriage all night long. Don't you imagine he will want to go to his inn and change, or eat breakfast, or perhaps even have a bit of sleep?"

"Oh—of course." Pippa slumped down into a chair with such a look of dejection that Lady Barstowe gave her a most interested survey.

"I declare, child, I don't know when I've seen you in such a taking. One would think you were waiting for a lover."

Pippa, who had been winding the end of her sash around her finger, sat perfectly still for a moment, then raised her eyes in astonishment to Lady Barstowe.

"You cannot be serious, Lady Barstowe? Why he is—is—"

"Yes?"

"He's been almost like a father to me. Why, I think of him always with the deepest respect."

"Very commendable, I'm sure. But I think I should

point out that he is but five and twenty, and much too young to have fathered a seventeen-year-old."

This somewhat tart rejoinder silenced Pippa for a few minutes while she pondered it. Of course she knew really how old Sir Anthony was, he had told her himself. But she had always thought of him as so much wiser than herself, therefore older, and never in the light in which he had just been presented by Lady Barstowe. A lover! How ridiculous! He was not—he was—well, of course, it was not impossible that he was *someone's* lover. Nothing more likely, now she thought of it; perhaps some young lady in London. Perhaps that was the real reason for his long stay there, not business at all! This was somehow a less than thrilling thought. She pictured to herself Sir Anthony smiling into the eyes of a tall, willowy brunet or a tiny, round, dimpled blond—and conceived an instant dislike of both.

Then she impatiently shrugged away the whole thought and looked up to meet the bland smile of Lady Barstowe. However, before they could pursue the conversation, the sound of carriage wheels was heard in front of the house and Pippa hurried to the window.

"He's here!" she cried out joyfully and ran to the front door.

Sir Anthony looked up in surprise as the door flew open, and she ran down the three steps, hands outstretched, with a welcoming smile that made him catch his breath.

"Sir Anthony! How good to have you back!"

He laughed happily and took her hands. "Well, well, how kind of you to make me so welcome. Do I dare hope that I have been missed?"

"Of course you have. You are my first friend, and naturally I did not like to see you go away."

Her openness caught him by surprise. He had forgotten how guileless she was.

"I was sorry to be forced to leave. But now let's hear all about you. Have you been enjoying Bath?"

"Oh, excessively. We have never stopped for a moment, it seems."

"I can see that it has done you good. You are in excellent looks. No, I must do better than that or Mr. Strangeways will laugh at me. You are looking very beautiful, child. It is obvious society agrees with you."

"Thank you, Sir Anthony, I—shall we—" She dropped her eyes in confusion and wished desperately that she had been able to show a bit more sophistication. He must think her still the same simpleton he had first met.

"Of course, we must go in. How silly of me to keep you standing here on the pavement. Maria Barstowe will be bound to give me a scold for such behavior."

She led the way inside and into the drawing room, where Lady Barstowe still calmly sat with her needlework.

"Well, Tony, I take it it's all the rage now in London to stand about talking on the pavement," she greeted him.

Tony grinned at Pippa as though to say "You see" and bent over Maria Barstowe's hand.

"I knew I should receive a sharp setdown from you. Will you not say welcome, my dear?"

"With all my heart, dear friend. We have missed you exceedingly. While we have been rusticating down here, I suppose you have been kicking up all sorts of larks in the city?"

"Only a few small ones, I assure you. London is very dull just now, even more so when I know you are here."

Pippa, watching this exchange, felt about eight years old. Why could she never banter with him gaily as Lady Barstowe did so easily? He seemed to like it very much, if the smile he was giving Lady Barstowe was anything to go by. *I wish she would not flirt with him while I am present,* Pippa thought resentfully. She stalked over to the window, aware that she was exhibiting childishness, and stood glaring out while they chatted easily together. Finally Lady Barstowe called to her.

"Pippa, are you still staring out the windows? I declare, you have spent the whole morning there. I had thought you were watching for Tony, but now I begin to think you are waiting for someone else."

"Of course I am not—I—" Pippa was greatly embarrassed. How could Lady Barstowe say such a thing? Now he would know how eagerly she had been awaiting his arrival, or worse, think she was a silly girl waiting for a young man to call.

"I had thought we might go for a drive. I have Strangeways's phaeton outside."

"Not for me, though I thank you," replied Lady Barstowe. "I am much too comfortable here. Besides, you know there is only room for two."

"Exactly. And I know that you are too lazy to bestir yourself. I counted upon your refusal, in fact, because I really want to have a quiet visit with my ward before the round of festivities for the day begins."

Pippa felt her face almost split with her smile at these words. "I'll get my bonnet," she said and whisked out of the room.

Tony cut around the corner expertly, and they were on the road to Beechen Cliff. He had opted against crossing the river and driving through Bath, saying they would be stopped too many times by acquaintances. Pippa, eyes glistening with excitement, and a most becoming flush to her cheeks, looked about with great interest, for this was a drive she had never taken.

"I declare that is a monstrously becoming—er—costume, Miss Cranville."

"Am I not a glass of fashion?" she said, laughing, but much gratified by his comment, for this was her favorite new outfit. Over the white-sprigged dimity, she was wearing a dark green silk faille spencer, the tiny jacket perfect for protection against the breeze of an open carriage. The ribbons of her poke bonnet were of the same green, and her auburn curls framed her face deliciously.

"I hope the pleasures of Bath have not so sated you that you do not look forward to your London Season," he said, rather obliquely, hoping to learn by her answer whether she had given her heart here in Bath.

"Oh, goodness, no! Though I find it such a delightful place, everyone is forever telling me how much more so is London."

"I am happy to hear it. Though, I fear, I have not yet solved the problem of London."

"Problem?"

"Yes, the problem of where you shall live and who shall be with you there."

"But I have a house. You told me that I will have my parents' house."

"Well, you can hardly live in it alone. And I have not yet come up with a respectable female relative to live there with you. It would be perfect if your Aunt Emma—"

"No," she interrupted hastily, "I fear she has not relented in the least. I have been writing her, you know, and she has not responded with a word."

"My dear child, I didn't know," he said in some surprise. "What prompted you to do so?"

"Oh—well, I"—she floundered uncomfortably—"please do not think it was anything so very extraordinary. I only felt that it must be very lonely for her now in that great house. Not that we had much intercourse when I was there, but at least I was a presence. Now she has no one."

"What a good child you are," he replied sincerely.

"Please do not refine too much upon it. I must admit that I have found it rewarding for myself also, and will continue to write, though she never replies."

"Explain, please."

"Well, though the first letter was done from compassion, I found it helped me order my thinking to write down my feelings and impressions."

"But you could do the same with a journal."

"I think I could not. For myself, I would put down anything without examining it. When I know it will be read, I must think of what I am saying very carefully and put it down so that it will be understood."

"And have you hopes that she will write to you?"

"No. But I feel, in some way, that it is a good thing for me to do. I think of her very differently now that I am away from her. Perhaps she is feeling the same thing."

"Your feelings do you credit, my dear, whether you want it or not. However, that does not solve our problem."

"Perhaps Lady Barstowe—"

"Yes, naturally I have thought of that, and I make no doubt she would oblige if I were to ask her, for she is unusually good-natured. But it would be asking a great deal, and I hate to do it. After all, she has her own house and is used to entertaining a great deal. It would not be fair to ask it of her."

"She has asked me to visit them. I need not spend the entire Season in London. I could make a short visit to them and not put them out too much, I think."

"Oh, I feel quite sure you could spend the entire Season with them and not put them out in the least. But I wanted to set you up in your own establishment, if possible, as I think your parents would have wanted."

"You are very good to concern yourself about me," she said shyly.

"I am but trying to fulfill my responsibility."

"But I would not be a burden to you. I know full well that you have your own business to take care of."

He turned to look at her for a moment in silence, then, "It is no burden," he replied succinctly.

The horses had slowed now, climbing the road to the clifftop, and Pippa and Tony both became very interested in the scenery. Presently they reached the top of the hill, and he reined in the horses and jumped down.

"Come along," he said, holding out his hand to assist her down. "Here is the finest prospect anywhere in Bath."

She gave him her hand and he helped her out, and then led her to a point where they could look out and see the whole city beneath them. She was gratifyingly impressed, pointing and exclaiming and telling him she had never seen so fine a view.

"I am happy that I have been the first to bring you here. I had thought one of your many beaux would surely have—"

"You have been hearing tales, Sir Anthony," she responded quickly with a laugh, "I cannot claim to have many beaux."

"Ah, I see. Then one in particular, perhaps?"

She could feel the warmth of a blush rising up her throat and spreading over her face, and looked away in confusion. The silence stretched between them excruciatingly as she sought an answer. Finally, desperately, she managed to laugh again.

"You force me to admit my partiality for Mister Strangeways, sir. Please spare my blushes and ask no more."

"Strangeways, is it? I might have known I could not trust him, though he is my best friend. No doubt I will be receiving a visit from him shortly?"

"No doubt. And I am more than a little inclined to accept him, for he is above anything handsome."

"Though I am constrained to agree, still I will be forced to decline his offer for you. You must remain yet awhile on the shelf."

"A dire fate. Do you think it possible that you are taking your duties as guardian too seriously?" she asked lightly, happy that she had managed to set a lighter tone to the conversation.

But he looked at her unsmilingly as he considered his answer for a moment.

"Yes, very seriously."

CHAPTER 17

"Ah, beautiful creature, you are pure enchantment tonight!" exclaimed Sidney Otway in a low voice as he bent over Pippa's hand and kissed it, rather longer than was strictly within the bounds of propriety. His warm, caressing voice and the obvious admiration in his eyes caused a responsive quiver in Pippa.

Mr. Otway was able to perform such an intimate gesture because Lady Barstowe and Sir Anthony were at that moment engaged with their hostess, the Duchess of Haverford. The duchess had invited them and a number of others to a dinner party with impromptu dancing to follow. All the furnishings had been removed from her largest drawing room for the dancing and there would be about ten couples to stand up. Most of the guests were young people, friends of Lady Fanny's, but the duchess had invited her old friend, Mr. Strangeways, and when she learned of the arrival of Sir Anthony, had sent around a note insisting he attend also.

Mrs. Otway was much in evidence, smiling knowingly at the assembled company when her son led Lady Fanny in to dinner, a proceeding watched by Pippa with a slight coldness about her heart, and no little bewilderment. She watched him at dinner, a lazy smile on his mouth as he sat with Fanny, leaning toward her, speaking softly into her small ear, and eliciting light, happy-sounding laughter from her. There was no escaping the fact that they seemed on very familiar terms and that the intimacies and warm glances Pippa had come to think of as exclusively her own were also shared with Lady Fanny.

But now, dinner over, the company assembled in the large drawing room, where the musicians were tuning their instruments and the guests were strolling about. Sidney Otway made his way to her directly as soon as the gentlemen joined the ladies after dinner. He took her hand and pulled her slightly apart from the group around the duchess and stood holding it for a moment while he surveyed her with most apparent approval.

She was wearing a blue silk gown of the exact shade of her mother's sapphires, creating a brilliant contrast with her sparkling auburn hair and causing her white complexion to seem translucent. She was not unaware that she was in fine looks tonight nor that she was the recipient of many admiring glances. She had been told so, most explicitly by Sir Anthony, as well as by Mr. Strangeways and Lady Barstowe. The duchess had stated bluntly, and loudly, that never had she beheld a prettier girl; so now Pippa was able to accept Mr. Otway's compliment without obvious embarrassment and to smile composedly at him.

"I thank you, sir."

"It was just on my lips to say you must always wear just such a shade of blue, but then I remembered other colors I have seen you in and thought just the same thing. I fear you are adorable in whatever you wear and I am doomed to be dazzled by the sight of you."

"Mister Otway, I think you flatter me overmuch. I must have a care not to take you too seriously," Pippa replied softly, the chill about her heart now completely melted.

"Sidney," said the voice of Mrs. Otway as she laid a possessive hand on his arm, "the musicians are ready to begin and I'm sure Lady Fanny must be wondering—forgive this interruption, Miss Cranville, I vow I could not blame any gentleman for forgetting his duties for so lovely a creature. I must get the name of your dressmaker!" During this gushing speech she had subtly tugged her son's arm and turned him in the direction of Lady Fanny, and now, with a smile and a bow, he spoke to Pippa.

"You will excuse me, Miss Cranville? And you must remember that I claim at least two dances. I will be back for them." And with that he walked away, Mrs. Otway smiling benignly after him. Pippa felt as though someone had thrown cold water in her face, and stood paralyzed and speechless with the shock of his abrupt departure. She had naturally thought that he had come to claim the first dance with her, though if her senses had not been so entirely disordered, she would have been aware, as everyone else seemed to be, that he would be required to dance first with his hostess's granddaughter.

She felt a warm hand on her elbow. "Miss Cranville, you will dance with me?"

She turned blindly to the voice of Sir Anthony and stared at him blankly for a moment before she was able to speak. "Why, of course—how very kind of you to ask."

"Kind! Whatever can you mean, child? I do myself a kindness when I dance with the most beautiful girl in the room."

"You always call me child—do you think I am a child?" she asked abruptly and as though she had not heard the rest of the speech.

"Well—I—of course I do not. It is only—oh, dear, how shall I put this? I think I feel that it is better to put more distance between us—more years, if you understand me." This rather incoherent speech was the result of being caught completely by surprise, for he had never consciously realized his motives and was completely unprepared for her question.

"No, I don't understand," she replied in the same manner as she had asked her first question, a jerky, barely civil way.

"Then I must make it clearer for both of us. You have caught me off guard, chi—Miss Cranville. I suppose I felt it would be less remarked upon if I seem to treat you in an avuncular way as I perform my duties as your guardian, which naturally put me much in your company. 'Miss Cranville' seems stiff and formal and not the way an uncle would address his niece."

"My uncle would call me Pippa, I think, or Philippa if you find the other too childish. I would prefer either address to 'child' or 'Miss Cranville.' "

"With your permission then I will call you Pippa. That's how I think of you anyway. And will you now call me Tony, as all my friends do?"

For the first time she lost her look of abstraction and looked directly up at him.

"Oh, no," she said definitely, "I could not. It would not seem proper."

"Perhaps you would prefer 'Uncle Tony'?" he inquired politely.

And now her mouth curved into a smile. "Oh heavens, no! It would sound ridiculous. Besides, I could never think of you as an uncle!"

"No? I wonder, if it's not too inquisitive, how do you think of me?" He tried to make the question perfectly casual, but he could not help awaiting her answer with great interest.

She pondered the question for a moment, then said, "Why, I suppose it is more as a—well—father, really."

Now it was Tony's turn to look blank. Though he himself had done his best to create the illusion of distance between them, he realized quite suddenly that he was less than happy to find that he had accomplished what he had set out to do.

"Hmmm—well, I see. And very right that you should, since I stand in place of father to you. I suppose if I were to do my duty properly, I should marry and provide a mother for you as well," he replied, somewhat more tartness in his voice than he was aware of.

"No, no!" she cried forcefully and spontaneously, "I mean—well, I have Lady Barstowe now, so you need not marry just to—"

"But if I should want to for myself, you would not object?" Tony could not help probing the subject.

"Why, I had not thought of—but of course, it would be most improper of me to object, Sir Anthony, to whatever you feel you must do. Should I offer you my congratulations?" she asked with a sinking heart, but a brave attempt at raillery.

"There is no need for that yet."

"Could I know the name of the lady you have in mind?"

"Now you are being provoking, Pippa. I have told you there is no one. Why are you pursuing the subject in this way?"

"I believe it was you who brought up the subject of marrying, sir," she replied waspishly.

"Now you are cross. Are you tired?"

Fortunately, before this unhappy conversation could be continued, they were interrupted by the approach of a smiling young man come to ask for the pleasure of the next dance with Miss Cranville. Pippa and Sir Anthony looked about, somewhat bewildered, only now realizing that the dance he had requested of her had come to an end and that they had stood talking through it, unaware of the music starting or the figures moving past them on the floor.

Tony gave Pippa and the young man a cold little bow and walked away. Pippa allowed herself to be led out to the floor and managed to nod and smile and speak but it was all mechanical, for her mind was completely taken up with images of the future Lady Seymour-Croft. The toast of London, no doubt, a brilliantly beautiful woman, dressed exclusively by French couturiers; a managing sort of woman, used to having her own way in everything, and not hesitating to manipulate everyone around her to get it. One of those cold, pale blond women who—

She was interrupted in these thoughts and realized that the young man had addressed a question to her and was waiting, with a puzzled expression on his face, for her answer.

"I beg your pardon, sir, the music is loud, is it not? I didn't quite catch—"

"I only said, Miss Cranville, that you seemed to be feeling the heat and would you like to sit down now?"

"Oh! Yes, you are right, it is somewhat warm. Would you mind very much if we—"

"With great pleasure, I do assure you." And he led her to the side of the room and found a seat for her, and then, taking her fan from her hand, proceeded to wave it in front of her face.

Sidney Otway, having opened the dancing with Lady Fanny, and then led out a protesting duchess for the next, looked about and saw Pippa. He came over and took the fan from the young man.

"My dance, I believe, Miss Cranville," he said smoothly, ignoring the faint protest from the young man, who stood there impotently for a moment, then went away.

"You take too much upon yourself, Mister Otway," Pippa protested. "I think it is my place to decide whether to dismiss my partners."

"Ah, you are cross. Are you tired?"

"I am *not* cross. Why must people be always saying that and asking if I am tired? Do I *look* so pale and drooping?"

"You are exquisite, as I'm sure you've been told endlessly this evening. It is just that I am not used to you being other than sweetly gracious."

"And unprotesting? I'm sure that is what you are really implying. But I do protest when there is need, Mister Otway. I am not entirely a doormat! And I feel there is a need to remind you that your manners at times are not all they should be."

"I stand reproved. Say you will forgive me, or I shall be forced to do something drastic!"

"Such as what?" she asked interestedly.

"I shall kneel before you with outstretched hands until you relent and say I am forgiven."

"Please do not do any such thing, sir," she said, her lips twitching with a smile in spite of herself.

"Then I am forgiven? You must say the words before I believe you."

"Fustian! Now you are trifling with me, sir, and I will have you know I demand to be taken seriously."

"Believe me, I take you very seriously indeed," he said meaningfully, his eyes caressing her.

"Do you? But then I think it is your habit to take many girls seriously, Mister Otway."

"Untrue! I protest, Miss Cranville. You know too well that I am at nonplus with you."

"And Lady Fanny?" The words were out before she could stop them, and she could have bitten her tongue with vexation to have so revealed herself.

"Ah, dear Fanny. But that is an entirely different matter, you must see that."

"It is no matter at all. Please forgive my mentioning it," she said hastily, taking back her fan and fanning herself vigorously.

"You have made me very happy by mentioning it, Miss Cranville. I can only hope it is a sign that you are not entirely indifferent to me."

"I cannot think why you should hope such a thing."

"Why because my feelings for you are far from indifferent, as you are well aware, fair one."

"So I had been led by you to think, Mister Otway," she said, looking directly at him and speaking with her usual openness. "But I now begin to doubt."

"Ah, we are back to Lady Fanny. Well, it is my mother, you see. She has set her heart on that young lady for a daughter-in-law," he said, laughing lightly at the absurdity of mothers.

"And you?"

"Well, one must marry sometime, I suppose," he said indifferently.

"And if one must, it is as well to reach for the duchess's granddaughter," she prompted him slowly.

"There! I knew you were a sensible girl as well as a beautiful one! I am never wrong in these things. But there is no need to discuss this now. I am here with the most glorious creature I've ever seen and—"

"And you must make hay while the sun shines?" she inquired sweetly.

"Yes, you darling girl," he whispered, leaning down close to her ear.

She stood up so abruptly, he was caught there for a moment, still bending over the chair. Someone tittered nearby and he straightened up hastily, a flush of anger on his face.

"And so must I, Mister Otway!"

"I—I—beg you pardon?"

"Make hay, Mister Otway. And I am wasting my time. You are much too green for reaping, I find."

And with that she walked away, furious and fuming, but with a feeling of triumph nevertheless. She found Lady Barstowe and plumped down on the sofa beside her.

"My dear, you seem in a taking. Has something happened to upset you?"

"Only that paltry creature, Mister Otway. It is nothing to signify," Pippa replied somewhat grandly.

"I hate to be the one to point out that I have always found him to be an odious young man, but the temptation is too strong. However, I made quite sure you would see it too before it was too late."

CHAPTER 18

After church the next morning, Sir Anthony declared that he thought a ride would do them all good, and went away to hire mounts. Lady Barstowe graciously assented to the plan since she had a delectable new riding dress.

They rode out Great Putney Street toward the Sydney Gardens reveling in the freshness of the air and the exercise. Pippa, though grateful to be in a saddle again, rode with the same air of distraction that she had shown since the evening before.

She had lain awake the night before, pondering the events of the evening, reliving each moment. Some of those moments made her ashamed, especially her final conversation with Sidney Otway, which she knew had been pert and improper. She wished very much that she had been able to maintain a more dignified position. However, in another way she couldn't help being secretly rather proud of that final speech, at least she was when she thought of how he had presumed to think that she was so lacking in morals that she would be willing to play games with him while he pursued Lady Fanny. She writhed with shame whenever she thought of his soft, insinuating voice saying he knew she would understand. No doubt he thought he had caught a green, countrified girl who would think such goings-on were all the crack and be properly grateful to him for his condescension. Oh! The unutterable nerve of him! She ground her teeth with rage, wishing that she had said even more to him than she had. All sorts of marvelously cutting remarks came easily now into her mind, phrases that would have reduced him to jelly!

Then her thoughts turned to the inescapable knowledge that he had very nearly been right in his assessment of her as easy game. *What a paper-skull I am that I had to have him spell the whole thing out for me before I understood! I am such a peagoose that I nearly deserve his opinion, for I behaved like a rustic with the straw still in my hair, coming to the city and falling for the first pretty face I see, blushing and sighing when he deigned to look at me.*

Thus castigating herself, she finally fell asleep, but not, fortunately, on a tear-soaked pillow. There were no tears, for she was not heartbroken, only angry with him for being a puffed-up, conceited young popinjay, and with herself for being such a clunch.

These thoughts were still preoccupying her mind as she rode along now. Melissa was in highest alt this morning and kept her mother and Tony laughing at her quips to such an extent that Pippa's silence was not so evident.

Not that they were unaware of it, or at least Lady Barstowe and Tony were. Lady Barstowe had confided to Tony her brief conversation with Pippa at the party the evening before and her speculations upon what had occurred. She made no doubt, she said, that Sidney Otway's true colors had finally become apparent to Pippa. She didn't know, of course, exactly what he had said or done, but it had been clear enough to show himself a coxcomb.

Tony had fumed impotently, declaring he had half a mind to go around to the Otways's and speak his mind to young Sidney. Maria Barstowe had dissuaded him from this course, saying that to her way of thinking the less said about the matter the sooner forgotten.

"You may take my word for it, there'll be no broken heart to mend here. I think her pride may be rubbed a trifle raw, but that's no great tragedy. It was not a bad experience for her to have, truly, and she's come out of it with little harm and a great deal more knowledge."

So Tony held his tongue, contenting himself with watching her covertly for signs of unhappiness. So far he felt there were none.

Suddenly Pippa spoke for the first time that morning. "I long for a good gallop. Is anyone game?" And with that she lightly whipped her horse and the little mare responded instantly and joyously, stretching her long legs to their fullest extent. Tony, with a glance at Lady Barstowe, who nodded in agreement, prodded his own horse and took off after Pippa. He soon caught her up and they galloped along side by side, Pippa bent forward intently, the wind whipping back her hair and the plume of her hat. The rush of air in her face seemed to blow the clouds of thoughts from her mind, and the freedom and speed of the movement to release her pent-up anger. When Tony began to pull up, she followed suit, and presently they drew up together, laughing and breathless.

"Glorious! What an inspired idea. Sir Anthony. This is my first ride since I left Ayleforth Hall, and I now realize that I have missed it very much."

"I should have thought of it long ago and had some of your own horses brought from the country."

"Oh, good heavens, do no such thing. It would be a quite unnecessary bother, not to speak of the expense. There is little time for riding here anyway, and when we want to do so in the future, why we can hire mounts again."

"Well, if you are sure. Though I think you should contrive to ride more often, if only to show off such an elegant riding dress," he said teasingly, eyeing the bright green costume fastened down the front with black military frogs, and the high-crowned beaver hat with gold tassels and a long green ostrich feather sweeping down one side. She blushed under his scrutiny, but her battered self-esteem lifted its head tentatively again in the warmth of his approval.

They prodded their horses and moved off down the road at a slow amble, to give the Barstowes time to catch up.

"Do your affairs go well in London, sir?"

"Well enough, if somewhat slowly," he replied non-committally.

"I take it very kindly that you would so put yourself out to come down here. I know it must be a great bother to you to make such a long trip for so brief a stay."

"Not at all. I have looked forward to coming. It is very pleasant here in Bath."

She longed to pursue the subject of London, specifically about his friends there, for the image of the blond goddess with a special *tendre* for Sir Anthony was still very much present in her mind. But after their sharp words about it the night before, she couldn't quite dare to be too explicit.

"You must miss your friends there, however," she prodded gently, in spite of herself.

"Oh, come now, surely you do not expect me to be pining away in two days?" he quizzed her teasingly.

"Well, if there were any degree of attachment you might very well do so."

"I think I am more attached to my friends here," he responded.

"Really? Who—" She stopped abruptly, much vexed with herself.

He laughed. "Well, there is Maria Barstowe—"

"Oh, yes, of course. You have been close friends for a very long time, have you not?" She tried to make her voice express a bright interest.

"A very long time," he agreed gravely, then added, "and with Mister Strangeways for almost as long, and with Melissa since she was a babe."

"Yes, of course," she replied, somewhat dashed to realize how recent was their acquaintance, for though *she* might consider him her first friend, *he* had many, all firmly established in his affections long before she came into his life. Of course, he had known her as a baby, but one could hardly call a few meetings between an eight-year-old and a newborn babe a friendship.

As though reading her thoughts, he said, "But you are my oldest acquaintance, you know, for I met you long before any of the others."

She turned to smile blindingly at him, grateful for his understanding, realizing once again how good he had always been to her.

"I wish you did not have to go away again so soon!" she said impulsively, though she knew it wrong of her to drag at him in this way.

"No more than I," he responded fervently, and then, with a sidelong glance at her, "but it is better so, believe me."

She mulled over this interesting remark for a few moments. But before she could come to any conclusions about it, they were joined by the Barstowes. They all agreed it was time to turn for home and that they had all developed astonishing appetites and would welcome some luncheon.

Lady Barstowe had invited Mr. Strangeways for dinner, along with Mr. Watkins, and afterward Pippa and Melissa entertained the company, taking turns at the pianoforte. It was very relaxed and intimate, with everyone in the very best of spirits and happy to be with one another.

The ladies all accompanied the gentlemen to the front door when they took their leave, and in the confusion of good-byes, Tony turned to Pippa and, reaching out, took both her hands in his own.

"Good-bye, Pippa. I know I leave you in good care with

Maria and Mister Strangeways, but I shall worry a bit just the same."

"You will?" she asked in her usual direct way.

"Yes. I want you to be well and happy."

"Thank you. You *will* come back soon?"

"In another fortnight," and impulsively, "I shall miss you too much to stay away longer." And with that he lifted each hand and kissed it, then, pressing them lightly, he released her and turned away. She could only stand there speechlessly and watch him go down the steps and enter the waiting carriage, still feeling the warm imprint of his lips on the backs of her tingling hands.

After they had dropped Mr. Watkins at his lodging, the two men rode along in a comfortable silence for a while.

"Lovely evening," commented Mr. Strangeways.

"Very. Maria Barstowe always manages to find the best cooks to be had."

"Its too bad that you must go away so soon."

"Hmmm."

"Are you sure it is necessary?"

"Now more than ever."

"Oh? How so?"

"I very much fear that I am in danger of losing my head over the girl."

"And is that such a bad thing? I'm afraid I find all that business of what people will say too silly to bother with. I think you would make a well-matched couple, and I shouldn't care, if I were you, what anyone said."

"You may be right, but it will never work out."

"And why not, if I may ask?"

Tony laughed ruefully, "Because she told me she thinks of me as her father!"

The next morning Pippa came down to breakfast to find Lady Barstowe there before her, sorting through a stack of letters and cards of invitations that had just arrived by the post.

"Why, Pippa, here is a letter for you!" Lady Barstowe exclaimed, holding it out to her.

Pippa knew, even before she took it, that it was from her Aunt Emma. How she could be so sure, she could not say. She reached out slowly to take it, broke open the seal, and read it with some trepidation. Then she handed it back wordlessly to Lady Barstowe, who read it aloud.

"Dear Philippa,

I have received your letters, and I thank you for writing to me. Never having had any great opinion of Bath, I must own myself astonished to read of your enthusiasm for the place, but naturally I am glad to know that you are having an enjoyable visit.

I must tell you that I used to know Althea Otway many years ago and found her to be an odious woman, and would advise you to avoid the family.

Everything here goes on as before, though more quietly. I have delivered your messages and have been charged with returning greetings from all.

Sincerely,
Emma Cranville"

Lady Barstowe and Pippa stared at each other silently for a moment.

"I confess I never expected her to write you," said Lady Barstowe.

"Nor I. But isn't it wonderful that she has? I think she must be more lonely now than she will admit, otherwise she could not have brought herself to write. I think these are the warmest words I've ever had from her."

"I give you credit, dear Pippa, for continuing to write her, or for writing her at all, after her treatment of you."

"Oh, she did not treat me badly really, or at least she

didn't *mis*treat me. She mostly ignored me, except after Sir Anthony arrived. Then there were some harsh words, but I think she resented having her life stirred up by him. She had lived so long in a sort of state of suspended motion, you see, and I don't think she wanted anything ever to change."

Melissa came in at that moment, paused to kiss her mother, and demanded to know what they were talking about. When she had read Aunt Emma's letter, she only tossed her head and said "Hmpf!" and helped herself to some toast.

"Now, Mama, what invitations do you have there?" she asked, crunching away on her toast, generously heaped with marmalade.

"I don't know yet, dearest, I became so interested in Pippa's letter, I haven't gone through them. Here"—she handed a stack across to her daughter—"you may go through them while I read my letters."

Melissa began opening them, passing them over to Pippa as she went, while Lady Barstowe opened her mail. She was in the habit of keeping up a lively correspondence with her friends scattered all over England, and from time to time she read the girls amusing bits from their letters.

She broke the seal on the last one and began to read. Suddenly she gasped.

"Good God!"

The girls looked up to find all the color draining from her face, her eyes wide in shock.

"Mama, what on earth—" Melissa jumped up to run to her mother at the same time that Pippa did so.

"Lady Barstowe, what is it?"

"My—my mother—she's—this is from my sister, telling me that my mother—oh, my God, I don't think I can bear—Melissa, darling, we must be very brave, your dear grandmama is extremely ill. Caro says she cannot last much longer and that we must come at once."

"Yes, darling Mama, of course we must."

"But—oh, heavens, my mind is in such a whirl. I must try to think calmly. Now the first thing we must decide is about Pippa."

"Dear Lady Barstowe, please do not concern yourself in the least. I will contrive to take care of myself quite well. You must concentrate now on your travel plans."

"But Pippa, where shall you go?"

"Go? But why should I *go* anyplace. I will stay here, of course."

"You cannot! Stay alone, unchaperoned, in this house? Why, it is not possible! Oh, if only Tony had not gone away this morning. I really am so distracted, I cannot think clearly at all."

"Perhaps Mister Strangeways—"

"No, no, that would never do! I know he would be perfectly trustworthy, but people would talk just the same."

"I didn't mean that he should come to stay here with me, but that we should send for him. After all, he is standing in place of guardian to me while Sir Anthony is away," Pippa explained patiently.

"Of course, how stupid of me. Ring for a footman, Melissa, and we'll send a note around to him immediately."

CHAPTER 19

Mr. Strangeways came around at once and found the house in an uproar, with distracted servants rushing through the hallways with clothes and various pieces of luggage.

He sent word upstairs that he had arrived, and in a moment a distraught Lady Barstowe came hurrying down to greet him.

"Dear lady, what is this? Has something happened?"

"Mister Strangeways, thank God you've come. A few more moments and I should have had strong convulsions, I am sure. It's Pippa you see, and Tony nearly to London by now, and I simply must go—"

"Lady Barstowe, please try to start at the beginning. I can see you are in a great taking, but I don't quite understand. What of Pippa?"

"Forgive me, I'm all to pieces. It is my mother, you see, she is dreadfully ill. In fact—well, at any rate I must go immediately to her, and Melissa also. I could take Pippa with us, but it seems a dreadful thing to put the child through: a family too distracted to pay any attention to her and a dying woman. On the other hand I cannot go off and leave her unattended here."

"No, of course you cannot," he agreed slowly, "Oh, dear, it *is* a problem."

"I have not liked to even speak of it in front of Pippa,

but I can see nothing for it but to send her back to her aunt for the time," Lady Barstowe said most reluctantly.

He didn't answer, but stood for a moment staring into space.

"It might be necessary, but I wonder if you could delay your journey by one day. We could send a message to her by a boy from my stable on a fast horse. Perhaps she would come *here*."

"That would be the answer, naturally, in normal circumstances, but I fear Aunt Emma could not be persuaded. She is a very unusual sort of aunt, with little fondness for her niece."

Pippa, running down the stairs at this moment in search of Lady Barstowe, heard her aunt named and stopped, dismay filling her eyes. It had already occurred to her that the only possible solution to this problem was that she go back home. She had been thinking of it just now while she helped Melissa pack her cases and knew she should steel herself to make the suggestion to poor Lady Barstowe immediately and thus relieve her of the worry. But now, hearing them speaking of it, she realized how very much she disliked the idea of going home.

"Ah, Pippa, I was just going to suggest we send for you to come down. We are discussing what it is best to do about you, and I suggested to Lady Barstowe that we send immediately to your aunt and ask if she would come here. What do you think?"

"Aunt Emma? Here? I don't think she would dream of—but, I am not so positive now as I would have been yesterday. After her letter this morning—she wrote to me, you see. I have been writing to her since I first arrived, but she has never answered till now."

"Don't you think if we wrote her of the emergency of the situation, she might be persuaded to come?" Mr. Strangeways pressed.

"I think it would be worth a try. But—oh, no, I cannot.

I must simply pack up and go back to her. I could not ask Lady Barstowe to delay her own trip for the time it would take for her to come—or even the time it would take to get her answer."

"Thank you, darling Pippa, for being so thoughtful. I should have expected you to behave just so. But I cannot leave before tomorrow noon at any rate. If we sent a man off immediately with a message, we should have her answer before then. If she refuses—well, then I'm afraid there will be nothing else for it, but that you will have to go back. I know I can ask Mister Strangeways to accompany you."

"Certainly you can, madam. I will do so happily."

"Then let us send for your stableboy, Mister Strangeways, and Pippa and I will compose the letter."

"If I may make a suggestion, I think the letter should come from you, Lady Barstowe, as an appeal for her help. Surely she cannot be such a monster of selfishness that she would not respond to you in your distress."

"Yes, you are right. I'll do it at once and it will be ready when the boy arrives."

Mr. Strangeways returned with the stableboy and a fast horse, and the message was duly dispatched to Ayleforth Hall. They felt he could make it there in no less than five hours and, after resting, could make the return journey in time to arrive midmorning of the following day.

Mr. Strangeways lingered for a while, begging to be allowed to contribute his services in some way, but finally left the family to themselves when it became apparent he was more hindrance than help now, since Lady Barstowe felt obliged to stay downstairs with him, feeling it was her duty to entertain any guest in her house. When he could not persuade her to go about her business and forget his presence, he took his leave, promising to return to take dinner with them.

The rest of the day was spent packing and consulting with the cook and butler regarding the disposition of the household after Lady Barstowe's departure, all depending, of course, on Aunt Emma's decision.

They sat down wearily to an early dinner with Mr. Strangeways, though there was little appetite displayed by anyone. The sense of being suspended in midair made for an atmosphere of stretched nerves and general abstraction. Lady Barstowe was obviously preoccupied with worry for her dying mother and guilt at her abandonment of Pippa. Melissa could barely keep within bounds her tendency to sixteen-year-old melodrama, and occasionally burst into tears for no apparent reason. Pippa was in such a state of apprehension and unhappiness that she could hardly speak at all and spent most of the evening staring frozenly into space.

Poor Mr. Strangeways, trying vainly to be of aid and comfort to all three, found himself longing for the solitary comfort of his room and his West Indian tobacco. When Lady Barstowe suggested they have an early night and retire, he leaped almost too eagerly to his feet and made his goodnights.

The early night was wasted, however, at least as far as Pippa was concerned. Her pillow, usually so comforting, tonight seemed to form itself into uncomfortable lumps that had to be continually rearranged, and she was too warm, and then too cold, and no position she could find seemed conducive to sleep. She kept trying to imagine Aunt Emma opening Lady Barstowe's letter and her reaction to it. She could almost picture her marching coolly to her escritoire and firmly writing her regrets that she could not accommodate Lady Barstowe, her recommendation that Pippa be dispatched forthwith to Ayleforth Hall, and signing with her sympathies to Lady Barstowe. This scene was so lifelike, it was almost impossible for Pippa to believe she was not actually witnessing it.

She then tried to picture her aunt exclaiming in sympathy with Lady Barstowe's plight and rushing upstairs to pack her cases for Bath, but she could not get a grasp on such a happening. It was entirely too unlikely a reaction for Aunt Emma, involving, as it must, the kindlier emotions that, in spite of her recent letter to her niece, Pippa could not associate with her aunt. The letter certainly betokened a weakening in her heretofore cold exterior, but it was a long way from a complete surrender of her defenses.

Oh, if only Sir Anthony had been there to take care of her, to tell them all what it was best to do, as he always had since Pippa had met him. Mr. Strangeways said he had sent off a letter to him immediately, which would hopefully reach him in two days. Surely he would come as soon as possible. Finally, with the comforting thought that he would be with her in a few days, she fell into a sleep, from which she woke from time to time to pull her covers more closely around her. Each time she was aware that she had dreamed the same dream, of being in an unfurnished room that slowly grew colder and colder.

"My dear child," exclaimed Lady Barstowe when Pippa came down for breakfast, "your eyes are positively glassy with tiredness. Didn't you sleep at all?"

"Not very much," Pippa admitted, then she gave a rallying smile. "But not to worry, I expect I shall have time for a great deal of rest in the next few weeks."

"Pippa, dear, I know it won't be so long as that. Even if you must go back to Ayleforth Hall for a time, it won't be for weeks! I promise you Melissa and I will come back as soon as may be—though, I suppose we might not be able to go about as much as before since we might be in mourning. But at least we will all be together, and I'm sure we could ask the duchess to take you when she is accompanying Lady Fanny to parties."

"Please don't concern yourself with such things, dear

Lady Barstowe. You surely don't think I am so selfish as to be thinking about parties when you are losing your dear mother. After all your kindness to me, I only wish I could have the happiness of doing something for you."

Melissa came in as pink-cheeked and bright-eyed as usual. It was obvious that her rest had been as unbroken as ever, and the possible loss of her grandmother, while affecting her youthful sensibilities, did not touch her heart. She helped herself to a hearty breakfast and chatted away volubly, speculating on what Aunt Emma would do and expressing aloud what Lady Barstowe and Pippa avoided saying out of tact for each other.

They welcomed her bright conversation, however, for it was but nine o'clock and the hours till noon and some relief from the suspense seemed to stretch away into infinity.

"I wonder what she'll do? Do you think she will come, Pippa? I don't. Nothing I have heard of her convinces me she would react as would be proper in an aunt with the least degree of attachment to her niece," Melissa stated with great conviction, cocking her head at Pippa like some saucy bird and obviously expecting a reply.

"No doubt you're right, Melissa," Pippa replied, trying not to inject the admission with any of the despair she felt.

"Let's see, the boy left—what?—very close to eleven yesterday morning. If he rode hard, he must have reached her by"—she stopped to count on her fingers—"not later than five in the afternoon," she finished triumphantly. This statement she directed to her mother, happy to prove that her governess's attempts to inculcate some arithmetic into her education had not been wasted. Lady Barstowe smiled indulgently, if somewhat tiredly.

"Yes, darling, surely he must have arrived by five."

"Well then," Melissa continued implacably, "she must have set him on his way back at a very early hour this morning—say by six, or five, even. Why he could be arriving at any moment!" She gave them both a sunny, encouraging smile. They responded, if somewhat wanly.

"And then, if her answer is what we expect it to be, Mister Strangeways will drive you home as soon as we are gone. Then, she must, in common courtesy, invite him to stay a few days, and by that time Tony will have contrived to come and he'll set everything straight in no time at all, you'll see."

"Oh, I do hope you are right," breathed Pippa fervently.

"I'm sure to be," declared Melissa with enormous confidence, "and you'll see, dear Pippa, it won't be so bad. Tony will not let her oppress you. He cares for you a great deal too much."

This assertion elicited a startled look from Pippa, and she was just about to open her mouth to probe further into this interesting subject when the sound of wheels was heard on the gravel of the driveway.

"Oh, here is Mister Strangeways. I'll go and bring him in," Melissa cried, jumping up immediately and running out of the room. Pippa and Lady Barstowe exchanged a rueful, understanding smile.

They heard an exchange of words and looked at each other, startled, as they realized at the same moment that both voices they were hearing were—female! Before they could comment, however, the breakfast room door opened and Melissa appeared, her eyes opened to their widest and a look of awe on her face.

Directly behind her was the commanding figure of Aunt Emma, who sailed calmly into the room and straight up to Lady Barstowe.

"My dear madam, I came as quickly as possible, though my carriage is so cumbersome that we made very poor time."

Lady Barstowe sat absolutely paralyzed with shock for

at least ten seconds, then gulped audibly and rose hastily to her feet to clasp the hand held out to her.

"Miss Cranville! We didn't th— I mean, we thought you would not—well, I mean I am so—oh, dear, you must forgive me, I'm all to pieces with surprise." She looked desperately at Pippa and Melissa, but realized at once the hopelessness of expecting help from either of them, as they were both still staring with open mouths at the lady. "Dear Miss Cranville, please sit down, you must be exhausted after such a journey," said Lady Barstowe, pulling herself together and leading Aunt Emma to a chair.

"I admit to some fatigue. Ah, thank you, and if you would be so good, I would appreciate some coffee. I seldom drink it, but now I feel the need for a restorative," Aunt Emma admitted, sinking into the chair held for her by Lady Barstowe.

"But of course you must have some coffee—and some breakfast—you must be famished!" Lady Barstowe went to pull the bell to summon the butler, casting a meaningful glance at Pippa on the way.

Pippa started out of her trance as she intercepted the look, and came around the table to her aunt.

"Aunt Emma, this is—this is very good of you. I cannot think how you contrived to get here so quickly."

"I left at four this morning and made John Coachman whip the horses all the way," said Emma simply. "By the way, Lady Barstowe, your stableboy will be back later in the day with your horse."

"Oh, it is not mine. Mister Strangeways very kindly lent it for this emergency."

"Ah, yes—Mister Strangeways. Philippa has mentioned him in her letters. Do sit down, Philippa, you make me nervous hovering in that indecisive way."

Pippa sank submissively into a chair, almost relieved to hear her aunt ordering her about in the old familiar way. Her appearance had so astounded Pippa that she had been unable to think clearly. Even now, though the shock had worn off somewhat, it was difficult to accept the fact that her aunt was actually in this room. It was almost impossible to keep back the burning questions she longed to ask: What had caused her aunt to behave so uncharacteristically? What had made her decide to come to Bath? But being unable to frame either of these blunt questions, she tried to make her mind function sensibly, and finally became calm enough to speak again.

"Yes, Mister Strangeways. You will like him very much, Aunt Emma. He is above anything fine. Sir Anthony left him in charge of me when he had to go away, and he could not have been kinder or more attentive."

Aunt Emma did not respond to this, but very deliberately finished the piece of bread and butter she was holding, then turned again to Lady Barstowe.

"I take it you are eager to be away, madam? Please feel free to make your arrangements to leave as soon as may be. I assure you, there is no need to delay any longer."

"How very kind," murmured Lady Barstowe. "It would be a great relief to me, as I see you understand, to be on my way immediately. I do hate to dash away the moment you are in the house, but I fear my mother—"

"Say no more. You run upstairs and finish your packing. Philippa and I will talk until you come down. It will be necessary for me to rest for a few hours as soon as you are off, but I'm sure my niece can occupy herself for a time. I took the liberty of sending my maid upstairs with one of your servants, and no doubt a room has already been prepared for me."

Lady Barstowe hoped very much that this was so, for so dubious had she been of the likelihood of Emma actually appearing that she had completely neglected to have a room made ready. She decided she had best go make sure of this and rose.

"Then I will do as you suggest and make ready to leave

at once. Melissa and I are both packed and need only to have our cases carried down. Come Melissa. We'll be back down directly."

Melissa rose obediently and followed her mother to the door, where she turned and dropped a brief curtsy to Miss Cranville and sent a flashing smile to Pippa.

Lady Barstowe turned back for a moment. "Miss Cranville, I can never thank you enough—"

"No need, madam, I assure you."

When the door closed after the Barstowes, Emma turned to her niece and their glances met briefly before they both turned away in some embarrassment. Neither knew quite how to treat the other under such circumstances. Emma took a sip of her coffee and cleared her throat.

"Well, child, I'm sure you are surprised to see me."

CHAPTER 20

Pippa was rather surprised by the openness of this question, but was pleased by it. It seemed to indicate the possibility that their relationship was on a somewhat different footing than had previously been the case.

"Very much, Aunt Emma, knowing your dislike of traveling and of Bath," she finally replied, opting for openness herself.

"True, and my first sight of Bath did nothing to change my feelings. Dirty, bustling place—far too many people, most of whom look as though they would be far better off at home attending to their affairs than gallivanting about imitating their betters," said Emma emphatically.

"You may be right, of course, but I must own that I have met only exceptional kindness everywhere here, and wonderful people," Pippa declared stoutly.

"Are you still interested in that Otway boy?"

This bluntness almost took Pippa's breath away, but she bravely faced the question.

"I think *interested* is much too strong a term to express my feelings about—"

"Nonsense! I can read between the lines as well as the next. Well, whatever your feelings were, I hope you are over them."

"Completely," replied Pippa, succinctly and conclusively, determined to resist all further attempts to draw her out on this issue. Aunt Emma, recognizing defeat, changed the subject.

"This—ah—Mister Strangeways, he is an elderly gentleman? I seem to recall—"

"Oh, no, not elderly! He is older than Sir Anthony certainly, but I would not call him elderly. At first glance he seems older because his hair is white, but his countenance is youthful, as you will see, and Sir Anthony tells me his hair has been white since he was a very young man. Perhaps you are thinking of his father, though I don't know if his father is still alive."

"Yes, perhaps I am. Ah, I believe I hear Lady Barstowe in the hall. We must go make our good-byes."

They found the Barstowes coming down the stairs, following several footmen laden with luggage. Melissa rushed to Pippa and hugged her fiercely.

"Did she eat you alive?" she whispered in Pippa's ear.

"Hush, silly child. Of course not," Pippa laughed at her, then pushed her back and began straightening the ribbon of her bonnet, feeling a rush of tears tighten her throat now that the moment for parting had actually arrived. "Now see you behave and help your dear mother," she scolded.

"Oh, Pippa, you and your extra year. I suppose you will always treat me as a baby," Melissa scolded back, through misty eyes. "But I shall miss you dreadfully, all the same," and she kissed Pippa hard and turned to run down the steps to the waiting carriage.

Lady Barstowe turned from Aunt Emma and took Pippa in her arms and held her close for a moment. "Dear child, be well. You know that I shall think of you and that we will come back as soon as possible."

Pippa could not speak for the lump lodged in her throat, but could only nod and try to smile as Lady Barstowe followed her daughter.

She waved the carriage out of sight, then turned back into the hall as Foukes, the butler, closed the front door.

"Well, Philippa, you must not grieve. You may be sure that Lady Barstowe is not the sort who will like being buried away in the country for long. She'll be back before you know it. Now, have you plans for this afternoon?"

"Only to receive Mister Strangeways. He will be coming around soon to see if we have had word from you."

"Ah, well, I won't wait. I must lie on my bed for a time. Perhaps he will take you for a drive or something. Now if you will excuse me—" With that she turned and mounted the stairs with a burst of speed quite unusual for her.

Pippa was left standing, staring after her. She felt a great deal of compassion for her aunt at that moment, seeing how eagerly she rushed off to her bed. *How tired she must be,* Pippa mused, *and after all, why should she not be, after being up at such an early hour this morning and traveling all that distance without stopping, just to come to my rescue. I must arrange some interesting expeditions for her with Mr. Strangeways and take her to call on the duchess soon. I'm sure those two will have a great deal in common.*

She wandered into the drawing room and sat down at the pianoforte, but then remembered that her aunt disliked having music played when she napped. She took up a book Melissa had left on the sofa, but found the words held no interest for her. She let the book drop into her lap and, leaning her head back against the sofa, let her mind mull over the events of the morning, and presently fell asleep, sitting upright.

It was there Mr. Strangeways found her when he was shown in by the butler shortly after eleven. He touched her lightly on the shoulder, and she started awake instantly.

"Forgive me, child, for waking you, but I must know what has happened. The house so quiet, you asleep here—has—did—?"

"Yes and yes. She came! Is that not the most astonishing thing ever? You cannot imagine our surprise when she walked in as we were having our breakfast."

"Good God! Did she drive all night?"

"Very nearly. She left at four this morning! I must tell you that I am nearly eaten away with curiosity to know what persuaded her to come."

"Why, I would guess that your letters softened her somewhat, and then, as I said before, she could not be so selfish as to not come to Lady Barstowe's assistance in such dire circumstances."

"Well, until the moment she walked in the door, I must admit that I never truly believed that she would come. You don't know what Aunt Emma was like!"

"Perhaps the picture was clearer to me, not being cluttered by too much knowledge," replied Mr. Strangeways, somewhat smugly. "But at any rate our problems are solved. I will send off word to Tony immediately, if you will give me leave."

Pippa led him into the library, where he seated himself at Lady Barstowe's desk and scratched away quickly. He folded the letter, sealed it, and rose.

"Now, what shall we do today? Will your aunt consent to a drive, do you think?"

"She went to bed as soon as Lady Barstowe was out of sight. Poor dear, she was very tired. But she said that you might take me, if you would not mind, sir?"

"Delightful, my dear, delightful. Run away and fetch your bonnet and we'll be off."

They drove away at a spanking pace and decided not to have a destination in mind but just to go where they willed. First he drove her to the other side of Bath to the Royal Crescent, where they watched a parade of soldiers in Crescent Fields, then by various roads out to Wick Rocks at the top of the Landsdown Hill.

After that he drove out the Great London Road as far

as Vauxhall Gardens, which Pippa had not yet visited. They got down to wander through this delightful place and take some refreshments. By this time Pippa was so enjoying her afternoon that she had nearly forgotten her Aunt Emma and all the anxious hours she had been through. But Mr. Strangeways had not. He was very curious to see for himself this aunt of Pippa's. He suggested that since it was close to five, it would be best to start back, in case Miss Cranville should wake from her nap and be worried about her niece.

"Is my aunt down yet, Foukes?" Pippa asked as they came in the front door being held by the butler.

"Yes, miss. I have just carried her a glass of wine to the drawing room."

"Good, I hope she is rested. Oh, shall I have Foukes bring you some wine also, Mister Strangeways?"

"That would be nice, yes."

Foukes went away to bring the wine, and Mr. Strangeways followed Pippa into the drawing room.

"Aunt Emma, I have brought Mister Strangeways to meet you," Pippa called out gaily as she opened the drawing room doors.

Emma sat very still for a moment, then slowly and deliberately raised her head. Pippa turned back to take Mr. Strangeways's hand to lead him forward and was arrested in midmotion by the expression on his face. The smile just forming on his mouth was stopped halfway; he stared for a second as the color drained from his face, and then his eyes rolled up in his head and he toppled backward in a dead faint. There was a sickening thump as his head hit the floor, which seemed to echo on and on in the silence of the room. Foukes appeared in the doorway with a glass of wine, which fell from his nerveless hand to crash beside the head lying at his feet, spattering Mr. Strangeways with red, bloodlike stains.

There was another instance of silence while three people stared down in horror at the body on the floor, and then a great deal of activity ensued.

Emma came forward and ordered the butler to gather his wits and call some servants to carry Mr. Strangeways to the sofa, and ordered Pippa to fetch her vinaigrette from her reticule on the table.

She then dropped to her knees beside the still form and felt at his neck for a pulse. Reassured that he still lived, she began dabbing the wine from his face with her handkerchief. When Foukes came back with two sturdy footmen, she was waving her vinaigrette beneath Mr. Strangeways's nose in an effort to revive him. She stood up and drew back while he was carried to the sofa, then went to his side again.

"Send for a doctor instantly," she said, without looking up. Pippa looked helplessly at Foukes, who nodded and withdrew with speed.

"It is my fault," whispered Pippa, feeling an icy chill spreading over her body when she saw that Mr. Strangeways was not responding in any way.

"How so?" asked Emma as she continued chafing his wrists and patting his cheeks between administrations of the smelling salts.

"I should not have allowed him to exert himself so much this afternoon. He came directly after you went upstairs, and we spent the entire afternoon driving all over Bath. We had a marvelous time, but it was selfish of me not to notice—"

"Pooh, I doubt an afternoon's drive brought on this—this—well, stop wringing your hands, child, and go see if that's the doctor at the front door."

Pippa had not heard anyone at the door, but she went out obediently, and there was Foukes letting in a short, stout little man with a bag, who was without doubt a doctor.

"Well, well, what's all this?" he exclaimed, rubbing his hands together.

"Doctor Graham, miss. Sir, this is Miss Cranville, whose house this is," said Foukes in stately tones, a note of reproof in his voice.

"Yes, yes, how de'doo, Miss Cranville. Now, you look perfectly healthy to me, so suppose we dispense with all this folderol and get to the patient!"

"Of course, Doctor Graham, come this way, if you will."

Emma rose from her place beside Mr. Strangeways as the doctor and Pippa came in. He questioned her tersely about what had happened, then shooed them both out of the room and closed the door firmly behind them.

They faced each other helplessly, while Foukes hovered with delicate tact nearby. Pippa wondered if her own face was as pale as Aunt Emma's. Emma turned to Foukes and told him to have someone make a room ready for Mr. Strangeways, for it would not be possible to allow him to leave tonight.

"Also send someone around to his rooms to fetch his manservant. And tell him to bring whatever he feels necessary to prepare his master for the night."

While Pippa was still wondering how it was possible for anyone to be so clearheaded in such a situation, she saw her aunt put her hand to her head and sway.

"Good heavens, Foukes, quickly, help me," she called after his retreating back, rushing forward herself to support her aunt.

Together they half-carried the fainting woman into the library across the hall from the drawing room, while Pippa, once they had her stretched out on a sofa, ordered yet another vinaigrette.

"And bring some brandy, Foukes," she called, busily chafing her aunt's wrists and patting her cheeks as she had just seen her aunt do to Mr. Strangeways.

Before Foukes could return, Emma's eyelids began to

flutter. She stared at Pippa dazedly for a moment, then started up violently, "I must—I must—" she muttered.

Pippa firmly pushed her back. "You must just lie still, dear aunt, for a little while. There is nothing we can do for Mr. Strangeways at the moment, since the doctor is still with him. Ah, here is Foukes with some brandy. We won't need the vinaigrette after all, Foukes."

She took the glass from his hand and held it to Emma's lips.

"No, no, I never—" Emma said with a frown of distaste as the fumes of the strong liquor reached her.

"I know, but this time it will do you good. You have had a terrible shock. After all, it isn't every lady who has a gentleman faint at her feet as they are being introduced. Now be sensible and take just a few sips."

She helped her aunt to sit up and held out the glass again, and this time Emma took it and forced herself to drink some of it. In a few moments some color began seeping back into her cheeks and her hands began to steady.

She laughed rather shakily. "Well, I think you were right, child. I do feel better."

Foukes, seeing that everything was now under control, slipped away to see to the tasks assigned to him, and Pippa sat quietly beside her aunt, from time to time handing her the glass, which Emma tamely took from her and drank until it was finished.

"Ah, there you are," said the doctor testily, entering the room. "Where are all the servants? I've been looking for you."

"Doctor Graham, please excuse us for not waiting outside for you. Aunt Emma felt faint so I brought her—oh, I did not introduce you. Miss Emma Cranville, Doctor Graham—"

"Why do people forever waste my time with these silly

formalities. I'm a very busy man. Now, what can you tell me about that gentleman?"

"Tell you about him? I don't quite understand, Doctor Graham," Pippa said in some bewilderment.

"I mean that I can't revive him and I want to know if he has ever had these spells before, has he had a recent illness, anything that you can tell me?" he barked, his round little face red with exasperation.

"Why, as to that I'm afraid I don't know what I can tell you," said Pippa slowly. "I have known him a very short while, and in our acquaintance I have never seen any signs of ill health, nor heard that he has had such spells before."

Pippa was in a quandary. She did know something about Mr. Strangeways, something in every way unusual. But whether she should speak of it to this strange man, she didn't know. Mr. Strangeways had told her in confidence and she had only told her aunt. She looked at Emma for some guidance. Emma stared back at her for a moment, then nodded, obviously encouraging her to tell what she knew of Mr. Strangeways.

Hesitantly Pippa began. "There is something that perhaps you should know—"

"Yes? Get on with it then," he snapped at her.

"He told me that many years ago he was in an accident—and apparently from that day to this he has been unable to remember anything that went before."

"Ah-ha! Do you tell me so?" The little man rubbed his hands together enthusiastically. "Well, I must say I've never had a case like this! Very interesting, to be sure. We know very little about the workings of the mind—could have been anything that set it off—some strange excitation of the brain causing a seizure, perhaps—well, we shall see, we shall see. Meantime let us not be standing around here doing nothing. Get the man carried upstairs to a bed. You have a room for him?"

"Yes, doctor, we've had a room prepared and have sent for his manservant to prepare him for bed. He should be here by now."

Pippa, glad to be of service at last, led the doctor out into the hallway, calling for Foukes.

Emma sat quite still for a moment, then reached out for the decanter and deliberately poured herself some more brandy. She drank it down, set the glass aside, and followed after them.

CHAPTER 21

Pippa, in her dressing gown, tiptoed down the silent hallway to Mr. Strangeways's room.

After he had been put to bed, Emma had sent the protesting manservant off to bed and, pulling up a chair by the bedside, prepared to keep watch during the night.

Pippa had tried to persuade her that after her long journey and the fainting fit she had experienced earlier, it might be wiser to let the manservant stay by him for the night, but her aunt had waved away such a suggestion dismissively.

"And what could he do for him if he should awaken? I assure you, I've had much more experience with illness than that servant."

Pippa couldn't help wondering where, since she herself had been unusually healthy all her life and could not remember ever being nursed by her aunt. She forebore to mention this; however she did try other persuasions on her aunt, with no success.

"Don't be foolish, child. I shall take no harm. I've had a good sleep this afternoon and feel quite refreshed and not in the least sleepy. You go along to bed and don't worry."

And Pippa had, reluctantly, gone to her room, convinced that she would not be able to close her eyes for a moment. But she had, and had only just opened them a few moments ago to find the sun streaming into her room.

She had jumped out of bed guiltily to go and check on the invalid.

She opened the door quietly and peeked in. Emma turned, her face sagging with weariness.

"Great heavens, Aunt, do not tell me you've spent the entire night—" whispered Pippa.

"He has not stirred, so there was nothing required of me but to sit here. I dozed from time to time—the chair is very comfortable."

"I will call his servant and you must go lie down for a while. Or would you prefer to come down for some breakfast?"

"I would prefer it if you would just sit here with him for a few moments, while I go wash my face and tidy my hair. I will change my gown, also, for I am sadly crumpled. Then when I come back, I would like you to go down and have a tray sent up to me here." This was all said in her usual, decisive tones of command, tones that brooked no debate. Pippa closed her mouth on any further protests and came forward to take the chair her aunt vacated.

When her aunt returned, Pippa went back to her room to dress, then went down and ordered a breakfast tray sent upstairs.

The day was as wearying and distressing as it could possibly be, for Mr. Strangeways remained unconscious, Aunt Emma remained implacably by his side, leaving only when the doctor visited, and Pippa was left alone to receive the usual morning callers. All of them exclaimed with astonishment at the sudden departure of Lady Barstowe and her daughter, and with horror over the news of Mr. Strangeways's strange malady. Pippa was exhausted at the constant retelling of all the circumstances to each new guest, by repeated trips upstairs to look in the sickroom, and by her reiterated exhortations to her aunt to go lie down for some rest.

After a lonely dinner, she went to the library in search

of a book to take to bed with her. She had no desire to remain downstairs alone and hoped that reading would make her sleepy. She looked into Mr. Strangeways's room for a moment to say good night to her aunt.

Emma, dark circles of tiredness under her eyes, held out her hand to Pippa. Tears started into Pippa's eyes as she clasped it in both her hands and held it tightly for a moment. In all their life together, this was the first such gesture she had ever made; indeed, Pippa had no memory of ever having held her aunt's hand before. She felt such a rush of affection for this strange, cold woman who had finally turned to her with warmth that she longed to throw her arms around her and hold her close for a moment. But she hadn't the courage yet to take such liberties. The new relationship was still too delicate to test that way. She contented herself with pressing the hand in hers as tightly as she could to show her aunt her feelings, and finally Emma pressed her hand back, then withdrew her own gently.

"Good night, child. I hope you will sleep. You must not worry, you know. I feel sure your friend will be all right. You see how healthy he looks. He breathes normally and his color is good. There cannot be too much wrong with him, I'm sure."

"But then why cannot you come to your bed also? I cannot bear to think of you sitting here again for another night. You must be deathly weary by now."

"No, strangely I am not. And I could not close my eyes. To think if he woke, all alone, in a strange room with no one beside him—no, I prefer to remain here. Now go along with you. Good night, child."

Pippa said good night, Emma heard the door close after her and turned back to look at her patient. He had not moved. She leaned back in the chair and closed her eyes. She was content to wait.

It was an hour later, and she was dozing lightly, when

some change in the pattern of his quiet breathing reached her through her sleep and her eyelids snapped open. She listened quietly, then sat forward and turned up the lamp a bit. She watched as he stirred, then sighed, then his eyes opened slowly and he stared at the ceiling. He turned his head at last and looked at her.

"Emma?"

"Yes, Perry?" she answered quietly.

"Why am I in bed?"

"You—you had a fall, Perry."

"Ah, yes, I remember now, the dratted horse. Did he break his leg?"

"I don't know, Perry," she said, her voice as steady as she could make it, while the tears streamed silently and unheeded down her cheeks.

"Too bad if she had to be put down—nice bit of horse-flesh. Must have landed on my head to go out cold like this. How long have I been unconscious?"

"For some time, Perry."

"And you came? But how—you had already gone to Ayleforth—did someone send for you? But that was not possible—no one knew about us—how did you—why, my darling girl, you are crying! You must not cry, just a tumble from a horse, you know. I'll be right as a trivet in a moment."

Emma finally reached for her handkerchief and wiped her eyes. She wondered what she should do now. Should she call the doctor to come before attempting any explanations? Suppose when he realized the true circumstances, he had another seizure? But she could not bear to leave his side now, and it would be hours before she could rouse someone, send for Dr. Graham, and wait till he had finished. No, she would go very gently, and it would be all right.

"Perry, my dear, look at me," she said now, leaning closer to him, "do you see nothing different?"

"Well, I don't recall that gown," he began, after studying her obediently for a moment.

"My gown! Oh—oh—oh, dear." With that she began to laugh, and with the laughter came more tears and a great cleansing release of emotions, melting the ice that had formed around her heart all those years ago.

"Emma—my God, Emma! What is it? You must tell me! Try to be calm, my darling. Whatever it is, it will be all right. I'm fine now, and we'll go back to Ayleforth Hall and I'll ask your brother for your hand, just as we planned. A few days' delay won't have ruined my chances surely. You still feel the same, don't you?" he asked anxiously, reaching for her hand and pulling her closer to him.

"Oh, Perry, dearest one, how shall I tell you? Look at me—don't you see, Perry? My hair is turning white."

"Why—why—"

"And so is yours, my darling. That was twenty years ago, Perry, when I left from here and went home to await your coming to see my brother. And I never heard another word from you or about you from that day to this. I thought you had changed your mind, I thought I had been mistaken in you, that you had only sent me away from Bath to get out of it—oh, everything terrible that it was possible to think. I waited, and I waited, and I finally gave up waiting."

"Twenty years! I have been—no, now I begin to recollect—just give me time to get my mind round this. I was here, visiting Carstairs—you were staying with the Broughs, then you went home. I was coming in a few days but then I had the accident with the horse. I suppose Carstairs, not knowing about you, simply summoned my father. When I came round, Emma, I was home—but I didn't know it and I didn't know my family. They told me who I was, and I had to accept what they told me and begin all over. I didn't remember anything—Emma, you must believe me! I didn't remember!"

"Hush, Perry. You must not excite yourself in this way. Of course I believe you," she told him soothingly.

"And you thought—oh, my God! I cannot bear to think of you waiting—and thinking those vile thoughts of me! Will you ever forgive me?" He was crying now, the tears rolling unchecked down his face to soak the pillow.

"I forgave you the moment you opened your eyes and said my name. I knew it all at that instant."

"Darling, darling girl, I love you. I have never stopped loving you—even though I couldn't remember you, something kept my heart intact all those years, as though it knew it was given already, for I was never able to fall in love. I thank God for it. Now we can marry—you will still have me, Emma?"

"Oh, Perry—dear heaven, what shall I do? I am an old woman now, Perry, I shall never be able to give you a child—" She pulled her hand away and drew back in genuine distress, her voice anguished.

Peregrine Strangeways pulled himself up in the bed; shakily but with great determination, he piled the pillows behind him for support, then, reaching forward, took both her hands and pulled her inexorably to him until she was lying across his chest, her head in the shelter of his neck, then he put his arms around her and held her close.

"Now here you are, where you have always belonged and where you shall always be from this day forward. I will never let you out of my sight again, Emma, for as long as I live. We will marry—"

"Perry, we shall be a laughing stock," she protested in a muffled gasp, though she did not remove her head from the warm resting place it had found.

"We shall marry," he continued firmly, "and after we have Pippa happily established, I shall take you off to the West Indies for a honeymoon."

Now she moved her face away to look up at the face so close to her own. "Then you remember about Pippa and—"

"I remember everything now. As though all the pieces of a puzzle have fallen into place in an instant. I think it was seeing Pippa the first time that started this whole process. She looks so much like you, you know—it was as though a curtain parted for a second—then it was gone. I kept trying to make it happen again. That is why I've kept coming back to Bath all these years. I was told I was thrown from a horse in Bath and I kept hoping that if I came back, something or someone would jog my memory—"

"Poor darling, to have suffered—"

"No, I must be honest, Emma, I did not suffer. But it was as though I dragged an enormous burden on my back that I was never allowed to see. It was tantalizing, always there, always out of sight, never to be put down. But it was worth carrying, now that I know it was you and that you still love me."

"With all my heart, my Perry, my beloved."

They looked straight into each other's eyes for an awe-filled moment, each finally accepting that the unbelievable had happened, then he very softly kissed the lips so close to his own. They stayed so, blissfully, for a moment, not wanting to disturb the sweetness of it, then drew apart, to wordlessly affirm the love shining in their eyes.

"Oh, Perry, I am a monster!"

"Confess—what have you done?"

"I've forgotten completely that you are an invalid. I should go now and get you some beef tea or something to help you regain your strength, rather than keep you talking and exerting yourself in this way."

"You are right," he agreed, pulling her closer still, "there has been enough talk for tonight!"

* * *

After her extremely early night, Pippa woke with the first light, and, slipping out of bed immediately, she put on her dressing gown and slippers and stole down the hall to Mr. Strangeways's room. She opened the door quietly and peeked in.

The chair, occupied by Aunt Emma for the past thirty-six hours still stood beside the bed, but was empty. Mr. Strangeways, who had lain unmoving on his back for the same amount of time, now lay curled on his side.

Pippa's first glimpse of these two changes caused her, at first, to gasp with surprise, then to sigh with relief. It was obvious that during the night Mr. Strangeways had finally regained his senses, had been attended to by Aunt Emma, and was now having a normal, health-restoring sleep.

She closed the door softly and went back down the hall to confirm her diagnosis of the situation. She opened Emma's door silently and peered around the edge. Yes, there lay Emma, also cosily curled on her side, one hand tucked beneath her cheek.

Pippa felt such an excess of love for this strange aunt after last night when she had turned for comfort to her niece that she tiptoed across the room to tenderly pull up the coverlet over the bared shoulder. She stood looking down at Emma fondly for a moment, wondering if she always looked this way in sleep. The permanent perpendicular frown lines between her brows smoothed away, the complexion dewy and glowing, the previously tightly held mouth softened and rosy and—good heavens!—turned up at the corners in a tiny smile!

CHAPTER 22

Pippa sat in a bright stream of sunshine that turned her dark red hair to gold, blinking contentedly as she ate her breakfast, savoring the feeling that all was right as possible in her world. She wished there were someone she could talk it all over with—if only Sir Anthony were there. She couldn't think of anyone else she could so completely bare her heart and feelings to without embarrassment.

But that would have to wait, for surely two weeks, until he could break away from his tiresome business in London and come for a few days' visit. In the meantime she could deepen her relationship with her aunt and they would grow closer and closer, and how proudly now she would take her about Bath and introduce her to all the new friends.

She thought again of that strangely youthful, sleeping face upstairs. *Why, she is beautiful! Maybe it was the smile; I can't recall ever seeing her smile before.* Pippa congratulated herself rather smugly on having wrought this transformation in her aunt by persisting in writing to her. It was clear that this gesture had finally softened the lady's heart. *She just didn't realize how much I needed her, and when the letters started coming, she began to understand and gradually she—*

These pleasant thoughts of her own goodness were interrupted at this moment by the object of them, and she beamed a brilliant smile of greeting at her aunt. The thought that she had helped her caused her to love her aunt more than she would have thought possible.

And Aunt Emma returned her smile! Not an unconscious, sleeping smile this time, but a full, in-the-daylight, meaningful one.

"Aunt Emma! Good morning! I had thought you would lie in quite late this morning after your long night."

"Long night?" Aunt Emma asked with just a trace of wariness in her voice.

"Oh, then Mister Strangeways recovered soon after I went to bed? Oh, I do wish you had called me—I would so love to have been there to help you."

"That's quite all right, dear child, I managed—er—quite well."

"How is he—in his senses, I mean? Does he remember—"

"Everything!" Again Emma's lips curved up in a smile; this time it was the same smile Pippa had seen on her sleeping face.

"But how wonderful! Do you tell me he has remembered those first twenty lost years I told you of?"

"He has indeed."

They were interrupted at this point by Foukes, who announced that Mr. Strangeways's servant was outside with a message for Miss Cranville.

"Bring him in, of course, Foukes," Pippa cried.

The manservant entered and bowed correctly, though his face still carried traces of his outraged sensibilities. He could not quite swallow his resentment that his rightful place had been taken at his master's side these past two days.

"M'lady, Mister Strangeways presents his compliments and requests that when you are finished your breakfast, you step up to his room."

"Thank you. Tell him I'll be up immediately. No, wait," called Pippa as he turned to go, "never mind, I will deliver the message myself." She turned to Emma. "You will excuse me, Aunt, but I simply cannot wait to see him."

"Certainly, certainly. Run along," said Emma calmly.

After knocking and being bade to come in, Pippa rushed across the room to his bedside and impulsively bent to kiss him resoundingly on the cheek.

"There! Now you know me for a forward chit who bestows her kisses freely where she will!"

He laughed and pulled her down to return the kiss. "Then I must take advantage of your bad character, mustn't I?"

"I must say you don't look ill in the least."

"Nor am I. In spite of all Jenkins's sulking I shall get up directly. He is determined to shave me in bed, and that I'll not stand for. He has been muttering all morning about not being thought good enough to nurse me. I doubt he'll ever forgive your Aunt Emma."

"Yes, he came to the breakfast room now with a face like a thundercloud. But never mind Jenkins! It's you I want to talk about. Aunt Emma tells me you have remembered everything, and I could not wait another moment to hear it. Now, tell me all!"

She pulled up the recently vacated chair and plumped herself down eagerly.

"Well, I was an ordinary sort of baby, I suppose, and probably an unspeakable little boy, up to every sort of mischief and—"

"Never mind all that part," she begged him impatiently. "Get straight to the good parts."

He laughed teasingly. "How do you know there is a part in any way out of the ordinary?"

"Oh, there must be! Such a romantic story must have a great deal out of the ordinary."

"Well, you are right, you minx. There is a romance. But perhaps you are too young for—"

"Mister Strangeways!' she said threateningly, "I vow I shall lose all patience with you in a moment!"

He chortled, happy at his success in sending her up, and then told her the whole story.

Of how he came to Bath to visit his friend, Carstairs, and met a beautiful young girl, also on a visit. Of how they met at balls and assemblies, and then secretly after a few days' acquaintance.

"We were both country bred and shy and despised that drawing room tittle-tattle that passed for entertainment in those days, and still today, Lord bless us. So we agreed not to tell anyone of our love, but that she would go back home and I would follow in a few days and ask for her hand in marriage, well away from all the gossips. But then, the day she left, I took a header from a horse and everything was knocked from my mind. Carstairs, knowing nothing else to do, summoned my father, and I was taken home to recuperate. And my poor love waited at home in vain for me to appear."

"How terrible! Oh, how terrible! The poor, dear creature. And now, I hope, you will go to her and tell her what happened. How she must have suffered!"

"You can have no idea, darling Pippa, of how much, and I hope you never will have cause to."

"What will you do? You must go to her at once!"

"Ah, fortunately that won't be necessary. She came to me," he said simply.

"Came to you? But how?" He could plainly see from her puzzled face all the thoughts racing through her mind as she reviewed the facts as she knew them and came to the only logical conclusion.

"Aunt Emma?" she breathed in a disbelieving voice.

"Yes, my darling Emma. It was her own sweet face I saw as I opened my eyes last night."

She sat staring at him, completely thunderstruck, her

mouth opening and closing helplessly as she tried to assimilate this totally unexpected news.

"But I—she—how could—great heavens!"

"I know it is difficult to accept it all in one gulp, child. Here, give me your hand. Now we will sit here quite quietly until you recover," he said, patting her hand soothingly.

She didn't even hear him, nor was she aware of her hand being held, but continued her thoughts, confused though they were.

"That's why she insisted—she wouldn't let anyone else nurse—and not a word—and she came—she must have—because of what I wrote of you in my letter—and I thought—and the way she looked last night while she slept—it wasn't my letters—well, in a way it was—"

"In every way it was, darling Pippa," Mr. Strangeways interrupted her firmly. "You must listen, Pippa. If it hadn't been for you"—here he paused to shudder—"none of this would have come about. It was seeing you that started something happening in my mind, for you look so like her, and then your writing to her of me and my strange story. She said at first she could not believe it, didn't want to believe it now, after all these years, it was almost too painful to bear. But from the moment she had the letter, she had no peace and only lived for the post, in hopes of having further news of me."

"Oh, my goodness, if I had only written more often."

"No, no, all came about just as it should. It was the lack of further news that caused her to come. She said she dropped Lady Barstowe's letter on the floor just where she stood as she read it and went upstairs and began packing as though she were walking in her sleep. There was never any question of her not coming. She *had* to come!"

"Of course she had to! So would I have done."

"Yes, I'm sure you would," he responded promptly, laughing at her again. "Now the important question is will you have me for an uncle?"

She jumped from her chair, hugged herself ecstatically, and began whirling and dancing around the room, only to return and throw herself upon him joyfully.

"Oh, this is beyond anything wonderful. I have an aunt and now I have an *uncle*!"

He laughed indulgently, "Here, silly child, you will strangle me. Scamper downstairs to your aunt, who I'm sure is waiting for you most impatiently by this time, and I will get up and dressed."

She rushed headlong down the stairs and straight into the arms of her Aunt Emma, who was standing at the foot of the steps as though getting ready to come up.

"Aunt Emma, oh, how happy I am! It is like a fairy tale come true. The fairy princess asleep all these years until her prince came and woke her!"

"You will not mind if we—"

"Mind? *I*? Oh, you cannot know me at all if you think that I could be other than overjoyed."

"Yes, my dear, that is exactly the problem, I fear"—Emma's eyes filled—"I do *not* know you as I should. I have done you a great wrong all these years and—"

"Please do not speak of—"

"No, child, you must let me, for my own sake. I know enough now about your generosity of spirit to know *you* have forgiven. But I must find forgiveness for myself, and I can only do that by explaining what happened to me all those many years ago. Something in me died then, you see, after waiting so eagerly for him to come. I had never loved before—oh, many schoolgirl infatuations, many flirts, but I had never fallen in love until I met Perry—"

Perry! thought Pippa with a small sigh of relief, for she had wondered if she would call him Uncle Peregrine during her meeting with him upstairs.

"—and from that moment I knew there could never be another for me," Emma continued, "so that when he did not come, I felt doubly betrayed. I decided then that nothing would ever touch my heart again. I was too fearful of being hurt by loving. When your father married and brought home his bride, I went to live for a time with my aunt, and then when your parents were taken, I came back to live with you. But I would not allow myself to love you. Besides, by then I could not had I wanted to—I was no longer capable of it, and content it should be so—until your letter came, telling me of Mister Strangeways."

"And then," Pippa took over rapturously, "not daring to believe, but unable to prevent the first stirrings of hope—"

Emma laughed somewhat shakily. "Oh, Pippa, you should be writing romances. Will you not let me be contrite with you—to beg your pardon for my behavior?"

"No, no, a thousand times, I will hear only happy things today, and now that you have called me Pippa—oh, dearest Aunt Emma!" And with that she flung her arms around her aunt in an excess of happiness and swung her around and around the entrance hall till they were both dizzy and laughing helplessly.

Several hours later an only slightly subdued party rode along in a landaulet ordered by Mr. Strangeways and driven by Emma's coachman. In spite of Mr. Strangeways's protestations of completely restored health, Emma had refused to countenance the idea that he was well enough to drive them himself in a phaeton.

They had tried to seat Pippa between them, but she had laughingly refused to be squeezed, and seated herself with her back to the driver. Their object was to drive Emma around Bath to reintroduce her to the city and to see and be seen by as many friends as possible. Pippa was eager to display her 'family' and was terrifically proud of her Aunt Emma, who looked so serenely beautiful sitting across from her, with her amber eyes contrasting so exotically with her nearly white hair. *Why, I wouldn't be surprised if she wouldn't have cut quite a dash in Bath society, had she chosen to come here without a previous attachment,* Pippa thought. *Such a face and such a slim, firm, upright figure.*

On Bath Street they encountered the duchess and Lady Fanny, just emerging from Smith's. When the duchess saw Pippa and Mr. Strangeways, she turned away from her carriage and waved to them, and they pulled in to the curb to greet her.

"How d'do. Lovely day for a drive," she called to them with an openly curious stare at Aunt Emma.

"Your Grace," responded Mr. Strangeways promptly, "you will allow me to present my fiancée, Miss Emma Cranville."

The duchess's glance swept from Emma to Pippa and back, and with hardly any hesitation at all she stepped forward, her hand outstretched. "Well, now, Miss Cranville, I wish you happiness, indeed I do," she said with enthusiasm. "I can see you are Pippa's relative, remarkable resemblance, and it is also plain to see that you are all very pleased with yourselves. You all look like cats who've been at the cream. Here, Fanny, come along and meet Pippa's aunt," she called to her granddaughter, who was directing the coachman in the stowing of parcels being carried out from Smith's shop by the subservient clerks. Fanny immediately turned and came over, greeting Pippa with her pretty smile and dropping a meticulous curtsy to Aunt Emma.

"Delighted, Miss Cranville. I collect you are here to replace Lady Barstowe. Have you heard from the Barstowes, Pippa? I vow I miss dear Melissa extremely already, do not you?"

"Indeed I do. Though I must confess so much has happened since they left, I've hardly had time to think at all. And of course I am so overjoyed to have my dear Aunt Emma with me," said Pippa all in a rush, the smiles dancing over her face and her hand reaching for Emma's.

"Here, now," interrupted the duchess, "why are we all dawdling about in the street? You will follow us to the Royal Crescent and we'll have some refreshment together—perhaps some wine to celebrate your engagement, Miss Cranville, about which I will expect to be told everything!" With this command she returned to climb spryly into her own carriage, begging Fanny not to be such a slowtop and ordering the coachman to take them home.

Obviously in great fettle, she ordered champagne as soon as they entered the house, and prattled away happily as they disposed themselves around the drawing room. Emma, after years of solitude, found herself somewhat dazed by the duchess and so unused to sustaining conversation that she was able to do little more than smile and nod and murmur "Yes, indeed" or "No, Your Grace."

"I have decided I must give you a dress party," declared the duchess, "must introduce you to everyone, and announce your good news, you know!"

Emma and Mr. Strangeways both protested at once against any such thing, but the duchess was not to be overborne.

"Nonsense, best thing to do. Everyone would think there's some havey-cavey business going on if you try to keep it a secret. Happy, ain't you?" They both nodded, nearly mesmerized by the duchess's rapid-fire delivery and positiveness. "Then no more to be said. Leave it all to me."

CHAPTER 23

The duchess made sure there could be no charges of havey-cavey business aimed at the engagement of Emma and Perry. She gave them dinner with thirty guests, followed by a ball where it seemed half of Bath was squeezed into her drawing rooms. She stood in the receiving line with her guests of honor, introducing Emma and announcing her engagement and cackling happily at the surprise this news encountered. Emma, after the first twenty minutes, became inured to it and left off blushing. She was magnificently gowned in pale orange gauze and diamonds, and was the recipient of the admiring glances of every man there.

Pippa's gown was her most grown-up evening dress and one she had saved for a very special occasion. Of a creamy silk with the faintest blush of pink, it had been created to match her mother's pearls. Low cut with short, puffed sleeves, it was starkly simple. Over it she wore a silk tunic, a sort of sleeveless coat, that hung straight from the shoulders down into a short train. It was edged all the way around with a fluted ruffle. She felt quite sure she had never looked so elegant in her life.

Mrs. Otway, gushing up to be introduced, was barely able to conceal her chagrin at not having been one of the intimate dinner guests.

"Dear Duchess, so sorry to have been already engaged for dinner," she said loudly for the benefit of those within earshot, "couldn't disappoint them, I'm sure you understand," she continued brazenly, squeezing the duchess's hand in both of her own in an intimate way and giving her a smile of complicity. This, as she knew very well, was perfectly safe, for the duchess would never be so bad mannered as to say anything to betray her in front of the company. She was not even aware that she could only display her own lack of breeding by relying on the good breeding of the duchess. The duchess now gave her a blank stare and pulled her hand away without a trace of the distaste she felt, and turned to present her to Emma.

Mrs. Otway repeated to Emma her regrets that she had been unable to attend the dinner.

"Yes, I'm sure you are," replied Emma dryly. "I believe we have met before, Mrs. Otway, in London wasn't it, the year of your own engagement?"

"Why, I do believe you're right! How stupid of me, but then one meets so many people in London," said Mrs. Otway with her usual crushing lack of tact. "Why, that was quite twenty years ago, and do you tell me that all this time you've remained—" But even Mrs. Otway was unable to finish such a disgracefully insulting sentence and, flushing darkly, turned hurriedly to Mr. Strangeways.

"My dear sir, you are a dark horse indeed. Had I but known you were on the lookout for a wife, I should have thrown out lures myself. Here I've been widowed for five years. . . ." Mr. Strangeways only smiled affably and passed the dreadful woman along to Pippa, who was so nearly in whoops by this time, she could do little but smile and shake her hand. She was afraid to open her mouth for fear she would laugh in the woman's face. She was very glad to note that Mr. Sidney Otway did not accompany his mother, though she had little hope that he would not appear before the evening was over.

Her fears were realized much sooner than she could have wished for. She stood to one side of the ballroom with Mr. Danston, watching Emma and Mr. Strangeways opening the ball, when she saw a lazily smiling Mr. Otway leading out Lady Fanny. As they turned in the figure of the dance, his glance met Pippa's, and he directed at her an intimate smile, as though they shared a great understanding. She refused to look away, staring back at him indifferently before deliberately turning her back to speak to Mr. Danston. Inwardly, however, she fumed with helpless rage at his effrontery. If he came to ask her to dance, what could she do but accept in order not to create an unbecoming scene? Oh, if only Sir Anthony were here to protect her from this detestable man. She would have no hesitation at all in confiding the story to Sir Anthony and no doubt that he would know how to deal with the situation.

However, after many dances had passed and he had not approached, she relaxed gratefully on a sofa beside her aunt, sure now that she had been wrong about Mr. Otway and that he did possess some traces of decency.

But she relaxed too soon, for as she chatted away to Emma and the duchess and Mr. Strangeways, who stood beside her, Mr. Otway came strolling up to them with great nonchalance.

"Ah, Miss Cranville, at last I find you free," he said gaily, his attitude clearly demonstrating his expectation that she would jump eagerly to her feet.

"If you are inviting me to dance, sir, I must decline, though I thank you," she said with icy politeness, turning again to Mr. Strangeways.

"Exhausted so soon, Miss Cranville? Why the evening has hardly begun. Ah, well, I won't mind sitting this one out myself. I have been meaning to ask if you would not accompany me to Sydney Gardens two nights hence. There is to be a grand gala with illuminations, and I thought it might be pleasant to make up a party—"

"I am expecting my guardian to be with us at that time, and naturally I will go with him," Pippa replied.

"Ah-ha! I see how it is—saving the little heiress for himself, in case his suit for the wealthy Miss Wantage should not prosper," said Sidney softly, leaning down close to her ear.

Pippa lifted startled, questioning eyes to his face, not sure she understood what he had just said.

"I'm af-fraid I didn't q-quite—" she stuttered in confusion.

"But surely you have heard of his pursuit of the beautiful Mary Wantage. It was the talk of London when last I was there. But I doubt he'll have any luck with that one—with her dowry she'll want a title for sure, not some merchant with pockets to let."

Mr. Strangeways, who had turned away to attend to the duchess, was distracted by a gasp from Pippa and turned back to see her with bosom heaving and a bright patch of red on each cheekbone.

"How dare you, Mister Otway," she said through teeth clenched tight in anger. "Sir Anthony is not—"

"Oh, well, business of some sort. Afraid I know little of such things—we've never had anyone in business in our family," Mr. Otway said carelessly, with a pronounced emphasis on the final possessive.

Before anyone could think of an answer to this, the duchess replied in her frostiest voice, "Very possibly, Mister Otway, but then the Seymour-Crofts are such an *ancient* and respected family that I'm sure they could open a linen-draper's shop and no one would remark upon it."

Not daring to cross swords with the duchess, Sidney bowed and held his tongue. Fanny was led back by her dancing partner at that moment and with a gay insouciance Sidney turned and requested the next dance with her. Before she could speak, the duchess interrupted again.

"You will excuse her, Mister Otway. I require my granddaughter to sit with me for a while."

Fanny shrugged her shoulders delicately, and obediently sat down in the space made for her between Emma and the duchess. Sidney's eyebrows drew together in a slight frown, but he only bowed to her again and turned to walk away with an admirable affectation of indifference. There was only the smallest discernible break in his stride when the duchess's voice reached him.

". . . don't care for that young man above half, Fanny."

Much later that same night, in the privacy of the Laura Place drawing room, Emma and Perry shared a glass of wine together after Pippa had climbed wearily up to her bed.

"I've never thought much of the Otways," Emma declared. "Althea Otway was a detestable, simpering young girl, pushy, you know, as all her family have been. And so I warned Pippa when I wrote her. I knew no son of Althea Otway could be right for my niece."

"They certainly seem to behave with singular stupidity. Only a depressing lack of wits could account for their behavior, especially that young coxcomb, Sidney. To have been insulting about Tony was the outside of enough, but to have done it in front of Pippa was a pea-brained thing to do. Pippa sets a great store by Tony."

"Perry, please tell me, just what *is* it that he does that makes it so imperative that he spend so much of his time in London?"

"Repairing his fortunes, my dear."

"Repairing—but what can you mean? His father often boasted of the fortune his son had made all by himself. Then he inherited from his mother, I know—or was it his grandmother? Whatever, he did inherit a quite respectable sum of money, I remember."

"That may be, but after he finished paying his father's debts, his pockets were to let for sure."

Emma began to look stricken. "Oh, Perry, I had not realized—he told me he had restituted all the money his father had lost that had been entrusted to him by Jonathan, but I couldn't know—"

"Of course you could not, my dear," said Perry, soothingly, "as I'm sure he would never have told you. But the fact is he invested his inheritance in cargos and sugar from the West Indies. And he built that into a very large fortune indeed. But you will recall that Jonathan left Pippa a great deal of money, and when Sir James died, it was discovered that he had lost it all. By the time Tony had repaid it, there was little left of his own money."

"Good God! How very dreadful to be sure. And I was so—so—rude to him, when he came to Ayleforth to tell me of it. And now he must start all over again?"

"Just so, my dear, just so. With the few pounds he had left, he is reinvesting and hoping to recoup."

"But surely this could be done without his actual presence, could it not? I mean, once having given over the money, one would just more or less have to sit back and wait, I should imagine."

"Very true." He hesitated for a moment, knowing that what he would say would be bound to embarrass her very much. Then he decided that there must never be less than complete honesty between them and that her character was strong enough to withstand the truth. "He has deliberately absented himself to avoid the possibility of people thinking he is protecting her fortune for himself."

As this struck home Emma blushed hotly. "And I—I was the first to say it," she admitted bravely, but with great shame.

"I know that, dear Emma. He told me of it. In fact that was what first made him aware of the danger. A penniless man, fending off suitors, would naturally give rise to that sort of speculation. It would be food for gossips, even if he stood well beforehand with the world, but if word got out of the state of his fortune—well, I'm sure we're both aware of the insatiable appetites of the Bath tittle-tattle set."

"Oh, that I could have been so despicable," she moaned softly to herself.

"Now, Emma, I won't have you berating yourself in this way. We have agreed—have we not—that we will not subject ourselves to this faultfinding? We both know that what we did, we could not help doing. I could no more blame you for becoming cold and hard in your grief than I could blame myself for having my memory blotted out and being helpless to come to you."

She gave him a smile, tremulous with tears of gratitude for his words, and reached silently for his hand.

Pippa lay in her bed, staring blindly at the flickers of light cast on the ceiling by the dying fire. She had been lying thus for some time, willing her mind numb so she would not think of the words she had heard from Sidney Otway this evening.

". . . the beautiful Mary Wantage." She finally heard again that insinuating whisper, in spite of all she could do to stop it, and impatiently threw back her covers and went to poke up the embers of the fire. She paced to the windows to stare into the darkness for a moment, then to her dressing table to look into the dim reflection of her own eyes. ". . . beautiful Mary Wantage," came Sidney Otway's voice again.

She turned away quickly, took up from the end of her bed her pale-green taffeta robe edged with swansdown and, pulling in on, went to sit before the fire.

Very well, she thought angrily, *Miss Wantage.* Beautiful *Miss Wantage.* Wealthy *Miss Wantage. Why should this be such a shock? I have suspected all along there must be someone in London to require his presence so often. And why should there not be, after all? He has been living there for many years. It would be wonderful, indeed, if he had not fallen in love with someone in all this time.*

She tried to conjure up a picture of Miss Wantage. Hair

like cornsilk, enormous blue eyes, pouting red mouth and—and—dimples, no doubt! She saw them, waltzing around a ballroom floor, Miss Wantage smiling up at him provocatively, his arm possessively around her slender waist—

She thrust the picture out of her mind abruptly and got up to pace around the room again, to the window, to the dressing table, and finally, wearily, back to her seat before the fire.

I am being ridiculous, she told herself. *He has a right to happiness, and if this is what he wants, I must be glad for him. It might very well be that when he comes down tomorrow, he will announce his engagement. And I will wish him happy!*

She pictured the scene to herself and practiced the words several different ways in her mind, determined to present a picture of joy and cheerfulness to him.

For never will I let him see for a moment that I—that I— She felt the tears welling up and spilling over to run down her cheeks. *No, no, I can't* bear *it,* she cried silently, *I* don't *wish him joy, I* don't *want him to marry her. I want him to*—marry me!

She sat quite still, even the tears stopped flowing, so surprised was she at the words that had popped out so shockingly from her mind. *Why, I love him! All along I have been in love with him! And now it is too late—no, not* now—*always it has been too late, for he must have known her before he ever came to Ayleforth Hall.*

And to be forced from the company of the enchanting Mary Wantage to attend the affairs of a gangling, ginger-haired girl dressed in boys' clothes! How he must have chafed at being compelled to take me in hand, a loathsome brat, just out of the schoolroom! He was even astoundingly kinder than I had thought, to have been so patient and good to me, when all the time he longed to be off back to London and the charms of Miss Wantage. Someone as beautiful and wealthy as she need not wait around for him to dance attendance upon her, either. Has admirers by the score, no doubt. But even she will not be dazzled by a title when Sir Anthony is there, I'm sure. She could not help knowing how much more worthy he is than her other admirers. Oh, there could be no question but that she would have him.

The pain of this thought brought her to her feet again, her hand balled up into a fist and pressed that area where her heart lay, as though if she pressed hard enough, she could ease the hurt. She paced around her bedroom, allowing the tears to run unchecked down her face and to splash on the green taffeta of her robe, making dark wet spots on the fabric.

After some moments of this she angrily dashed the tears from her wet cheeks. *I will* not *cry*, she decided. *I hope I am not so poor spirited that I can only cry when I can't have what I want. He will come and tell us about his engagement and I will smile and say what is necessary. I will be very unhappy, but never, never for one moment will I allow anyone to see, most of all him. I have been enough of a charge on him already, and I will not spoil his happiness by behaving in such a way as to cast a shadow over it.*

But I can't stay here in Bath. I can't pretend day after day and in crowds of people. I must go home, back to Ayleforth Hall. Tomorrow I will ask Aunt Emma to take me there, and I can ride with Jem and try to forget about it. And when he comes to tell me he is getting married, I can do everything that is proper, without an audience.

"Do you not think, Perry, that it would help if I wrote Sir Anthony—to apologize and reassure him that I know the entire story now and that I look forward to his making us a long visit as soon as may be?" asked Emma, as Perry lit a candle for her to take upstairs with her.

"Well, my dear, I'm sure it will not hurt in any way, though I doubt he will come for more than a day or so."

"But why not?"

"Because there is now a further complication. He told me—the last time he came—that it was a good thing for him to stay away as much as possible since he was falling in love with her."

"With Pippa?" Emma said in amazement.

"Now why should that come as such a surprise? She is nearly as beautiful as you, they are very near in age after all, and neither is attached."

"Why—why, I don't really know. I suppose it is difficult for me to think of her as other than a child still."

"She is the same age that you were when I saw you first, and I didn't hesitate to fall desperately in love with you the moment I saw you."

"Oh, Perry, can you remember? I saw you walk into the room and thought you were the most beautiful man I'd ever seen. Even when you turned and stared at me so, I couldn't drag my eyes from you, though I thought I would faint away."

He snatched her hungrily into his arms with a soft moan and kissed her until she pulled away with a happy, breathless little laugh.

"Darling, we must be more careful. Suppose one of the servants—"

"Nonsense. Serve them right if they're going to go creeping about the halls at this hour of the night," he declared, reaching for her again.

But she evaded him and hurried up a few steps with a decidedly girlish giggle.

"No, Perry. I could not answer for myself if I allowed us to go on. Good night, my darling." And she blew him a kiss and resolutely turned away. After a few steps, though, she stopped and turned again.

"Perry," she said thoughtfully, "has Pippa ever given any indication that she is aware of his feelings?"

"No, I can't say she has."

"Do you have any idea of her own feelings toward him?"

"Only what he told me," said Perry, laughing at the memory of it.

"Well, what did he tell you?"

"That she thought of him as a father!"

"Good heavens! Well, I think I shall have to make my own inquiries."

"Now, Emma, I never think it is good to meddle in this sort of thing."

"Hmmm," was her only response to this advice as she again turned away, giving him an absentminded wave as she went.

He watched her out of sight, then, shaking his head resignedly, he commented with great feeling, "Women!"

CHAPTER 24

Emma, sorting through the morning post, could hardly keep her eyes on her task, so striking was the picture opposite her. Pippa, in a pale yellow round gown of jaconet, sat in a spill of lemony sunlight, quietly sipping coffee. Her auburn hair hung in loose ringlets on her shoulders and seemed to create a shower of golden sparks around her head at each small movement.

"My love, that is an excessively becoming gown. I think the bodice *à l'enfant* is such a perfect style for young girls," said Emma.

The eyes lifted for a moment, accompanied by the barest sketch of a smile in acknowledgment of the compliment, and Emma was struck by—unhappiness, was it? that she saw there.

"Why, Pippa, is something wrong?"

The chin came up. "Of course not. Why do you ask?"

"Oh, it seemed to me that you were less than your usual cheerful self this morning. Perhaps you are becoming overtired from all this Bath gaiety."

"Yes, Aunt," agreed Pippa, just a shade too quickly, causing Emma to give her a sharp look. "I have been thinking of that myself. I wonder how you would feel about going back to Ayleforth Hall."

Emma could only stare at her for a moment, she was so taken by surprise. It was the last thing she would have expected Pippa to want.

"Well, my dear, I must own myself at nonplus," she finally managed. "Are you sure you really want that? It is very quiet there, as well you know. I fear after all the good times you've been having here, you would find home sadly boring."

"I should like that, I believe," said Pippa quietly.

"Will you be content to leave after the gala—say day after tomorrow? I doubt we could be ready before then in any case."

"Oh—well, the gala. I'm not so sure—"

"But, my dear, you were so looking forward to it, and I must admit, so was I. It's been years since I've seen any illuminations."

"Of course, Aunt Emma, how selfish of me. We'll go afterward." She went back to her coffee.

Emma studied her covertly for a moment, then went on with the sorting of the post.

"Ah! Here's something to cheer you up. A letter from Sir Anthony, telling you of his arrival, I'm sure."

Pippa took the missive silently, broke open the seal, and read. A small frown appeared, but was immediately replaced by a look of indifference. She passed the letter, without comment, to Emma.

"Not bad news, I hope," said Emma lightly, though she was perfectly sure it must be to have caused the frown.

She read that Sir Anthony sent his regrets that he would not be able to attend them in Bath as planned, due to certain affairs that required his attention. He wrote that he would come for sure on the following weekend, and looked forward very much to the visit.

"Oh, how really too bad!" exclaimed Emma. "To be kept in town just now and miss the gala."

"No doubt he will have just as enjoyable a time in London," said Pippa enigmatically.

"But how could he, child, when he must attend to his

affairs, as he says himself. Very tiresome for him, I'm sure."

"Ah, well, there are affairs—and affairs," said Pippa with an attempt at a light laugh that came out rather shakily.

"Now what *can* you mean by that?" Emma asked, genuinely puzzled.

"Well, Sir Anthony has many friends there. Invited everywhere, no doubt. A more than eligible young bachelor must be in great demand. It is a near certainty that every time he comes down here, he breaks the heart of some fair lady—not to speak of her mother!"

"Why, Pippa! Such cynicism is most unlike you! I've never heard you speak of Sir Anthony so. I'm sure I've only ever heard of all the time and care he has given to your own affairs."

"Yes, I agree. And I think I must not be a further charge on his time. I'm sure he has many more interesting things to do with it than be at the beck and call of a young girl. He probably feels that now I have you with me, he need not be quite so much in attendance as before. And quite right too! You and I go on very well together. We don't n-need him anym-more."

In spite of the defiance and determination evident in this speech, the quaver at the end did not escape Emma's notice. *Now, what is this?* she thought, *What has happened? Is she only upset that he cannot come, or could it be something to do with young Otway. Perhaps she was more hurt by him than I had realized. I had not thought her feelings were so much engaged as far as that young man was concerned, but possibly they were.*

"Pippa," she began tentatively, "I hope you had not formed any degree of attachment for Sidney Otway—"

"Sidney Otway!" Pippa replied in such accents of loathing that Emma could not help smiling.

"Well, that seems very definite. I hope you will not think

my question too interfering. I assure you I only asked because I very much hoped you would reply as you did. I cannot like Mister Otway, but sometimes a green, unsuspecting girl can become involved deeply before she realizes the true character of such a man. He is handsome and an accomplished flirt and knows well how to attach the feelings of young women without commitment on his own part."

"You may rest easy, dear Aunt. I behaved somewhat foolishly in the beginning, I admit, but I hope I'm not such a peagoose that I can be bamboozled forever!"

The trip back to Ayleforth Hall took place as planned on the day after the gala. The gala itself had been a less than pleasurable affair in spite of all that Emma and Perry could do between them to stimulate the atmosphere by gay badinage and rather exaggerated amusements at trifles. Pippa remained quiet and thoughtful, not even aware of the pall she was casting on the evening.

Nothing could have been more fetching than her tunic dress of celestial blue gauze, but her air of abstraction finally routed all but the staunchest of her admirers, who had surrounded her on her first appearance in the Gardens. Robert Danston and young Mr. Watkins could not be dislodged, though both were too shy to whisper any declarations of adoration into her ears as they walked about.

In spite of the illuminations, Emma was very happy to have the evening over with. She herself, now that she was reunited with her beloved Perry, did not mind where she was and would as soon be back to Ayleforth Hall with him as anywhere. And with Pippa in her present mood there was little joy to be found in taking her about in society. Therefore the following morning found her briskly ordering the packing of their cases and reassuring the servants that Sir Anthony would be in Bath on the weekend to close the house, pay their wages, and deal with the house agent.

Mr. Strangeways had written to Tony to tell him that Pippa wished to go home and that it would be necessary for him to come to Bath and attend to these details, but they hoped he would see fit to come then to Ayleforth Hall, as he was sorely missed by all. He also told Tony that he and Emma were of a mind to marry as soon as may be, seeing there were no obstacles in the way of it, and for a certainty they had waited long enough! They would not, however, set a date until they could consult with him about his free time, for he must attend as best man for his old friend.

Ayleforth Hall seemed just as it always had been, beautifully kept grounds and every evidence of unflagging care and attention inside the house.

Pippa quickly changed her traveling costume for a riding dress and hurried off to the stables to saddle her mare for a ride. She felt driven somehow to gallop full out for a very long time. The thought of such a ride had been in the forefront of her mind as a comfort and shield as they left the house in Bath and were driven through the now familiar streets, streets that had held so much promise of happiness when first she'd seen them. But she dared not dwell too long on those memories, for her throat felt as though she had swallowed a door knocker, so big was the lump that rose in it.

Pippa was not accustomed to exhibiting her innermost feelings after a life that had, until very recently, held no confidantes. Her instinct, therefore, in this most unusual situation, was simply to close it away in her mind and try to come to terms with it by herself. Also, there seemed to her something shameful to herself in such feelings. She felt that people would only pity her if they knew of it, or think she was a silly, infatuated girl, who knew no better than to fall in love with a man who stood in place of a father to her. A sophisticated, worldly man who *everyone* knew was nearly engaged to the beautiful Miss Wantage and had no time for the schoolgirl passions of his ward.

Pippa took the path in back of the stables and soon let the horse have her head. Though well exercised during Pippa's absence, she had had little chance for a real run and seemed as eager as Pippa to feel the rush of air past her face.

She spent three days thus: riding out in the morning after an early breakfast, long before her aunt or Mr. Strangeways came down, wandering through every part of the estate, and coming home exhausted only in time for dinner.

She tried to make herself as pleasant as possible at the dinner table and sometimes entertained at the pianoforte afterward, but it was only too apparent to the watchful older people that all was not well with Pippa.

She always excused herself early and retired to bed, whereupon Emma and Perry would discuss what could be wrong with her.

"It's that young whelp, Otway," growled Perry.

"I should own myself astonished to learn it was any such thing. In fact I think I can safely say I know it is not that, for I asked her straight out while we were still in Bath—the day before the gala, as a matter of fact, when it seemed to me she was acting mopey—and nothing could have been clearer than her feelings about him. She had very definitely taken him in immense dislike. I can only think it was because he was insulting to Sir Anthony."

"Yes, but that doesn't explain this depression of spirits."

"I think she is missing him."

"Sidney Otway!?"

"Upon my soul, Perry, how can you be such a paper-skull! I mean Sir Anthony."

"Oh—well, I suppose she does. But it's not like her to pout this way. I'm sure she understands that he must be in London about his business."

"Hmm. I'm not so sure she thinks he *is* attending to business there. She said something the day his letter arrived in Bath about there being affairs and *affairs*. It wouldn't surprise me to learn she feels he would rather be with his friends there than with her. He's very nearly the first friend she ever had, and I think such knowledge would hurt."

"But what knowledge? Where could she have gotten such an idea? I know of no special people in London that Tony feels strongly about. Of course, it's perfectly possible there *is* someone, I suppose."

"Well, if there is or if there isn't, I wish he would come soon and dispel, if he can, some of this gloom."

Tony arrived on Saturday evening after dinner, just as the tea tray was carried into the drawing room. Pippa had made her goodnights and was on her way to the door when it opened to admit him. They both stood absolutely still for a moment, then in a lightning transformation, that caused both Emma and Perry to stare in astonishment, Pippa's chin came up, a gay smile lit her face, and she advanced to Tony, her hand out in greeting.

"Well, sir, you've finally managed to drag yourself away from the gaieties of London and visit your poor country friends. We are honored indeed!"

Tony's answering smile faded somewhat at her tone of false raillery, so unlike any voice he had ever heard her use before. It was a perfect copy of all he despised most in experienced young society misses: artificial and arch. He rallied after an instant, however.

"Pippa, my dear child, I have been worried by your

sudden withdrawal from Bath. I hope it was not ill health that caused it."

She gave a trilling little laugh. "Ill health indeed! How dare you, sir? Do you imply that I look pale and wasted?"

"Why—why, certainly not. I only—it was—" His voice trailed off, his bewilderment now complete.

Emma and Perry had watched this exchange with mouths agape, their puzzlement as great as Tony's. After a few days with a Pippa who, however hard she tried, could not disguise the fact that her spirits were sadly depressed, they found it hard to grasp this sudden change. Now, seeing Tony at a complete standstill, Emma recovered her aplomb and came to his rescue.

"Sir Anthony, we are so happy to welcome you to Ayleforth Hall once more—I, in particular, welcome you," she said, meeting his eyes squarely, her voice filled with meaning.

He accepted it fully as the apology he knew it to be. Since Mr. Strangeways had written to him all the particulars of their unusual reunion in Bath, he had come knowing that he would meet a different Aunt Emma than the one he had known before, but even so he was astonished. Indeed, it was difficult to believe this radiant-eyed woman was the same Aunt Emma who had treated him with such indifference and disdain at his first meeting with her.

He took both her hands in his and kissed them separately, then stood looking into her eyes for a moment. Finally he nodded approvingly.

"Well done, Miss Cranville. May I wish you happy?"

"You may indeed, Sir Anthony, and I thank you. For your wishes and for all you've done to make it possible for you to offer them."

There was a small, embarrassed pause, then Perry came forward to welcome Tony and ask if all the business in Bath had been concluded satisfactorily.

"I was sorry not to be able to attend to it for you, but I was sure the house agent would not want to deal with me."

"No problem at all. I arrived there early this morning, cleared everything away, and was on my way here by noon."

"My dear man, you must be starving! Emma, do order up some supper—"

"No, no," Tony laughed, "I did stop for a bite and to bait my horses not two hours ago. I couldn't eat again, I assure you." He turned again to Pippa. "I was somewhat worried about my ward. I could not imagine her giving up the life in Bath for any other reason than illness—but I can see I needn't have worried about that. You are in good health, as even I can see."

"Excellent health, Sir Anthony. But it all began to pall, you see, especially after dear Lady Barstowe and Melissa were called away."

The original smile with which she had greeted him remained on her face, as it had throughout his speech with Emma and Perry. By now it had become little more than a painful rictus. She seemed to realize it and, tossing back her curls vivaciously, tapped his wrist playfully, and treated them all to another gay little laugh.

"But you are a naughty man, sir, to arrive so late. You find me on my way to my bed, entirely exhausted from a day in the saddle. You *will* forgive me, I'm sure. Perhaps we'll meet at breakfast."

And with that she dropped him a curtsy and whirled away to the door. She turned with one last ravishing smile and whisked out the door.

She had intended to run lightly up the stairs, showing them all, if they should be attending, the picture of a happy, healthy young woman eager for her bed. But her legs were trembling and her heart was tumbling about as though it had been cut loose from its moorings, making it impossible to carry through such a plan. She cast a quick look over her shoulder; they were not visible and could not see her. She put out a shaky hand to the banister and crept slowly upstairs.

CHAPTER 25

The following day was a frustrating one for Tony. He had come down early to breakfast to be met with the news from Grigson that "Miss had breakfasted an hour earlier and gone out riding."

He had spent a great deal of the day pacing about the lower rooms and gardens. Finally acknowledging to himself that the girl was deliberately evading him and would not return before dinner, he made his way to the stables and asked for a horse to be saddled for himself. He met Jem, closemouthed as ever, who denied all knowledge of Pippa's whereabouts. He spent over an hour casting about through the various rides on the estate without encountering her, and finally gave up in exasperation.

She made an appearance at the dinner table, sparkling, teasing, and wholly unapproachable. When the ladies retired, leaving the gentlemen to their wine, Tony tried to discover what Mr. Strangeways knew of this strange behavior. But Perry held himself to be as puzzled as Tony.

"She's been like this—well, not quite like this, I admit, but different—since a few days before we left Bath. I had a mind that it was that Otway boy, but Emma assures me it's no such thing, though she can't think of a better reason. However, if I were you, Tony, I'd discuss it with her before you leave."

They rejoined the ladies; everyone disposed themselves comfortably before the fire and waited for the tea tray to be brought in. Pippa took a token sip of the cup handed her and rose.

"Well, if you will excuse me, I think—"

"No, Pippa, I will not excuse you," interrupted Tony. "I've been waiting all day for a chance to speak with you."

"To speak with me!" She raised her eyebrows in mock astonishment. "Why, how thrilling you make it sound, to be sure, Sir Anthony. I assure you I am not unaware of the honor you do me. Do proceed."

Tony's lips tightened grimly. "Privately, I think, if you don't mind."

"Dear me, you quite frighten me, Sir Anthony, I'm not sure that I—"

He rose and strode rapidly to the door, which he held open, and waited. "In the library, if you please," he said in a tone that brooked no argument.

There was little she could do, short of a downright refusal, which might create an emotional atmosphere she knew herself incapable of handling. Her carefully controlled facade was as fragile as glass, but she felt sure she could maintain it for the length of his visit if she limited their time together to a short dinner hour and only the most innocuous sort of conversation.

Therefore, she crossed the room with a bright smile.

"You will excuse us then, Aunt Emma—'The Guardian' speaks, and I must obey." She led the way down the hall and into the library. He closed the door decisively behind them.

"I hope, sir, that you are not going to scold me, for I dislike it excessively," she informed him, seating herself on the sofa, and paying more attention than was entirely necessary to the arrangement of her skirt.

"Scold you! I should like to shake you! I don't know what you mean by this display of superficiality you are treating me to."

"I'm sure I don't take your meaning at all, Sir Anthony. I hope I am never superficial."

"And I hope I am not so blind as you seem to think I am," he retorted.

"Oh, surely not, how could you be?" she replied with a sweet smile.

In spite of himself his lips twitched at this neat riposte, but he turned away to hide it.

"Sauce! And I refuse to be diverted by it. I have something I must discuss seriously with you. Mister Danston came to see me in Bath on Saturday morning. Perhaps you will know why?"

"How could I?" she asked in some amazement.

"I thought it possible you would be aware, though he assured me he had not spoken to you on the subject."

"*What* subject?"

"Well, I see you do not know. Very proper of him, to be sure."

"Please tell me what you are talking about or I shall have strong convulsions," she begged him.

"Mister Danston came to request my permission to pay his addresses to you."

"What? Good heavens—why I—he cannot—I vow I have never been so surprised in all my life!"

"Well, he is a very shy young man, but he has behaved just as he ought, though even I must admit such punctilious manners are rare these days. Well, what do you say? You have had your first proposal."

"Surely you cannot think I—" She stopped abruptly, and then, after a moment's thought, asked, "What did you say to him?"

"What would you have me say to him? I told him that of course it would depend on your wishes. That I would consult you about it and then give him an answer."

"You would have no objections?"

"How could I have with such an exceptionable young

man? He is of very good family—why, my own father picked him out for you! He has an unusually large fortune, a country estate that will be his one day, a large mansion in London. You would have carriages, jewels, any extravagance you could dream of, and—"

"I beg you not to be so ridiculous! I have no interest in hearing a catalog of Mister Danston's good points. He is very nice, of course, but we would not suit—why, he's only a boy!"

"I believe he is several years older than you, actually," began Tony.

"I wish you will not keep on in this irritating way. I have no interest at all in Robert Danston!"

"I assure you I had no wish to irritate you. Surely you must see that I had to tell you of this? In fact I expect this will only be the first of a great many proposals. It is necessary that I ascertain if there is any strong degree of attachment on your part," he explained with as much patience as possible.

"There is no degree of attachment at all. It was very silly of him, if you ask me. Why, he's never so much as—as—" She stopped in confusion, wishing very much that she had never started the sentence.

"Oh, I doubt very much that he would without first asking permission," he said gravely.

Pippa could not help laughing at this, though she was trying her best to maintain a dignified composure.

She stood up. "Well, that is settled then? You will tell him that, though I am aware of the honor he does me, I cannot accept."

"Just as you wish," he answered with a bow.

"Then if our talk is concluded, I will wish you goodnight, sir." She went to the door.

"Pippa!"

She paused with her hand on the doorknob, but didn't turn for a moment. The pleading sound of his voice had almost undone her. She swallowed hard, counted to five, and turned.

"Was there something more, Sir Anthony?" she asked brightly.

"What is it, Pippa? Won't you tell me—we are still friends, I hope. Has someone hurt you?"

"Hurt *me*? Why, whatever can you mean?"

"Young Otway—" he began hesitantly.

"I declare I am at a loss to explain why you must all keep bringing up Mister Otway to me. I lost my head for a very short time, he made me angry, I showed him my displeasure, and that was an end of it! The only time I think of him is when one of you mentions him, and I wish you will not do so anymore, for I am heartily sick of discussing him."

He studied her through this outburst. Indignation, yes, but genuine, and not a sign of any disposition to tears. Not Otway then.

"Then I am at a loss to explain your conduct."

"I hope you will not tease yourself about it any further, Sir Anthony. I'm sure I beg your pardon if my behavior displeases you in some way. I have been but a short while in society, as you very well know, and no doubt my manners will improve with time and attention," she replied haughtily, if somewhat breathlessly at the conclusion.

"No amount of time spent in society would suffice to improve this hoity-toity attitude you have adopted."

"Then I hope you will not feel compelled to subject yourself to it any longer. I would not want to keep you from your perfectly mannered London friends!" She felt her temper rising in a hot flood, knew she should not let it, but was helpless to stop.

"At least they *are* my friends," he snapped, his own patience shredding. "They don't blow hot and cold from day to day so that one never knows where one stands with them!"

"Then you must give yourself the happiness of going back to them. I'm sure they must miss you quite dreadfully when you must waste your time coming down here to pick the straw from my hair."

"I had not—until now—considered it a waste of time!"

"But now you have discovered your mistake? Then go back! I don't need anyone to give me any town bronze. I'm not even sure I want it. And if I do, I'll apply to Aunt Emma or Lady Barstowe!"

Without giving him time to reply, she whirled about and ran across the room, jerked the library door open so hard that it banged against the wall, and fled upstairs.

He stood there in total confusion. What on earth had happened? He had had every intention when he brought her in here of getting to the bottom of this mystery, of cajoling her back into her former charming ways, of recapturing her friendship. How could he have let matters disintegrate in such a way that she could provoke him into a quarrel?

He had never seen her angry before, and the picture she had presented, red flags of anger in each cheek, bosom heaving, eyes sparkling, made her even more beautiful than he had ever thought her before. If only he could have pulled her into his arms and kissed her until that wild, heaving anger changed to a different kind of passion.

Good God! What am I doing? he thought in dismay. *I must* not *allow myself to think of her in this way. Lord knows it's difficult enough loving her, without teasing myself with such dreams.* He turned abruptly and made his way back to the drawing room.

Emma and Perry looked up smilingly. Both were much too well-bred to allow him to see a trace of curiosity.

"Now, Tony, I'm sure you'll have a glass of brandy," said Perry, rising to fetch the decanter.

"Yes, thank you, old friend, I think I am just about

ready for it," answered Tony, running his hand through the carefully arranged locks his valet had spent quite twenty minutes arranging before Tony came down to dinner.

"Do sit down here, Sir Anthony," invited Emma, patting the sofa beside her. "You'll find the fire feels quite good this evening. I noticed a distinct chill in the air before dinner."

"Miss Cranville, I wonder—I don't quite know how to put this—but I must admit I'm in a puzzle about Pippa. We had been quite good friends, you see, and now—well, she seems to be angry with me for some reason that is quite unfathomable. I tried to get her to tell me, but—"

"What did you speak of just now, Sir Anthony?"

"I told her I'd had a visit from young Danston, who'd offered for her."

"Danston? Well, he's certainly a suitable young man for a Cranville. Did she—"

"She was completely uninterested. Then I asked her to tell me if Otway had hurt her in any way—"

"Otway? Hmmm—yes, well, we asked her that also—"

"Don't I know it! She let me know in no uncertain terms that she had a decided aversion to any further discussion of him."

"And is that why you feel she is angry with you? If so, you must not mind it. I think it was only because he angered her and she has taken him quite in disgust. The anger was not directed at you, I'm sure."

"I wish that were all," he exclaimed, "but there was much more. She seems to have some bee in her bonnet about my friends in London. She invited me to go back to them and not worry about her anymore."

"Oh, here, Tony, you must have misunderstood her. Why, she idolizes you, that I would swear to," Perry protested.

"I hardly think so, old fellow. No doubt there were the

beginnings of friendship and a great deal of gratitude at first, but now she seems to have turned around completely. She rang quite a peal over me just now, and I'm afraid I rather lost my temper and said things I should not have, which only goaded her further. I think the best thing I could do would be to go away and let the whole thing cool down for a while."

"Oh, you must not go so soon," pleaded Emma, reaching out to pat his hand soothingly. "Young girls sometimes get into these takings quite suddenly, and as suddenly it is gone. Give us a few more days at least. Why, you and I are hardly acquainted yet."

"You are very kind, Miss Cranville. Well, you may be right. At least we will see how things stand tomorrow. If there is no change, I think I must leave, for my presence might only exacerbate the situation further."

Perry began asking him about his business in London and how it was prospering, and Emma turned away to stare into the flames. She had been studying Pippa for days and felt convinced she knew what was causing this strange behavior in her. Or as sure as she could be. The sad thoughtfulness since the day of Sir Anthony's letter in Bath, the withdrawn quality since their sojourn here, the brittle attitude when Sir Anthony appeared, and now this quarrel. She was in love with him, whether she realized it or not, though by all the signs she did realize it and for some reason thought it impossible that he could ever return her love. From all the hints she had thrown out about "affairs" and "London friends," it seemed possible that she had heard some bit of tittle-tattle in connection with him. *Now, what could it be?*

"Sir Anthony"—she turned to him during a lull in the gentlemen's conversation—"how is it that such a handsome young man as yourself has never married? I'm sure many traps have been set for you among the London mamas."

"Lord, madam, I hope I'm not such a clodpole as to be unable to avoid 'em. The truth is that I've never met anyone I'd feel like tying myself to for life—that is—well—" He threw a harried glance at Perry, begging for rescue.

"Emma, dear," began Perry.

"No, Perry. I would like to say this. I know that I seem to be a nosy old lady and that I should not badger you, but sometimes two people can get at cross purposes and ruin their whole lives, simply for the want of someone who could set it straight, if he but would. I don't want to look back, years from now, and realize that if I had cared a little less for good breeding and a little more for people, I could have made two people very happy."

"Emma, I don't think this is something we should interfere with," began Perry warningly.

"You are not, Perry. I am. Sir Anthony, it has seemed to me in the last few days that the problem with Pippa is that she is in love."

"In love," he repeated after her dully.

"Yes. With you."

"With—"

"You!" she reiterated firmly.

"Oh, but I—but I—"

"You are unable to return her feelings?" she asked softly. This was very cunning of Emma, for she already knew that he did love Pippa, since Perry had told her Tony had confessed it to him. But she didn't want Tony to know that Perry had betrayed his confidence, and she also recognized that Tony would never pursue what he thought to be a hopeless suit. She hoped by telling him first that Pippa loved him, she would give him courage to confess his love to Pippa. She felt the whole business of his financial standing would fall by the wayside, become something two young people in love would find a way to deal with.

But she had not reckoned with Tony's stubbornness.

"I would be sorry to learn that you are right about Pippa, Miss Cranville. It would be entirely unsuitable. But I am happy to be able to tell you that I think you are mistaken in this. I think I must now seek my bed, if you will forgive me." He bowed stiffly and left them.

CHAPTER 26

A slim figure in nankeen trousers and a rather ill-fitting coat slipped silently down the dark staircase and across the hall. The bolts were silently withdrawn and the door as silently opened to allow the figure to slip through and close the door soundlessly behind. Without hesitation the figure sped down the steps and around the house, heading for the stables.

Presently Miss Philippa Cranville, dressed again in men's clothes, walked her horse around the stables and mounted to ride off into the dark, moonless night.

Pippa's flight from Tony the evening before had led to a crying bout in her room and then a return of the anger she had originally felt. Hoity-toity attitude indeed! How dare he speak so to her! And she didn't blow hot and cold. She had maintained the friendliest of demeanors at all times. Just because she didn't follow him around like a little puppy dog anymore. Oh, yes, that was it! He had grown used to a show of reverence from her, liked the idea of the flirting, adoring Miss Wantage in London and the awed, adoring little girl in Bath. *Well, I have changed! I am not a little girl anymore and I refuse to behave in such a bird-witted way any longer!*

Naturally, I hope I shall always show him my gratitude for all he has done for me, but I hope I can do so without groveling, however gratifying such a posture may be to him.

Oh, why doesn't he just go away? Well, I won't see him anymore! I'll—I'll go away! She had jumped up from her bed to find her purse. Twenty pounds! Well, that was certainly enough to last a few days. He would understand well enough that she had left to avoid him and would stay away until he was gone. And this time she wouldn't make the mistake of stopping at some house where he might have acquaintance!

But she had realized suddenly that she couldn't go jauntering about the country on horseback, unattended. In the small villages around here such a sight would be much speculated upon, and if he chose to make inquiries, he could catch up with her in no time at all. But she could dress again as a boy! It had worked admirably the first time for everyone but him. She had scrabbled about in the bottom of her closet until she had unearthed the rather crumpled clothes from her previous adventure, decided she would leave just before first light, and made ready for bed. But sleep had evaded her and she had lain, watching the window for the first signs of dawn.

When she had ridden far enough into the woods to feel completely safe from discovery, even the excitement of the adventure could not keep her from nodding off in the saddle. When the sun was up, she found a nice little nest beneath a tree and cuddled into it for a nap.

It was well into the afternoon before she was roused by a noisy fight between two jays and sat up to rub her eyes and feel the first terrible pangs of hunger. *What a noddicock I am*, she thought. *Why didn't I think to bring some bread or something?* A ramshackle way to set off, to be sure, not so well-thought-out as her first flight. Well, she would just have to ride on till she cleared these woods and came to the road that bounded the property on the other side. There was a village not too far away where she could buy something.

She fetched her horse, saddled it, and presently rode

away, the only sign of her occupation her purse, lying on the grass beneath the tree, where it had fallen from her pocket during the night.

There was no alarm when she did not appear the next morning, though Grigson informed them that Miss must have gone very early indeed, for she'd not been there for breakfast.

Tony sat for a while with Emma, walked about the grounds with Perry, and ate a luncheon he did not want. What he wanted was to see that little minx again and give her a taste of his displeasure. For he had also become angry after going up to his bed the night before.

Ungrateful little hoyden! Well, he *would* go back to London and be damned to her! *From now on I will leave her to her aunt and we will communicate by letter. Just because she has developed a* tendre *for some young whelp and found it unreturned, she must make everyone around her miserable!* First thing tomorrow he would tell her what he thought of such childishness and be off. Well—no, he could not do it first thing, for without a doubt she would follow her previous habit of disappearing for the day and leaving them all to kick their heels for her until dinner. Well, at dinner then, and off first thing the following morning!

He had tossed around in the bed for the entire night, only falling asleep in the early hours. His mood was not improved by the lack of sleep, nor by the information that, just as he had predicted, she had taken herself off at an early hour. Damned discourteous thing to do—also cowardly. As the day wore on he became more incensed by her actions and, finally with a muttered oath, strode off to the stables.

She was skulking about in the woods no doubt, and he would find her and drag her back. Enough was enough. He followed the obvious path behind the stables, and from time to time he thought he saw a hoofprint in the dirt of the path and felt sure he was on her trail. But then it occurred to him that she rode this way frequently, and the print could be days old. Still he kept going, his anger leading him, while his calmer self told him of his foolhardiness. Fate did not assist him by showing him the wallet lying on the grass beside the path, but doggedness kept him going until he came to the road on the far side, and here he was given some assistance by a passing cart. The farmer told him the nearest village was two miles down the road and he decided to head for this, since no other indication was offered.

He found the village boasted an inn, and as he rode into the yard he could clearly hear Pippa's voice raised in protest inside.

He walked to the door and stood quietly, leaning against the door post, an interested observer of the quarrel.

"You'd no call to be eating an honest person's food and then saying you can't pay for it!" said the indignant personage who was obviously the landlord.

"But I *will* pay for it. If you'll just be patient, I'll ride back and find my purse. It must have fallen out and—"

"Fallen out is it? That for a likely story if ever I heard one. And I hope I'm not such a bird-wit as to be taken in by the likes of you."

"Perhaps I can be of some assistance here, Landlord. If you will tell me what the young gentleman owes, I will lay out the ready," said Tony, unable to hide his grin. To have found her so easily, and in such circumstances, was surely enough to make anyone feel good.

She whipped around at the sound of his voice and gaped at him in dismay.

"How did you—?"

"Find you?" he asked coolly, "Well, by now it has become almost a habit, has it not? Here you are, Landlord.

Now—er—sir, if you will join me, we'll ride back together."

He took her by the arm, to insure there would be no tricks, and led her outside. She followed him meekly enough, still too much astonished by his sudden appearance to have found her tongue. They mounted, and he led the way back down the road.

They jogged along silently together until they reached the path leading back through the woods to Ayleforth Hall, when she pulled up.

"If you don't mind, I would prefer to ride back alone," she said coldly.

He raised his eyebrow at her cynically. "I'm sure you would, but it happens I do mind. I've something to say to you, and since you make a habit of donning male costume and taking off into the night at any unpleasantness, I think it better if we keep together."

"Oh, dear, am I to be read a lecture on my cloddish behavior again."

"Yes, since the first one obviously fell somewhat short of the mark."

"I simply wanted to be by myself until—"

"Until I had gone away?"

"If you must have it—yes."

"Well, I am going away. I'll be off back to London first thing in the morning, and I won't put you to the trouble of running away again. If I have something to communicate, I'll write it to you in a letter."

"If you can find the time while dancing attendance on—" She broke off abruptly.

"I don't know what you can possibly mean. I am in the process of trying to build a business and have no time for dancing attendance on anyone—other than you, of course."

"Oh, come now, Sir Anthony, you cannot expect that your activities in London have gone entirely unnoticed.

You may take my word for it that even Bath has had the news of your—"

"My what? What news? What on earth are you nattering about now?"

"I'm not nattering, and I'll thank you not to use that tone with me. I may be just a country girl and not up to all the starts of an accredited beauty like Miss Wantage, but I won't be spoken to like that!"

He stared at her for a moment, his brain spinning. "Miss Wantage? What do you know of Miss Wantage?"

"Don't you have a friend in London by that name?"

"Yes—yes, I do, as a matter of fact."

"A close friend?"

"Why, yes, I think you could say we are close friends."

"Well, then! I am informed that all London is buzzing with amusement at your pursuit of her," she said scornfully.

"My pursuit of—of—Mary Wantage!" He began to laugh unrestrainedly. "Tell me, child, where have you heard this *on dit*?"

"I was told it in Bath. And don't call me child."

"By whom?"

"Why, everyone knows of it."

"Then everyone knows more than I. Now really, Pippa, I think whoever repeated this story to you was teasing you. Mary Wantage has been engaged for a year to the Earl of Liversey. He is a very good friend of mine, and he would be horrified to learn that the gossips have it that I am trying to cut him out."

"She's engaged? But she—you—he told me—"

"Who told you?"

"Sidney Otway."

"And you believed that young coxcomb? But why didn't you just ask me about it?"

She had no answer for this. She rode on, her head hanging, trying not to let the tears come; whether they were tears of humiliation or happiness, she could not have said.

"Pippa, why are you crying? What is it?" he asked in alarm.

She only shook her head and turned away, but now she could not hold the tears back, and her shoulders began to shake with sobs.

"Why, Pippa! What on earth—dear child, you must not cry!" he exclaimed, pulling up his horse and jumping down to come to her side.

Her horse had stopped when she dropped the reins to cover her face with her hands, and Tony lifted her down from the saddle and stood holding her arms, wondering frantically what to do with her.

"Please, my dear, only tell me what is the matter and we will try to set it right. You must not cry," he begged her.

"Oh—oh—I am sorry. I did not mean to—but—b-but—" And with this she put her head down on his chest and began to cry in earnest. He patted her shoulder in a helpless sort of way, and then began trying to extricate his handkerchief from his sleeve.

"There, there, you must not—oh, my God!—please, dear child—here now, take my handkerchief," he pleaded with her. She took it and pressed it to her eyes, which did something to prevent the further destruction of his already soaking shirtfront, but nothing to stop the small, hiccupping sobs. Tony's arms automatically went around her and held her closer, and pulling her up, he transferred her face from his chest to his shoulder and pressed his cheek to her hair, making all the comforting noises one does in such a situation.

In the process he began pressing small kisses on the top of her head and his hand soothed back the tangled, dark red curls from her wet face. He cupped the sweet chin in his hand and turned her face up to his. Murmuring "There,

there, dear Pippa" and "darling child," he was all the while, without even realizing what he was doing, raining small kisses on her closed eyes and cheeks. Presently the murmurs became "Darling Pippa" and "Dear, precious girl," and the soft mouth, so irresistibly close to his own, seemed to demand its own kiss. His lips brushed feather light against hers, and then, unappeased, came back again more firmly. This was, apparently, the correct treatment, for the sobs stopped almost immediately.

Since it is against all human nature to stop doing what is so distinctly pleasurable, the kiss lasted for some considerable length of time. But since it also becomes necessary to breathe, they presently drew apart for a moment, Pippa with a look of dazed surprise, Tony with a dawning horror at what he had allowed to happen. He loosened his arms around her and began to apologize.

"My God—you must forgive me—I lost my—"

But Pippa's expression was slowly changing from surprise to joy, and with a smile and no hesitation she brought her arms up to clasp him firmly around the neck and, pulling his head down, gave him back his kiss with enthusiasm.

He resisted for only a moment, then it was beyond his power to hold out against the demands of his senses, and of his heart, and with a wild moan, he snatched her up against his chest and forgot himself entirely.

Presently, only partially satiated, they drew slightly apart to look into each other's eyes, an absolute necessity for lovers between kisses.

"Pippa—oh, Pippa, my darling—"

"Yes, dearest Sir Anthony?"

He laughed shakily, "Do you think, darling girl, that you could bring yourself to call me Tony now?"

"T-Tony," she responded obediently, "I—I love you—very much."

"And I you—oh, Pippa, and I you, with all my heart."

These declarations demanded immediate proof, which they each received with passionate kisses.

He released her, though reluctantly. "Now, my dear, we must behave sensibly for a moment. I never meant for this to happen—"

"You did not want to love me?" Disbelief was apparent in her voice.

"No, no—I mean yes—well, you must know I already did love you, for a long time now."

"Oh, Tony, truly," she breathed, leaning toward him again.

But he gently pushed her back. "Listen to me, Pippa. We must try to think seriously about this. Though I loved you, I never meant for you to know—at least not until—well, you must know my circumstances make it impossible for me to even consider marriage."

"Circumstances? What can you mean?"

"I have lost my fortune, Pippa, to put it simply. My father invested unwisely, and in order to repay his debts I—"

"But that is no problem, darling Tony, I have a great deal of money, you told me so yourself."

"That has nothing to do with it. Surely you cannot think that I would marry you and live on your money?"

"But you will make your own back, and in the meantime we could be together."

"No," he said firmly, "it would not answer at all. We must simply wait. Besides, you are very young, too young to be making such a decision. You haven't even had your Season yet. Why, you will meet hundreds of young men in London, and should be free to consider—"

"You cannot mean that," she said laughingly.

"Well, of course I am not so unnatural as not to hope that you will prefer me. But I am quite serious that we must wait."

She stamped her foot rebelliously, her amber eyes flashing. "Of all the nonsensical things I've ever heard. How can you be so selfish?"

"Selfish?" he repeated bewilderedly.

"Yes. You want it to be just as you think is right in the eyes of the world. You're not even thinking of what *I* want. It's all silly humbug, like pride and that sort of thing," she exclaimed, a wealth of scorn in her voice.

Tony stared at her in astonishment at such a view of male character.

"I'm sorry, Pippa. I hope I will always, in every other way, put your wishes before my own, but in this you must trust me to know what is best."

She glared angrily at him for a moment, then a thoughtful look appeared in her eyes and slowly they dropped to the path; her lips curled up at the corners in a secret smile. She had had much experience in ordering events as she wanted them. He had forgotten how she had run away from Ayleforth Hall when she didn't choose to meet Robert Danston.

Naturally, I won't remind him of that, she decided hastily. *I will simply sit down quietly and figure out what will be best to do to change his mind. I'm sure to think of something.*

Meekly she went to him and patted his cheek. "Of course, my darling, you know best. Now could you be done with the serious things and kiss me some more—a great deal more, if you please?"

No gentleman could deny such a politely worded request from a lady, not even Tony.